"SLAY HIM!"

said the mounted soldier. "He does but try to fool us with talk."

"A good thought," said the man afoot. And the trooper drew sword and dagger and hurled himself upon Hasselborg.

Tumbling backwards to get out of the range of the wicked blades, Hasselborg got out his own sword just in time to parry a slash.

The dismounted man, finding that Hasselborg could stop his crude swings, changed tactics. He stalked forward, blade out horizontally; then suddenly caught Hasselborg's sword in a *prise* and whipped it out of his grasp. Out shot the blade again; the soldier's legs worked like steel springs as he hopped forward and threw himself into a lunge. The point struck Hasselborg full in the chest, just over the heart. . .

More intergalactic adventures to look forward to...

The KRISHNA SERIES from L. Sprague de Camp and *Ace Science Fiction:*

THE QUEEN OF ZAMBA

L. SPRAGUE de CAMP

ACE BOOKS, NEW YORK

THE QUEEN OF ZAMBA

I.

Victor Hasselborg shook the reins and spoke to his aya: *"Hao,* Faroun!" The animal swung its head and blinked reproachfully at him from under its horns, then started to move. The carriage wheels crunched on the gravel of the Novorecife drive.

Beside him on the seat, Ruis said: "Give him a looser rein, Senhor Victor. And you must learn not to speak to him in so harsh a tone. You hurt his feelings."

"Tamates, are they as sensitive as all that?"

"So—yes. The Krishnans carefully grade the tones in which they speak to their beasts—"

The drumming of the aya's six hoofs mingled with Ruis's chatter to put Hasselborg into a slight trance. He smiled a little as he thought: No comic-book hero he, with ballet suit, ray gun, and one-man rocket. Instead he was about to invade the planet Krishna in this silly native outfit with its divided kilt, wearing a sword, and driving a buggy!

It had been some weeks before by subjective time that Hasselborg had drawn on his client's expensive cigar and asked: "What makes you think your daughter has gone off Earth?"

He watched Batruni narrowly. Although at first he had been ready to dislike the man, he was now beginning to think the textile manufacturer a friendly, generous, well-intentioned sort, if inclined to be lachrymose.

1

Yussuf Batruni shifted his paunch and blew his nose. Hasselborg, visualizing hordes of germs flying out of Batruni's nostrils, shrank back a little.

Batruni said: "She talked about it for months before she disappeared, and she read books. You know, *The Planet of Romance, The Martian's Vengeance,* and trash like that."

Hasselborg nodded. "Go on."

"She had enough money for the trip. I fear I gave her more than was good for a young girl alone in London. But she was all the family I had, so nothing was too good—" His voice caught and he shrugged sadly.

"I'll go over her belongings," said Hasselborg. "Meanwhile, do you think she went with somebody?"

"What do you mean?"

"I said, d'you think she went with somebody? And I don't mean your Aunt Susie, either."

"I—" Batruni stiffened, then checked himself. "Excuse me. Where I come from, we take care of our daughters' virtue, so I cannot help— But, now that you bring it up, I am afraid the answer is yes."

Hasselborg smiled cynically. "The Levant ought to advertise its virgins the way Egypt does its pyramids. Who's the man?"

"I do not know."

"Then how d'you know there is one?"

"There are only—little things. Nothing you can put a finger on. On my last trip to London, when I asked her about her young men, she evaded. Talked about other things. That was a big change from the times before, when I would learn every detail of the young man's appearance and habits whether I was interested or not."

"Don't you suspect anybody in particular?"

"No, just a vague general suspicion. You are the detective; you draw the inferences."

"I will," promised Hasselborg. "As soon as I've looked over her apartment, I'll wire Barcelona for the passenger lists of all the spaceships that have left in the last month. She couldn't get away under an assumed name, you know, because her prints would be checked against the European Central File as a matter of routine."

"That will be good," said Batruni, looking out of the window into a fog that had so far defied the efforts of the fog sweepers. His great Levantine nose showed in profile. "Do not spare the expense, and when you find where she has gone, follow her on the very next ship."

"Wait a minute!" said Hasselborg. "To chase somebody on another planet takes preparation: special equipment, training—"

"The very next!" said Batruni, beginning to wave his hands. "Do you think I like sitting around? Speed is of the utmost importance. I will pay you a bonus for speed. Have you never heard of the early bird, Mr. Hasselborg?"

"Yeah, and I've also heard of the early worm," said Hasselborg. "Nobody gives him a thought."

"Well, this is no joke. If you cannot hurry, I will go to—" He broke off in a fit of sneezing.

Hasselborg held his breath to let the germs settle, then said: "Now, now, I assure you I won't waste a minute. Not a microsecond."

"You had better not," said Batruni. "And if you can return my Julnar—ah—unharmed, I will add fifty percent to the fee."

Hasselborg cocked an eyebrow, thinking that if you could only strap a howdah to Batruni's back, he'd fit perfectly into a circus parade. "I get your point. However, Mr. Batruni, while I can trail runaways, I can't bring back the infirm glory of the positive hour, nor can I put Humpty Dumpty together again."

"Then you don't think there is any chance—?"

"About as much chance as there is of having an Irishman turn down a drink when you offer it to him. However, I'll do my best."

"Fine," said Batruni. "By the way, Mr. Hasselborg,

you do not talk like a Londoner. Are you Swedish?"

Hasselborg pushed back the brown hair that drooped untidily over his broad forehead. "By descent only. I'm a North American; born in Vancouver."

"How did you happen to settle in London?"

"Why—" Hasselborg became wary, not wishing to go into the sordid details of his fall and partial resurrection. "After I left the Division of Investigation to go into private work, I specialized in insurance frauds. And Europe offers a good opportunity for that kind of work now." He laughed apologetically. "Investigating them, I mean. Follow me?"

"Yes." Batruni looked at his watch. "My plane leaves in an hour, so you must excuse me. You have the photographs, the key to her apartment, the list of addresses, and the letter of credit. I do not doubt that you will live up to your recommendations." However, he said this with a rising inflection that did imply a doubt.

Hasselborg, as he stood up, worked the little trick that he sometimes used on dubious clients: he pushed back his hair, straightened his scarf, took off his glasses, pulled back his shoulders, and stuck out his big square jaw. By these acts he changed in a couple of seconds from a nondescript, mild-looking person with an air of utter unimportance to a large, well-built character whom an evildoer would think twice about meddling with.

Batruni smiled with renewed confidence as he shook hands.

Hasselborg warned him: "I'm no miracle-working yogi, you know. If she's gone outside the Solar System, it'll take years to bring her back. There's no extradition from most planets, and once I get her aboard the Viagens Interplanetarias she'll be under Earth law and I can't drag her by main force. It would cost me my license at least."

Batruni waved a hand. "Never mind that. I will take care of your future if you get me my darling. But to wait all those years—" He seemed ready to blubber again.

"You could put yourself in a trance, couldn't you?"

"And wake up to find those bad Socialists had stolen all my factories? No, thank you. It is not the time—the doctors tell me I have another seventy-five years at least —but the suspense. It will not be so long for you."

"The Fitzgerald effect," said Hasselborg. "If you're not back from Aleppo when I shove off from London, I'll leave a report for you. *Mah salâmi!*"

Viagens Interplanetarias wired back a list of names from Barcelona, and the name of Julnar Batruni turned up on the list for the *Juruá*, bound for Pluto with four other Londoners in addition to other passengers. Of the Londoners, one was a well-known spinster sociologist, two a minor World Federation official and his wife, and the remaining one a radio announcer named Anthony Fallon.

Hasselborg trotted around to the BBC offices, where he unearthed the Personnel Director and asked about Fallon. He learned that Fallon was in his early thirties— a little younger than Hasselborg himself—a native of London, married, with a varied background as a World Police trooper, a cameraman on a scientific expedition to Greenland, a hippopotamus-farmer, an actor, a professional cricket player, and other jobs. No, BBC had no notion where he was now. The blighter had simply called Personnel one fine day, told him he was resigning, and walked out. (That was two days before the Juruá left Barcelona.) And really you know, this is England, where a chap can go where he pleases without some copper checking up on him.

Finding the Director of Personnel stuffy, Hasselborg inquired among the staff, adding details to his picture of Fallon. The man, it transpired, had cut something of a swath among the female help; he'd apparently led not a double but a quadruple or quintuple life. The men liked his tall tales without altogether believing them; on the other hand they thought him a bit of a cad and a trouble maker. Good thing he'd gone. (These uninhibited guys have all the fun, thought Hasselborg sourly.)

Hasselborg wrote up his visit on his shorthand pad and went to Fallon's address, which turned out to be an ordinary Kensington flat. A pretty blonde girl opened the door. "Yes?"

Hasselborg got a jolt—the girl looked like his lost Marion. "Are you Mrs. Fallon?"

"Why, yes. What can I—"

"My name's Hasselborg," he said, forcing what was meant for a disarming grin. "May I ask you a few questions about Mr. Fallon?"

"I suppose—but who are you really?"

Hasselborg, thinking that the direct approach would work here as well as any, identified himself. The strong Briticism of her speech made him almost forget her resemblance to his ex-wife. The girl was of medium height, sturdily built, with substantial ankles, wide cheekbones, rather flat features, and a vivid pink-blue-and-gold coloring.

After some hesitation, she asked him in. Most people did, since they were more thrilled than resentful over being investigated by one of those fabulous creatures, a real sleuth. The only trouble was to keep them on the subject; they wanted to know about your romantic adventures and wouldn't believe you when you assured them that investigation was a dull and sordid trade, which brought you into contact with a singularly unlikable lot of people.

She said: "No, I've no idea where Tony went. He just told me he was going on a trip. Since he'd done that before, I didn't worry for the first week or two, and then I learned he'd quit his job."

"Did you ever suspect him of—uh—playing around?"

She smiled wryly. "I'm sure he did. You know, tales of how he had to stay late for spot broadcasts, which later turned out never to have taken place."

"Do anything about it?"

"I asked him, but he only flew into a temper. Tony's a very peculiar man."

"He must be, to leave a girl like you—"

"Oh," she smiled deprecatingly. "I'm afraid I bored him. I wanted the usual things, you know—a real home and lots of children."

"What did you intend to do when he went this time?"

"I hadn't decided. I can't help liking him in a way, and he was wonderful when we first—"

"I understand. Did he ever mention a Syrian girl, Julnar Batruni?"

"No; he was cagey. You think he went with her?"

Hasselborg nodded.

"Where to? America?"

"Farther than that, Mrs. Fallon. Off Earth."

"You mean millions and millions—Oh. Then I suppose I shan't see him again. I don't know whether to be relieved—"

Hasselborg said: "I'm trying to find Miss Batruni and, if possible, bring her back. Want me to try to fetch your man, too?" (He found himself, he couldn't imagine why, hoping she'd say no.)

"Why . . . this is all so unexpected. I'd have to think—" Her voice trailed off again.

"Mind if I take down some data?" The shorthand pad appeared. "What was your maiden name?"

"Alexandra Garshin. Born in Novgorod, 2103. I've lived in London most of my life, though."

Hasselborg grinned, "Tony's the only Cockney in the case." After a few more questions he said: "While I don't usually mix business with pleasure, it's nearly dinner time, and I think we could pursue the subject better over a couple of reindeer steaks. What say?"

"Oh! Thanks, but I couldn't impose on you—"

"Come on! Old man Batruni'll be paying for it." Hasselborg looked studiedly friendly and harmless, hoping that his expression would not seem to be to the un-prejudiced observer like that of a hungry wolf. Or at least a coyote.

She thought, then said: "I'll come; but if you ever meet my parents, Mr. Hess . . . Hass—"

"Vic."

"Mr. Hasselborg, don't say I went out with you on such short acquaintance."

"Cocktail?" he said.

"Thank you, a blackjack."

"One blackjack and a glass of soda water," he told the waiter.

She raised eyebrows. "Teetotaler?"

He smiled regretfully. "No. Narasimachar treatment."

"You poor man! You mean you're really conditioned so a good drink makes you gag?"

He nodded. "Sad, too, because I used to like the stuff. Too well, that was the trouble, if you follow me." He wouldn't go into the story of his moral collapse after Marion— "When I get a case where I've got to drink with the boys for professional reasons, boy, then the going is rugged. But let's talk about you. Are you fixed for support while I chase your errant spouse beyond the cranky comets and behind the mystic moons?" He washed down a couple of pills with his soda water.

"Don't worry. I've got a promise of a job, and if the worst came to the worst I could go back to my parents —if I could stand hearing them say 'I told you so.' "

The physician laid down his last hypodermic and said: "Really, that's all I can think of." He counted them off on his fingers. "Tetanus, typhus, typhoid, small pox, yellow fever, bubonic, pneumonic, malaria. It's a wonder you're not dead from all the shots you've had lately. Maybe you'd like to be shot for whooping cough?"

Hasselborg met the doctor's gaze squarely, although he guessed that the word in the doctor's mind was "hypochondriac." "Thanks, I've had it. Got those prescriptions? Wish I could take time to have my appendix jerked."

"Is something wrong with your appendix?"

"No, but I don't like wandering around some strange planet with one inside me that *might* go wrong. For all I know, I'm going some place where, when you get sick, they chop off a finger to let out the evil spirits. And I hope my teeth hold out; just had 'em checked."

The doctor sighed. "Some chaps with everything wrong can't be bothered with elementary medical care, while the healthiest individual I've seen in years— But I suppose I shouldn't discourage you."

Hasselborg went out to Woolwich for an hour's pistol practice at the range; then back to arrange with a colleague to take over his two pending fraud cases. Then home to his apartment to hang on the telephone until he got through to Yussuf Batruni, who waxed emotional all the way from Aleppo: "My boy, my boy, it is noble of you—"

Then he took Alexandra Garshin Fallon out to dinner again, saying: "Last date, chum."

"So soon?"

"Yep; I'd rather wait till a later ship, but I'm only the third engineer of my soul; Joe Batruni's the captain. I drop you right after we sheathe our fangs and go home to pack."

"Let me come around to help you."

"No. Sorry." He smiled to counteract her hurt look. "I can't, you know; might give away trade secrets."

"Oh," she said.

He knew that wasn't the real reason. The reason was that he was falling in love with her, and he was not sure he could keep his mind on packing if—

Just as well he was going, he thought. The idea wormed into his mind that it would be so easy to fail to find Fallon and his light-o'-love, and then come back and have Alexandra to himself— No! While he didn't consider himself a Galahad of purity, he still had his code. And although he had witnessed most of the delinquencies of mankind in the course of his career, and had partaken of some of them, he was still a bit of a fanatic on the subject of wife-stealing. With reason.

He laid out on his bed one Webley & Scott six-millimeter twenty-shot automatic pistol, one blackjack, one set of brass knuckles, one pair of handcuffs, one pocket camera, one WF standard police fingerprint recording apparatus, one pencil flashlight, one two-way pocket radio set, one portable wire-recorder set, one armor vest, one infrared scanning and receiving apparatus—pocket size—one set of capsules containing various gases and explosives, which would accomplish anything from putting an audience to sleep to blowing a safe, one box of knockout drops, a pick-lock, a supply of cigars, a notebook, and pills: vitamin, mineral, longevity, headache, constipation, cold—and ammunition for all this equipment: HV cartridges, camera film, notebook fillers, and so on. The most valuable of the equipment he stowed in his pockets until his suit began to look lumpy. The rest he packed.

Alexandra came out to Waddon to see him off, saying: "I wish I were going with you."

He supposed she did not know she was turning the knife in the wound, so he smiled amiably. "Almost wish you were, too. Wouldn't do, of course. But I'll think of you. If you get tired of waiting around for Tony and me, you can always go in trance or—" He meant—ditch Fallon and go her way, but thought better of saying so.

"Speck in my eye." She dabbed at the optic with a handkerchief a little larger than a postage stamp. "Gone now."

"Look here, could I have that handkerchief?"

"What for?"

"Why—uh—just to take along." He grinned to hide his embarrassment. "In spring, when woods are getting green, I'll try and tell you what I mean. In summer, when the days are long, perhaps you'll understand the song."

"Why Victor, you're *sentimental!*"

"Uh-huh, but speak it not in Gath. It would ruin my professional reputation." They shook hands formally, Hasselborg finding it hard to keep up his pose of guileless geniality. "Good-by, Alexandra."

The Barcelona plane whizzed down the catapult strip and off the field in a cloud of smoke.

II.

While Hasselborg pondered the case on his way to Barcelona, it occurred to him that the fugitive pair might have resorted to some human version of the old shell game, like arranging with another pair of passengers to switch identities after they got to Pluto and then returning to Earth or one of the other inner planets under their assumed names. They might get away with such a dodge, because their prints would not be checked once they had left Barcelona. Having no wish to spend years chasing them through the Galaxy as if they were a pair of rather unholy grails, he looked up the investigating firm of Montejo and Durruti in Barcelona and arranged for them to cover all incoming spaceships until further notice.

Then he sent a last-minute post card to Alexandra— not exactly a professional thing to do, he told himself, but she might be dead before he returned—and boarded the *Coronado* for Pluto.

There were nine passengers besides Victor Hasselborg, who found himself bunking with one Chuen Liao-dz. They were all squeezed into the little honeycomb of passenger compartments in the nose, below the control compartments and above the cargo and the vast mass of fuel and machinery that occupied nine-tenths of the craft.

After an ineffective effort to unpack his belongings at

the same time that Chuen unpacked his—without disclosing the professional equipment—Hasselborg said: "Look here, chum, suppose I lie on the bunk while you unpack; then we trade off?"

"Thank you," said Chuen, a short, thick, dish-faced man with coarse black hair turning gray. "You turn crank on the end of your bunk, and the end comes up like a hospital bed. What's your line, Mr. Hasselborg?"

"Insurance investigator. What's yours?"

"Ah—I'm economic official to the Chinese government. A very dull person, I assure you. First trip?"

"Uh-huh."

"Then—ah—I suppose you know your instructions for takeoff?"

"Sure. Lie down when I hear the warning bell, et cetera."

"That's right. You'll find exercise compartment down the passageway to the right. Better sign up for one hour out of every twenty-four, subjective time. It'll keep you from going mad from boredom."

That proved no overstatement. With every cubic centimeter accounted for, there were no ports to look out of and no deck space for strolling. Even the minute passenger list ate in two shifts in the tiny compartment that served as lounge the rest of the time for whichever half of the passengers had been lucky enough to preëmpt the available seats.

When the ship had risen above the plane of the ecliptic and had cut its acceleration back to 1.25 G, Hasselborg played cards, pulled on weights in the exercise room—just big enough to let him do so without barking his knuckles—and pried into the lives of his fellow passengers. Some proved garrulous and transparent; others opaque and taciturn. He found his roommate, oddly enough, to be loquacious and opaque at the same time. When Chuen was asked what official business he was on, he would reply, vaguely:

"Ah—just looking into possibilities of high-grade im-

ports and exports. No, nothing definite; I shall have to
decide on the ground. Only goods of highest quality for
a given mass can be handled, you know—"

Hasselborg decided, more in fun than in earnest, that
Chuen was really a plain-clothes agent either of China
or of the W.F. If such were the case, however, it would
do no good to say: "See here, old man, aren't you a
cop?" One of the more dismal facts about the profession
was that you had to spend so much time playing dumb.

This monotonous half-life, bounded by bare
bulkheads and punctuated by bells that reminded the
sluggish appetite that the time had come for another
meal, continued for days until the warning bell told him
they were nearing Pluto. Hours later the pressure of de-
celeration let up and the loud-speaker in the wall said:
"Passageiros sai, por favor!"

Suitcase in hand, Hasselborg followed Chuen down
the inclosed ramp that had been attached to the ship's
side. As usual there was nothing to see; space travel was
no game for a claustrophobe. The ramp moved slightly
with the weight of the people walking down it.

An air lock shut behind him, and a young man sat at
a desk checking off names on a register. Hasselborg
handed over his passport, saying:

"Tenha a bondade, senhor, to let me speak to the head
passenger *fiscal."*

Then, while the inspector went through his bag,
Hasselborg identified himself to the head passenger
agent, a Brazzy like most of the Viagens people.
Hasselborg reflected that, public and internationally-
owned corporation though the Viagens was supposed to
be, with all jobs strictly civil service, somehow the citizens of the world's leading power always got a dis-
proportionate share of them.

The agent politely insisted on speaking English to
Hasselborg, who, not to be outdone, insisted on speaking the Brazilo-Portuguese of the spaceways to the

agent. Hasselborg, giving up the contest first, asked:

"I believe two passengers named Fallon and Batruni came in on the *Juruá*, didn't they?"

"Let me think—I can check the register. Was not the Batruni that beautiful girl with the dark hair?"

Hasselborg showed a photograph to the agent, who said: "Ah, yes, that is her. *O Glória-Pátri*, such a woman! What did you wish with her?"

Hasselborg grinned. "Not what you're thinking, Senhor Jorge. Is she still here?"

"No."

"Thought not. Where'd she go?"

The agent looked wary. "Perhaps if you could tell me of the circumstances—"

Hasselborg cleared his throat. "Well, Miss Batruni has a father who's anxious to get her back, and Mr. Fallon has a wife who's perhaps less anxious but who is still interested in knowing where he went. And obviously they didn't come all the way out here just to admire the view of the Solar System. Follow me?"

"But—but Miss Batruni is of age; she can go where she likes."

"That's not the point. If she can go where she likes, I can also follow her. Where'd she go?"

"I prefer not to tell you."

"You'll have to, chum. It's public information, and I can raise a stink—"

The agent sighed. "I suppose you can. But it goes against all the traditions of romance. Will you promise me that when you find them you will not spoil this so-beautiful intrigue?"

"I won't promise anything of the sort. I won't put gyves on the girl's wrists and drag her back to Earth at gun point, if that's what you mean. Now, where—"

"They went to Krishna," said the agent.

Hasselborg whistled. As he remembered it, of all the hundreds of known inhabited planets, Krishna had natives the most like human beings. That was to

Hasselborg's disadvantage, since the elopers could take off from the landing station without oxygen masks or other special equipment and lose themselves among the natives.

Aloud he said: *"Obrigado.* When does the next ship leave for Krishna?"

The agent glanced at the compound clock on the bulkhead. "In two hours fourteen minutes."

"And when's the next after that?"

Senhor Jorge glanced at the blackboard. "Forty-six days."

"And when does it arrive at Krishna?"

"You mean the ship-time or the Solar-System time?"

Hasselborg shook his head. "I always get confused on that one. Both, let's say."

"Ship-time—that is, subjective time—you arrive in twenty-nine days. Solar-System or objective time, one thousand four hundred ninety-seven days."

"Then Fallon and Miss Batruni will have arrived— how many days ahead of me?"

"Krishna time, about a hundred days."

"Yipe! You mean they take off sixteen days ahead of me; I take twenty-nine days following them; and I arrive a hundred days after they do? But you can't do that!"

"I am sorry, but with the Fitzgerald effect you can. You see they went in the *Maranhão,* one of the new mail-ships with tub acceleration."

Hasselborg shuddered. "Some day somebody's going to make a round trip on one of your ships and arrive back home before he left."

Meanwhile he thought: to invade an unfamiliar planet required more preparation than he could manage in a couple of hours. On the other hand, he could imagine Batruni's reaction if he arrived back on Earth to spend a month boning up. The magnate would resemble not merely an elephant but a bull elephant in *must.* Still, for such a fee a chance was worth taking. He asked:

"Is there a bunk available on the one that's leaving now?"

"I will see." The agent buzzed the clerk in the next compartment and held a brief nasal conversation with him. "Yes," he said, "there are two."

"If you'll visa me, I'll take one of them. Have you got a library with information on Krishna?"

Senhor Jorge shrugged. "Not a very good one. We have the *Astronaut's Guide* and an encyclopedia on microfilm. Some of the men have their own books, but it would take time to round them up. You wish to see what we have?"

"Lead on. I'd also like a look at the register of the *Maranhão*, to compare signatures." The real reason was that he wouldn't put it past this superannuated Cupid to give him a bum steer in order to protect the so-beautiful intrigue.

However, the register checked with the agent's statements. Moreover, the library was not very informative. Hasselborg learned that the surface gravity on Krishna was 0.92 G, the atmospheric pressure 1.34 A, the partial pressure of O_2 1.10 times that of Earth—with a high partial pressure of helium. The people were endoskeletal, bisexual, oviparous, bipedal organisms enough like human beings so that one could pass himself off as the other with a little skillful disguise. In fact there had even been marriages between persons of the two species, although without issue. They had a pre-mechanical culture characterized by such archaisms as war, national sovereignty, epidemics, hereditary status, and private ownership of natural resources. The planet itself was a little larger than Earth but with a lower density and a higher proportion of land to water, so that the total Krishnan land area was nearly three times that of the Earth.

Senhor Jorge opened the door. "You had better come, Mr. Hasselborg; you have only twenty minutes. Here is your passport."

"Just a minute," said Hasselborg, looking up from the viewer and reaching for his pen. He dashed off three short letters to be photographed down and go back to Earth by the next ship: one to Montejo and Durruti calling them off their job, and one each to Yussuf Batruni and Alexandra Fallon stating briefly whither he was going and why.

When he boarded the ship, he found that space was even more limited than on the first lap of the trip. He had as roommates not only Chuen Liao-dz but also a middle-aged lady from Boston who found the idea most repugnant. He thought, if I were Fallon, now, she'd really have something to worry about.

They arrived.

In contrast to Pluto, the ramp was open to the mild, moist air of Krishna. Great masses of clouds swept in stately procession across the greenish sky, often cutting off the big yellow sun. Even the vegetation was mostly green, with flecks of other hues. Walking down the ramp, Hasselborg could see, stretching like a gray string across the rolling plain, the high wall that marked the boundary of Novorecife.

The next contrast to Pluto was less pleasant. An official person in a fancy uniform said:

"*Faça o favor*, passengers going on to Ganesha and Vishnu, into this room. Those stopping off at Krishna in here, please. Now, line up, please. Place your baggage on the floor, open, please."

Hasselborg noticed what looked like a full-length X-ray fluoroscope at one side of the room. More uniforms appeared and began going through the baggage and clothes with microscopic care, while others herded the passengers one by one into the space between the X-ray machine and the fluoroscope to look at their insides. Some of the passengers made heavy weather, especially the lady from Boston, who was plainly unused to Viagens ways.

However, the guard assigned to Hasselborg's pile had barely begun his job when he jumped up as if he had been jabbed from behind with a sharp instrument "*Alô!* What is this?" He had turned over the top layer of clothes and come upon the professional equipment.

Two guards rushed Hasselborg down the hall, while two others followed, one carrying his baggage. They ushered him into an office in which a fat man sat at a desk, and all four talked so fast that Hasselborg, despite a fair command of the language, could hardly follow. One of the guards went through Hasselborg's pockets, making excited noises as he came upon the pistol, the camera, and other items.

The fat man, whose name according to the sign on his desk was Cristôvão Abreu, Security Officer, leaned back in his swivel chair and said: "What are you trying to get away with, senhor?"

Hasselborg said loudly: "Not a thing, Senhor Cristôvão. What am I supposed to do, click my heels together and salute? What are *you* trying to get away with? Why are your men hauling me around in this undignified condition? Why do you treat incoming passengers like a bunch of steers arriving at the abattoir? What—"

"Quiet yourself, my friend. Don't bluster at me; it will not excuse your crime."

"What crime?"

"You should know."

"Sorry, chum, but I don't. My papers are in order, and I'm on legitimate—"

"It is not that, but this!" The fat man indicated the wire recorder and other apparatus as if they had been the parts of a dismembered corpse.

"What's wrong with them?"

"Don't you know they're contraband?"

"*Mão do Deus!* Of course I didn't know. Why are they?"

"Don't you know that the Interplanetary Council has

forbidden bringing machinery or inventions into Krishna? Don't tell me anybody can be so ignorant!"

"I can be." Hasselborg gave a short account of the hurried departure that had brought him to Krishna without proper briefing. "And why are these gadgets forbidden?"

Abreu shrugged. "I merely enforce the regulations; I don't make them. I believe there is some social reason for this policy—to keep the Krishnans from killing each other off too fast before their culture is more advanced in law and government. And here you come with enough inventions to revolutionize their whole existence! I must say— Well, I know my duty. Mauriceu, have you searched this one thoroughly? Then take him to the office of Góis for further examination." And Abreu went back to his papers with the air of having swatted one more noxious insect.

Julio Góis, assistant security officer, turned out to be a good-looking young man with a beaming smile. "I'm sorry you have had this trouble, Mr. Hasselborg, but you gave the Old Man a terrible turn with your apparatus. He was on duty here ten years ago when some visitor introduced the custom of kissing to Krishna, and the excitement from that hasn't died down yet. So he's sensitive on the subject. Now, if you will answer some questions—"

After an hour's interrogation, Góis said: "Your papers are as you say in order, and I'm inclined to agree that if you hadn't been honestly ignorant, you wouldn't have tried to bring your devices in openly. So I'll release you. However, first we'll sequester the things in that pile. You may keep the little club, the knuckle-duster, the notebook, the pen, the knife— No, not the pencil, which is a complicated mechanical device. Take an ordinary wooden pencil instead. No, the breastplate is one of those wonderful new alloys. That's all I can allow you." He switched to English: " 'Tis not so deep as a well, nor so wide as a church door; but 'tis enough, 'twill serve."

"Huh," said Hasselborg, "how do I catch these people without the tools of my trade?"

Góis shrugged. "You'll have to use the brain, I think."

Hasselborg rubbed his forehead as if to arouse that organ. "That puts me in a spot. Do you know where Fallon and Miss Batruni took off for when they left Novorecife?"

"They were headed for Rosid, in the principality of Rúz, which is a dependency of the Kingdom of Gozashtand. Here's a map—" Góis ran a fingernail north from the green spot that symbolized Novorecife, the Viagens outpost.

"Were they traveling under aliases?"

"I don't know. They didn't confide in me."

"What does one need to travel around Krishna?"

"Some native clothes, weapons, and means of transportation. Our barber can give you the antennae and dye your hair. What will you go as?"

"How do you mean?" asked Hasselborg.

"You can't run around without means of support, you can't say you're a Terran spy for fear they'd kill you, and you have to use the disguise. Most nearby rulers are friendly to us, but the common people are ignorant and excitable, and there's no extraterritoriality. Once you leave Novorecife, we wash our hands of you, unless you disobey the regulation about inventions."

"What do you suggest for a cover? I can be an insurance salesman, or a telelog repairman, or—"

"*Os santos, no!* There's no insurance or radio here. You'd have to go as something that exists, like a palmer—"

"A what?"

"A religious pilgrim. However, that might get you into religious arguments. What's your church?"

"Reformed Atheist."

"Just so. Some of the Terran cults are established here, you know; missionaries got in before the ban went into effect. How about a troubadour?"

"That's out. When I sing, strong men pale, women faint, and children run screaming."

"I have it, a portrait painter!"

"Huh?" Hasselborg sat up with a jerk. He was about to say that he hated all painters, but that would involve explanations to the effect that his former wife had run off with one to live in a shack on the California coast. Instead he said: "I haven't painted anything but roofs for years." (He had been trained in sketching when he was entering the Division of Investigation but chose not to admit it.)

"Oh, you needn't be good. Krishnan art is mostly geometric, and their portraits are so bad by our standards that you'll be a sensation."

"Wouldn't they recognize my technique as exotic?"

"That's all right too; the Terran technique is a fad in Gozashtand. The Council hasn't tried to keep Earth's fine arts out of Krishna. Take a few days to practice your painting and learn Gozashtandou while you have your new equipment made. I see by your letter of credit that you can afford the best. I'll give you an introduction to the Dasht of Rúz—"

"The who of what?"

"I suppose you'd say a baron. He's Jám bad-Koné, a feudal underling of the Dour of Gozashtand."

"Look," said Hasselborg, "at least let me take my pills. I have to keep my health, and nobody'll know what's in them. Do you follow me?"

"Góis smiled. "Perhaps we can allow the pills."

When Hasselborg reached the barber shop, he found his shipmate Chuen in the chair ahead of him. The barber had already dyed the man's hair a poisonous green and was affixing a pair of artificial antennae to his forehead by means of little sponge-rubber disks, which merged with the skin so that it was almost impossible to tell where one left off and the other began. The barber said:

"Those should stay for at least a month, but I'll sell you a kit to glue them back on if they should work loose. Remember to let your hair grow longer in back—"

Hasselborg also noted that the barber had glued artificial points to Chuen's ears, so that altogether the man now looked something like an overfed leprechaun. "Hello, Chuen; going out among the aborigines, too?"

"Indeed so. Which direction you taking?"

"They tell me my subjects have gone north. How about you?"

"I don't know yet. You know, I am afraid green hair doesn't become me."

"Better be glad they don't wear those haystack wigs they wore on Earth back in the time of James the Second. Aroint thee, scurvy knave!" Hasselborg made fencing motions.

Gozashtandou proved an easy language for a man who already spoke a dozen. Mornings Hasselborg spent posting solemnly around the bridle path on the back of an aya, while a member of the Viagens staff trotted with him and told him over and over to keep his elbows in, heels down, et cetera. These beasts had an unpleasantly jarring trot, especially since the saddle was right over the middle pair of legs. When he learned that his particular aya had also been trained to draw a carriage, he eagerly bought a light four-wheeled vehicle with a single seat for two. Two or three hundred years before on Earth, he recalled, men had driven a variety of these contraptions and called them by a multitude of special names: buggy, brougham, gig, surrey—something only an antiquarian would know about. At least, one aya and a carriage should in the long run be as cheap and convenient as, and more comfortable than, an aya to ride and a second to carry his gear.

Afternoons he put in an hour or two with another staffer who flourished a dummy sword and yelled: "No, no, always you wave the blade too wide!"

"That's how they do it in the movies."

"Do they try to kill people in the movies? No, they try to give the audience a thrill, which is different—"

With Chuen he practiced Krishnan conversation and table manners. The main tools were a pair of little spears to be held like chopsticks. Chuen, of course, had a great advantage here. Góis, watching Hasselborg's fumbles, turned beet-red containing his mirth.

"Go ahead and laugh," said Hasselborg. "I should think the Council would at least let us show 'em knives and forks."

Góis shrugged. "The Council has been very strict since the tobacco habit invaded the planet, *amigo meu*. Some consider the Council unreasonable for saying that by letting these people have knives and forks we'd be inviting an interplanetary war, but—"

"Are the Krishnans as dangerous as that?"

"Not so much dangerous as backward. The Council reasons that it will be time enough letting them have an industrial revolution when they have more civilized ideas about politics and the like. I don't think they know what they want; the policy changes from year to year. And some say the stupid Council will always find reasons to stop progress on Krishna. Progress— Ah, my friends, I must get back to Earth before I'm too old to see its wonders."

At this outburst Hasselborg exchanged a quick glance with Chuen, who said: "What's your opinion of the regulation, Senhor Julio?"

"Me?" said Góis in English. "I am but a poor, infirm, weak, and despised young man. I have no opinions." And he changed the subject in a marked manner.

Hasselborg stayed on a week after Chuen left, working on his orientation. Since the authorities would not let him take along the photographs of Julnar and Fallon, he practiced copying them with pencil and brush until he achieved recognizable likeness. He balked at

Góis's suggestion that he load himself down with a complete suit of armor but finally compromised on a shirt of fine chain mail. He also bought a sword, a dagger with a fancy guard, a big leather wallet like an Earth woman's handbag with a shoulder-strap and many compartments, and a native dictionary of Gozashtandou-Portuguese and Portuguese-Gozashtandou, like all Krishnan books printed on a long strip of paper folded zigzag between a pair of wooden covers.

Then one morning before sunrise, while two of Krishna's three moons still bathed the landscape, he set out from the north gate. He felt a little foolish in fancy hat and monkey jacket but philosophically told himself he had lived through worse things. Góis had been adamant about letting him take his rubbers. Hasselborg, much as he dreaded wet feet, had to admit that rubbers over the soft-leather high Krishnan boots would have looked a little bizarre.

That young man was there to see him off. Hasselborg said: "Have you got that letter of introduction?" He half expected a negative, since Góis had been putting off writing the thing on one excuse or another.

"Sim, here . . . here it is."

Hasselborg frowned. "What's the matter? Sit up all night writing it?" For Góis had a nervous, distracted look.

"Not quite. I had to choose the right wording. Be sure not to break the seals, or the dasht will get suspicious. And whatever happens, remember that Julio Góis esteems you."

A funny sort of farewell, thought Hasselborg; but he simply said: *"Até à vista!"* and tickled his aya's rump with his whip until it went into a brisk trot on the road to Rosid.

III.

Victor Hasselborg rode for several Earth hours alone, mumbling sentences of Gozashtandou to himself. A couple of Earth hours after sunrise, the sun finally broke through the tumbled clouds. Hasselborg pulled up alongside an enormous two-wheeled cart drawn by a bishtar, an elephantine draft-animal with a pair of short trunks, and asked the driver how far it was to Avord.

The driver leaned over, then jerked a thumb towards the rear of the cart. "Twenty-five hoda, master."

Hasselborg knew it was over thirty, but these fellows always deducted a little to make the hearer feel good. The fellow looked like a thinner version of Chuen in his Krishnan disguise, with the same slant-eyed, flattened face, more like that of a Mongoloid like Chuen than a Caucasoid like Hasselborg. Maybe, he thought, that was why Chuen had been sent on his mysterious errand. Fortunately the bishtar driver seemed to find nothing odd about Hasselborg. He merely asked whether it was likely to rain.

Hasselborg said: "If the gods so decide. Thanks for the information." He waved and trotted off, pleased with having passed his first inspection.

He passed other travelers from time to time—riding, driving, or on foot. This was evidently a major highway. Góis had told him that the dasht had it patrolled to keep the danger of robbers and wild beasts to a minimum. Even so, towards the end of the day, a deep animal roar came over the plain, making his aya skitter.

He put on speed and soon sighted the cultivated strips that meant he was nearing Avord. The sun had disappeared into the towering clouds or good, and Hasselborg had felt a sprinkle of rain. Now the clouds were getting black and the wind was bothersome. Perhaps he should put up the collapsible top. He stopped the vehicle and struggled with the contraption for a while; it was evidently one of those one-man tops that could easily be erected by one man, four boys, and a team of horses. Finally the thing yielded, and Hasselborg whipped his animal to a gallop as he drew close to the village.

The houses of Avord were of plaster or concrete, with outside windows few, small, and high. Hasselborg found the inn where Góis had said it would be, and identified it by the animal skull over the door. He hitched his beast and went inside, where he found a big room with benches and a stout, wrinkled fellow with ragged antennae, whom Hasselborg took to be mine host. He rattled off:

"May the stars favor you; I am Kavir bad-Ma'lum. I wish a meal, a bed, and care for my aya."

"That will be five karda, sir," said the innkeeper.

"Four," said Hasselborg.

"Four and a half."

"Four and a quarter."

"Done. Hamsé, see that the gentleman's baggage is stowed and his animal stabled and fed. Now, Master Kavir, will you sit with two of my regular customers? On the left is Master Farrá, who owns one of the outlying farms. The other is Master Qám, on his way from Rosid to Novorecife. What would you? We have roast unha, ásh stew, or I can boil you up a fine young ambar. Eh?"

"I'll take the last," said Hasselborg, not knowing one from the other and wishing he could inspect the kitchen to see if it measured up to his standards of sanitation. "And something to drink."

"Naturally."

Master Farrá, a tall, weather-beaten Krishnan who scratched a lot, asked: "Whence come ye, Master Kavir? From Malayer in the far South? Both your accent and your face suggest it—no offense, of course. I can see ye're a man of quality, so we're delighted to have you sit with us. Well?"

"My parents came from there," said Hasselborg cautiously.

Qám, a small dried-up man with his hair faded to jade, said: "And whither now? To Rosid for the game?"

"I'm headed for Rosid," said Hasselborg, "but as to this game—"

"What's news from Novorecife?" said Qám.

"What are the *Ertsuma* up to now?" said Farrá. (He meant Earthmen.)

"Is it true they're all of one sex?"

"Be ye married?"

"Has the dasht had any more woman trouble?"

"What's this about Hasté's niece at Rosid?"

"What do ye for a living?"

"Like ye to hunt?"

"Are ye related to any of the folk of Rúz?"

"What think ye the weather'll be tomorrow?"

Hasselborg parried or evaded the questions as best he could, until the sight of the landlord with a wooden platter afforded him relief. The relief proved short, however, for the ambar turned out to be some sort of arthropod, something like a gigantic cockroach the size of a lobster, half buried under other ambiguous objects and an oily sauce that had been poured over all. His appetite, ravenous a minute before, collapsed like a punctured balloon.

Evidently the local people ate the thing without qualms, and with these jayhawkers staring at him he'd have to do likewise. He gingerly broke off one of the creature's legs and attacked it with one of the little eating spears. He finally gouged out a pale gob of muscle, braced himself, and inserted the meat into his mouth. Not quite nasty; neither was it good. In fact it had little taste, so the general effect was like chewing on a piece of old inner tube. He sighed and settled down to a dismal meal. Although he had had to eat strange things in the course of his career, Victor Hasselborg remained in his tastes a conservative North American with a preference for steaks and pies.

The innkeeper had meanwhile set down a dish of what looked like spaghetti and a mug of colorless liquid. The liquid proved both hot and alcoholic. Hasselborg's conditioned revulsion almost brought up his gorge, but he steeled himself and gulped.

The "spaghetti" was the worst trial, proving to be a mass of white worms, which wriggled when poked. Nobody at Novorecife had asked him to eat a dish of live worms with chopsticks. Cursing Yussuf Batruni and his addlepated daughter under his breath, he wound up half a dozen of the creatures in a bunch on the sticks. However, when he raised them toward his mouth, they sloomped back into the dish.

Luckily, Qám and Farrá were arguing some point of astrology and failed to notice. The former, Hasselborg observed, also had a dish of worms, now reduced to a few survivors who twitched pathetically from time to time. Hasselborg concentrated on the insect and its accessories, gloomily thinking of the billions of bacteria he was forcing into his system, until Qám picked up his dish and shoveled the rest of the worms from the edge with his spears into his mouth. Hasselborg followed suit, only mildly comforted by the knowledge that the germs of one planet seldom found an organism from another a congenial host. Outside, the rain hissed on the flat roofs.

When the main course was over, the innkeeper set a big yellow fruit before him. Not bad, he thought.

He wiped his mouth and asked: "Did either of you see a man who went through here toward Rosid about ten ten-nights ago?"

"No," said Qám. "I wasn't here. What sort of man?"

"About my height, but less heavy, with a dark-skinned girl. They looked like this." Hasselborg brought the pencil drawings out of his wallet.

"No, nor I either," said Farrá. "Asteratun, have ye seen such people?"

"Not I," said the innkeeper. "Somebody run off with your girl, Master Kavir? Eh?"

"My money," corrected Hasselborg. "I paint for a living, and this rascal took a portrait I'd made of him and went away with out paying. If I catch him—" Hasselborg slapped the hilt of his rapier in what he hoped was the correct swashbuckling manner.

The others giggled. Qám said: "And ye be for Rosid to paint more pictures in hope ye'll be paid this time?"

"That's the general idea. I have introductions."

Farrá, scratching his midriff, said: "I hope ye've better luck than that troubadour fellow last year."

"What was that?"

"Oh, the dasht became convinced the man was a spy from Mikardand. No reason, y'understand; only that our good Jám mortally fears spies and assassins. So, ye see, the poor lute-plucker ended up by being eaten at the games."

Hasselborg gulped, mind racing. There had been something in his indoctrination about the public spectacles of certain Krishnan nations on the Roman model.

He drank the rest of the liquor, which was making his head buzz. He'd better locate a good lawyer in Rosid before he began snooping. Of course he was a lawyer too, but not in Krishnan law. And a lawyer might not be of much avail in a land where a feudal lord had what in European medieval law was called the high justice and could have you killed on his say-so.

"Excuse me," he said, pushing his stool back. "After a day's ride—"

"Certainly, certainly, good sir," said Qám. "Will you be back for supper?"

"I think not."

"Then I hope you leave not too early in the morning, for I should like to ask you more questions of far places."

"We'll see," said Hasselborg. "The stars give you a good night."

"Oh, Master Kavir," said Farrá, "Asteratun gives us the second bed to the right at the head of the stairs. Take the middle, and Qám and I will creep in on the sides later. We'll try not to rouse you."

Hasselborg almost jumped out of his skin as he digested this information. Whatever was making Farrá scratch, the thought of spending a night in the same bed with it filled the investigator with horror. He took Asteratun aside, saying:

"Look here, chum, I paid for a bed, not a third of a bed."

The innkeeper began to protest but, by a lengthy argument, a claim of insomnia, and an extra quarter-kard, Hasselborg got a bed to himself.

Next morning, Hasselborg was up long before his fellow guests, not yet being used to the slower rotation of this world. Breakfast consisted of flat doughy cakes and bits of something that appeared to be meat; organs from an organism, no doubt, but that was all you could say for them.

He washed down a handful of pills, wrapped himself in his cloak, and sallied forth into the drizzle. Faroun looked hurt at being hitched up and driven forth into the rain. He kept peering back at Hasselborg with an indignant expression, balked, and had to be stung with the buggy whip to make him go.

In thinking over the evening's conversation, it struck Hasselborg that Qám's questions had been unnecessarily pointed, as if designed to unmask one who was not what he seemed. Hasselborg wondered if the lamented troubadour, too, had had a letter of introduction.

That reflection started another train of thought: How about those quotations from Shakespeare with which Góis liked to show off his culture? Wasn't there a place in *Hamlet* where somebody gave somebody else a letter of introduction that actually contained instructions to kill the bearer forthwith?

Hasselborg suddenly wanted earnestly to know what was in that carefully sealed letter to the Dasht of Rúz. When he reached Rosid—

The drizzle stopped, and the sun threw a yellow beam down from time to time between great bulks of cloud. Hasselborg rolled a grimly appreciative eye at them. Whatever fate awaited him, at least he might this time avoid catching his death of cold.

He drove hard to make his destination in plenty of time to find himself a safe roost. About noon Krishnan time he pulled up, dismounted, hitched his animal to a bush, and sat on a convenient boulder. As he ate the lunch Asteratun's cook had put up for him, he swept his eye over the gently rolling terrain wih its shrubby vegetation. Small flying things buzzed around him, and a creeping thing something like a land crab scuttled past his feet. A group of six-legged animals fed on the crown of a distant rise.

He was seeing Alexandra's face in the clouds when the faint drumming of animal feet brought his attention back to earth. A pair of riders on four-legged camel-like beasts were approaching. There was a jingle of armor, and he could see slender lances held upright like radio antennae.

With a flash of alarm, he hitched his sword and his dagger around to where he could get at them quickly, though he feared that against two armored men a tyro like himself would have no chance to buckle a swash. True, the look of the men suggested soldiers rather than bandits, but in a country like this the line might be hard to draw.

Hasselborg saw with displeasure that they were going to rein up. Their armor was a composite of plate and chain with a slightly Moorish effect: chain mail over the joints connecting squares and cylinders of plate. As one of them stopped and signaled his mount to kneel, Hasselborg said:

"Good day to you, sirs; may the stars protect you. I'm Kavir bad-Ma'lum."

The man who had dismounted exchanged a brief glance with his companion and advanced towards Hasselborg, saying:

"Is that so? What's your rank?"

"I'm an artist."

The man turned his head back over his shoulder and said: "He says he's an artist." He turned back to Hasselborg. "A commoner, eh?"

"Yes." Hasselborg regretted the word as soon as he spoke it. If these birds were going to turn nasty, he should have claimed the rank of *garm*—knight—or better.

"A commoner," said the man afoot to his companion. "A fair aya you have."

"Glad you like him."

Although the man smiled, as nearly as Hasselborg could interpret Krishnan expressions the smile was predatory rather than friendly. Sure enough the man's next words were:

"We do indeed. Give him to us."

"What?" Hasselborg instinctively reached for his shoulder holster before remembering that his beloved weapon was not with him.

"Surely," continued the man. "Also your sword and those rings and any money you have. You're well-starred that we let you keep your garments."

"Forget not the carriage," said the mounted man. "He looks strong; he can pull it himself, ha-ha!"

"I'll do nothing of the sort," said Hasselborg. "Who are you two, anyway?"

"Troopers of the dasht's highway patrol. Come now, make us no trouble, or we'll arrest you as a spy."

The mounted man said: "Or kill you for resisting arrest."

Hasselborg thought that even if he gave up his goods, they might kill him anyway to prevent complaints. A firm line might be equally risky, but he had no alternative.

"I wouldn't if I were you. I have an introduction to the dasht from an important *Ertsu,* and if I disappeared there'd be a terrible howl."

"Let's see it," said the dismounted soldier.

Hasselborg drew the letter out of his wallet and held it up for the soldier's inspection. The latter put out a hand to take it, but Hasselborg jerked it back, saying:

"The address is enough. What do you want the letter for?"

"To open, fool!"

Hasselborg shook his head as he put the letter away. "The dasht likes his letters untampered with, chum."

"Slay him," said the mounted trooper. "He does but try to fool us with talk."

"A good thought," said the man afoot. "Spear him if he tries to run, Kaikovarr." And the trooper drew sword and dagger and hurled himself upon Hasselborg.

Tumbling backward to get out of range of the wicked blades, Hasselborg got his own sword out just in time to parry a slash. *Clang! Clang!* So far so good, though the trooper addressed as Kaikovarr was guiding his shomal off the road and around toward Hasselborg's rear.

The dismounted man, finding that Hasselborg could stop his crude swings, changed tactics. He stalked forward, blade out horizontally; then suddenly caught

Hasselborg's sword in a *prise* and whipped it out of his grasp. Out shot the blade again; the soldier's legs worked like steel springs as he hopped forward and threw himself into a lunge. The point struck Hasselborg full in the chest, just over the heart.

IV.

Hasselborg thought he was a dead man, until he realized that his hidden mail shirt had stopped the point and that his foe's blade was bent up into an arc. Then his highly educated reflexes came to his rescue. He braced himself and pushed back against the push of the sword, wrapped his left arm around the blade, and heaved upward. The soldier's sword flew out of his hand, to turn over and over in the air as it fell.

The soldier's mounted companion shouted: *"Ao!"* but Hasselborg had no time to devote to him. His right hand had been seeking a pocket. As he stepped forward, the dagger in his opponent's left shot out to meet him. Even faster, Hasselborg's own left seized the fellow's wrist and jerked it forward and to the side, so that the soldier took a step that brought him almost body to body.

Then, Hasselborg's right hand came out of his jacket pocket with the knuckle duster. A right hook to the jaw landed with a meaty sound, and the soldier's knees buckled. After another punch, Hasselborg dropped the brass knucks and snatched his own dagger, forgotten till now.

A blow from behind knocked him to his knees over the body of the soldier. That lance! He rolled over, dragging the feebly struggling soldier on top of him, and found the man's neck with the point of the dagger.

The shomal was mincing around as its rider tried to

36

get into position for another lance thrust, which he found difficult now that Hasselborg was using his companion for a shield. Hasselborg yelled:

"Lay off, or I'll slit your pal's throat!"

"Gluck," said the soldier. "He's killing me!"

The mounted man pulled back a pace. Hasselborg got to his knees again, still holding the dagger ready.

"Now what'll I do with you?" he said.

The soldier replied: "Slay me, I suppose, since you dare not let me go."

"I can't." He was thinking of a scheme which, though corny, might work on the naive Krishnans.

"Why not?" The soldier's lugubrious expression and tone brightened at once.

"Because you're the man."

"What mean you?"

"My astrologer told me I'd get into a fight with a guy like you, whose death horoscope was the same as mine. When were you born?"

"Fourth day, eleventh month of the fifty-sixth year of the reign of King Ghojasvant."

"You're it, all right. I can't kill you because that'd mean my own death on the same day, and conversely."

"Mean you that if I slay you I doom myself to death on the same day?" asked the man gravely.

"Exactly. So we'd better call it off; follow me?"

"Right you are, Master Kavir. Let me up."

Hasselborg released him and quickly recovered his own weapons lest the soldiers start more trouble. However, his victim pulled himself up with effort, tenderly rubbing the places where he had been struck.

"You all but broke my jaw with that brass thing," he grumbled. "Let me look at it. Ah, a useful little device. See, Kaikovarr?"

"I see," said the other soldier. "Had we known you wore mail under that coat, Master Kavir, we'd have not wasted our thrusts upon it. 'Twas hardly fair of you."

Hasselborg said: "It's just as well, though, isn't it?

Looks as though we'd have to be friends whether we want to or not, because of that horoscope."

The dismounted soldier said: "That I'll concede, as the unha said to the yeki in the fable." He sheathed his weapons and walked unsteadily to his kneeling shomal. "If we let you go with your goods, you'll make no mention of our little now-difference?"

"Of course not. And likewise if I hear you're in trouble, I'll have to try to help you out—what's your name, by the way?"

"Garmsel bad-Manyao. Hear this: It was reported that you were asking questions at Asteratun's Inn last night—a rash deed in Rúz, though with that letter I suppose you're in order." He turned to his companion. "Let's be off; this place is ill-starred for us."

"The gods give you a good journey!" said Hasselborg cheerfully. They growled something hardly audible and trotted away.

No doubt Qám had reported him to these birds, Hasselborg thought as he watched them grow small in the distance. This local spy-mania would complicate matters. If questions were dangerous *ipso facto*, he couldn't walk in on the local shamus for a cozy chat as to the whereabouts of Fallon and his paramour.

He finished his lunch, the excitement of his recent encounter subsiding as he pondered his next move. Then he resumed his ride, still thinking. To do a good job, he reflected, he should have a tum-tum tree, but Krishna seemed to lack them.

Hours later, as he approached Rosid, men could be seen working in the cultivated strips. He also passed side roads and more traffic, people walking or riding and driving the remarkable assortment of saddle and draft animals domesticated on Krishna. Some of these beasts pulled carriages of ingenious or even fantastic design.

The sun was nearing the horizon in one of the marvelous Krishnan sunsets when the cheerful sight of a row of gallows trees, complete with corpses, told Hasselborg he was entering the outskirts of the city, reminding him of the verse:

"The only tree that grows in Schotland
Is the bonnie gallows tree—"

In the distance, the sun touched the onion-shaped domes of the city proper with orange and red.

Hasselborg spotted another house, bigger than the suburban bungalows, with an animal skull over the door.

This time the innkeeper proved a silent fellow who made no effort to introduce Hasselborg to his other guests. These guests huddled in small groups and talked in low tones, leading Hasselborg to suspect that he'd stumbled upon a place frequented by questionable characters. That bulky fellow in the corner with the horn-rimmed glasses, for instance, might be another innocent passerby; or again he might be a plainclothes cop keeping an eye on Rosid's underworld.

Hasselborg got a wall seat. He ate a palatable if still mysterious meal alone, until a young man who had been idling at the bar came over and said pleasantly; "Sarhad am I; the stars give you luck. You're new here, I think?"

"Yes," said Hasselborg.

"Mind you?" The youth seated himself beside Hasselborg before the latter could reply. "Some of our old-timers wax tiresome when they drink. Now me, I know when I've had enough; too much spoils your hand in my trade. Foul weather we've had, is't not? Hast seen old sourpuss's daughter? Some hot piece, and they do say she's—"

He rattled on like that until the hot piece herself brought his dinner. Since she was the first Krishnan female he had had a chance to scrutinize from close range, Hasselborg took a good look. The girl was pretty in a wide-cheeked, snub-nosed, pointed-eared way. Her costume, what there was of it, showed the exaggerated physical proportions that Terran artists depicted on girl-calendars. Hasselborg wondered idly whether the artists had first got the idea from photographs of Krishnan women. The Krishnans were obviously mammals even if they did lay eggs.

Sarhad dropped a chopstick. "A thousand apologies, master," he said, squirming around and behind to pick it up.

Something aroused Hasselborg's ever-lively suspicions, and he slid his right hand towards his dagger. A glance showed that Sarhad, while fumbling for his eating-spear with one hand, was busily exploring Hasselborg's wallet with the other.

Hasselborg grabbed Sarhad's right arm with his left hand, whipped out his dagger with his right hand, and dug the point into the young man's lower ribs, below the edge of the table.

"Bring your hand out empty," he said softly. "Let me see it."

Sarhad straightened up and looked at him, his mouth opening and closing like that of a goldfish whose water needs changing, as if thinking that he ought to say something but not knowing quite what. Then his left hand moved like a striking snake and drove the point of a small knife into Hasselborg's side, where the mail-shirt stopped it.

Hasselborg pushed his own dagger until Sarhad said: "*Ohé!* I bleed!"

"Then drop your knife."

Hasselborg heard it fall, felt for it with his foot, and kicked it away. All this had happened so quietly and quickly that nobody else appeared to have noticed.

"Now, young master," said Hasselborg quietly, "we're going to have a little talk."

"Oh, no we're not! If I yell, they'll be all over you."

Hasselborg made the head-motion meaning "no" and said: "I think not. Dips operate alone, so you have no gang; and you'd be dead before they could interfere and so would get no satisfaction from my demise. Finally, the brotherhood of criminals considers it an unfair business practice to commit a crime in a hideout like this for fear of bringing danger upon all. Do you follow me?"

The youth's naturally greenish complexion became even more so. "How know you so much? You look not like one of the fellowship."

"I've been places. Keep your voice down and keep smiling." (Hasselborg emphasized the point with a dig of the dagger.) "This inn caters to the brotherhood, doesn't it?"

"Surely, all men know that."

"Are there others in Rosid?"

"It's true. The big robbers frequent the Blue Bishtar, the spies collect at Douletai's, and the perverts at the Bampusht. While if you'd have an orgy of the *rramandu* drug, or crave to feast on the flesh of men, try the Yemazd."

"Thanks, but I'm not that hungry yet. Now, I want to know about local police methods—"

"*Iyá!* So the haughty stranger has a game—"

"Never mind that; I'm asking the questions! Who's the chief of police?"

"I know not your meaning . . . *ao!* Prick me not; I'll answer. I suppose you'd wish the commandant of the city guard—"

"Is that part of the army?"

"But of course; what think you? Or else the captain of the night watch. They've but now elected a new one, Master Makaran the goldsmith."

"Hm-m-m. Is there any central office where they keep records of your colleagues and other matters having to do with the law?"

"I suppose the archives of the city court—"

"No, not records of trials. I mean a file of records of individuals—with a picture and description of each one, a list of his arrests, and the like."

"I've never heard of aught like that!" cried Sarhad. "Do they thus at the place whence you come? A terrible place it must be, in all truth; not even Maibud god of thieves could make an honest living, let alone a poor mortal cutpurse. How manage they?"

"They get along. Now, where can I buy some artist's supplies?"

The youth pondered. "Oho, so you're one of those who falsify copies of old pictures? I've heard of such; fascinating work it must be. You'd not like an assistant, would you?"

"No. Where—"

"Well, let me see, keep you along Novorecife Pike until you pass through the city wall, then continue for two blocks to the public comfort station, then turn right for one block, then left for half a block, and you'll see the place on the left. The street's called Lejdeú Lane. I remember not the name of the shop, but you can tell it by the—you know, one of those things painters hold in one hand while they mix their hues on it—over the door."

Hasselborg said: "I suppose you could enjoy your meal better without my dagger pricking your skin. If I put it away, will you be a good boy?"

"But surely, master. I'll do aught that you command. Are you absolutely sure you crave no partner? I can show you your way about here, as Sivandi showed Lord Zerré through the maze in the story—"

"Not yet," said Hasselborg, who thought he could trust Sarhad about as far as he could knock him with a feather. He ate with his left hand, keeping his right ready for trouble.

When he finished, he hitched his wallet around and said: "Has anybody around here heard of another stranger from Novorecife coming this way about ten ten-days ago? A man about my height—" He went into his description and produced the sketches.

"No," said Sarhad, "I've seen none like that. I could ask around, though I doubt 'twill help, because I keep close track of new arrivals myself. I make the rounds of the inns, and watch by the city gates, and keep myself generally informed. Little goes on in this city that Goodman Sarhad knows not of, I can tell you.''

Hasselborg let him chatter until he finished. Then, rising, he said: ''Better get that prick taken care of, chum, or you'll get infected.''

''Infected? *Ao!*'' Sarhad for the first time noticed the darkened stain on his jacket. ''The cut's nought, but how abut paying me for my coat? Brand-new; only the second wearing; just got it from Rosid's finest tailor—''

''Stow it; that's only a fair return. The stars give you pleasant dreams!''

Next morning Hasselborg, not trusting these great clumsy locks, checked his belongings to make sure nothing had been stolen. Then he set out afoot. The city gate was decorated with heads stuck on spikes in what Hasselborg considered questionable taste. A couple of spearmen halted him. They let him through after he had waved the letter to the dasht and signed a big register.

He strolled through the city, taking in the sights, sounds, and smells—though the last could not very well be avoided, and caused him to worry about picking up an infection. He was almost run down by a boy-Krishnan on a scooter and then had to jump to avoid a collision with a portly man in the robe, chain, and nose-mask of a physician, whizzing along on the same kind of vehicle.

At the artists' shop, he asked for some quick-drying plaster—he meant plaster of Paris but did not know the Gozashtandou for it—and some sealing wax. With these purchases he returned to his hotel, signing out again at the gate. The calendar girl, having let herself in with a pass key, was doing his room. She gave him a good-morning and a smile that implied she would be amenable to further suggestions. Hasselborg, having other fish to fry, merely gave her the cold eye until she departed.

When alone, he put on his glasses, lit his candle, and

got out his bachelor sewing kit and his little Gozashtandou-Portuguese dictionary. With the plaster he made molds of the three big waxen seals on his letter to the dasht. Then he broke open the seals, carefully so as not to tear the stiff glossy paper, and detached the fragments of the seals from the ribbon that enwrapped the letter by heating the needle from his kit in the candle flame and prying the wax loose from the silk.

He held the letter towards the light from the little window and frowned in concentration. When he had puzzled out the Pitmanlike fishhooks of the writing, he saw that it read:

Julio Góis to the Lord Jám, Dasht of Rúz:

I trust that my lord's stars are propitious. The bearer is a spy from Mikardand who means you nought but ill. Treat him even as he deserves. Accept, lord, assurances of my faithful respect.

V.

Hasselborg, reading the letter through again, did a slow burn and suppressed an impulse to crumple the letter and throw it across the room. That dirty little— Then his sense of humor came to his rescue. The fishes answered with a grin, "Why, what a temper you are in!" And hadn't he been up against this sort of thing often enough not to let it get his goat, or whatever they had in lieu of goats on Krishna?

So, Góis *had* been getting ideas from *Hamlet!* Hasselborg shuddered to think of what might have happened if he'd handed the letter to the dasht without reading it first.

What now? Gallop back to Novorecife to denounce Góis? No, wait. What had possessed Góis to do such a thing? The man had seemed to like him, and he didn't think Góis was off his wavelength. It must be that Hasselborg's presence on Krishna threatened Góis' interests; just how would transpire in due course. If so, if Góis were involved in some racket or conspiracy, his superiors like the pompous Abreu might be also involved. In any case, these Brazzies, while good fellows for the most part, would stick together against a mere *Americano do Norte.*

Could he forge a new letter? It would take a bit of doing, especially since he was not sure that his written Gozashtandou would fool a bright native. By consulting

45

his dictionary, however, and experimenting with a pencil eraser, he found that he could erase the words for "spy" and "ill" and substitute "artist" and "good" for them. He did so, folded the letter, and tied it up. Then with the candle he melted gobs of sealing wax on the ribbon where it crossed itself and used the plaster molds of the original seals to stamp new impressions on the wax just like the old.

Before he mounted his noble aya and galloped off in all directions, however, a little reflection was in order. He went to work with needle and thread on the cuts in his coat left by the affrays of the previous day while he pondered. Since Góis had tried this treacherous trick, he had probably also lied about the direction in which Fallon had gone. As Hasselborg could neither be sure of the direction nor return to Novorecife for more instructions, he would have to do it the hard way. He would have to make a complete circuit of the Terran outpost: rivers, mountains, bandit-infested swamps, and all, investigating all the routes radiating out from Novorecife until he picked up the trail of the fugitives. Of course, if his circuit failed to find the trail, he would have a good excuse to—stop it! he sternly told himself. This is a job.

Meanwhile he had better try the dasht, as originally intended, on the chance that he might be able to pick up a lead at the court. Then a quick getaway with an introduction to some bigwig in Hershid. . .

A brisk, cool wind flapped the pennons on the spires of the onion-shaped domes of the palace and drove great fleets of little white clouds banked deep across the greenish sky. This green-and-white pattern was reflected in puddles around the palace gate. The wind also whipped Hasselborg's cloak as he stood talking to the sentry at the gate. The guard said:

"His High-and-Mightiness will take your letter within, and in an hour he'll come back to tell you to come round tomorrow to learn when the dasht'll give

you an audience. Tomorrow he'll tell you the schedule's
not made up for the next ten-night, and to return next
day. After more delays, he'll tell you to be here twenty
days from now. So ye'll just sit and drink until your
money's gone, and when the day arrives ye'll be told that
at the last minute they gave your time to some more
worshipful visitor, and ye'll have to begin over, like
Qabuz in the story who was trying to climb the tree for
the fruit and always slipped back just afore he reached
it. I envy you not."

Hasselborg jerked the strap of his wallet so that the
coins inside jingled, saying: "D'you suppose a little of
this might help, if you follow me?"

The sentry grinned. "Mayhap, so that ye know how to
go about it. Otherwise ye'll lose your coin to no advantage—"

The guard shut his mouth as the black-clad major-
domo waddled back to the gate, wheezing: "Come at
once, good Master Kavir. The dasht will see you forthwith."

Hasselborg grinned in his turn at the sight of the
guard's drooping jaw and followed his guide across the
courtyard and through the vast entrance. They passed
Krishnans of both sexes in bright clothes of extreme cut,
the women in gowns like those of ancient Crete on earth,
and walked through a long series of halls dimly lit by
lanterns held in wall brackets in the form of scaly,
dragonlike arms. Occasionally a page whizzed by on a
scooter.

Hasselborg was beginning to wish for a bicycle when
they halted at the entrance to a big official-looking
room. At the far end he saw a man talking to another
who sat on a raised seat—the dasht, no doubt. The
major-domo whispered to another functionary. Other
Rúzuma sat at desks along the walls or stood around
as if for want of anything better to do.

The standing man bowed, put on his hat, and went
over to one of the desks to talk to a man there. Then a

drum rolled briefly, a horn went *blat,* and the functionary at the door cried:

"Master Kavir bad-Ma'lum, the distinguished artist!"

Who ever said he was distinguished? thought Hasselborg. Maybe they were trained to do that to impress the yokels. During the long walk, the figure of the dasht grew larger and larger. Hasselborg realized that he was a big fellow indeed, in all directions, with plump ruddy features and bulging green eyes behind thick-lensed spectacles; except for the glasses, altogether like the Krishnan version of a jolly medieval baron.

When Hasselborg reached the end of the line down the middle he doffed his hat, knelt, and cried: "I abase myself before Your Altitude!"

Evidently he had done it right, for Jám bad-Koné said: "Rise, Master Kavir, and advance to kiss my hand. With this recommendation from my good friend Master Julio, all doors shall be open to you. What's your business in Rosid?"

Jám's hand was noticeably dirty, so that the thought of kissing the germ-infested object almost made Hasselborg squirm. Still, he managed the ceremony without a visible tremor, saying:

"I have some small skill at portrait painting, may it please Your Altitude, and thought you or some of your court might like their pictures painted."

"Hm-m-m. Have you mastered the new *ertso* style?"

"I'm tolerably familiar with the methods of the *Ertsuma,* Your Altitude."

"Good. I may have a commission for you. Meanwhile feel free to frequent the court. By the way, how's your hunting?" "I—I've had but small experience—"

"Excellent! My gentlemen pine for amusement, and you shall attend my hunt on the morrow. If you're truly not good at it, so much the better; 'twill afford the rest of us some honest laughter. Be at the lodge an hour before sunrise. It's been a pleasure meeting you."

Hasselborg gave the formula and backed along the

line until he came to the crossline that indicated that he could turn and walk out forwards. As he did so, the drummer gave five ruffles and the bugler a toot after each. The doorman shouted:

"A message from His Supreme Awesomeness, the Dour of Gozashtand!"

Hasselborg stood aside to let the messenger by, then went in search of the Charon who had brought him in. He walked slowly, partly to appear at ease, and partly to watch the others to observe how they behaved. There was even a remote chance of stumbling upon Fallon and Julnar; at least one should keep one's eyes open. . . .

He got lost for a while, wandering from room to room. In one room a pair of bare-breasted women were playing Krishnan checkers while other people kibitzed; in another, a group of Krishnans seemed to be rehearsing for a play. Finally Hasselborg entered a room where Krishnans were snaffling food from a buffet table. He tried some of the stuff cautiously, although the heavy perfume used by the Krishnans kept his appetite down.

"Try some of this," said his neighbor, a man in white satin. "You're the portrait painter, aren't you?"

"Why yes, sir, how did you know?"

"Gossip, gossip. My good sir, with neither war nor jury duty at the moment, how else can one occupy one's time?" Presently they were in friendly chit-chat about superficialities.

"I'm Ye'man," the Krishnan explained, as if everybody should know the patronymic and titles that went with his given name. "This ugly wight on my right is Sir Archman bad-Gavveq the glider champion. Paint him not; 'twill curdle your pigments, as the salt demons curdled the Maraghé Sea in the myth. You should hear Saqqiz read his poem on the theme; a masterpiece in the old epic style—"

When he could get a word in, Hasselborg asked: "Who's the lady in the transparent blue outfit with hair to match?"

"That? Why, that would be Fouri bab-Vazid, of course. You know, old Hasté's niece. Could you not tell by the Western hue of her hair? There are various stories of the whys and wherefores of her staying here; whether that she's enamored of our good dasht, or promoting her uncle's cult, or spying for the dour—But you'll hear all that in due course. You'll be in on the hunt? We should have a good fall, not like last time, when the field crossed the reach and the drum led porridge up the chimney—"

Since his companion's speech seemed to have become suddenly unintelligible, and since mention of hunting reminded him that he had preparations to make, Hasselborg excused himself and sought the exit. He found the major-domo in a kind of sentry box just inside the main entrance to the palace, whence he could keep an eye on the gate.

He said: "Thank you for your courtesy," and dropped a couple of silver karda into the man's hand. As the latter's expression implied that he'd guessed the size of the tip about right, he continued:

"I should like to ask you some questions. The dasht just invited me to go hunting tomorrow, and being new here and no hunter anyway, I don't know how to go about it. What do I need, and where's this lodge, and what's he going to hunt?"

"You'll need a hunting suit, sir, which you can get any good tailor to make you, though he'll have to hasten. His Altitude will probably hunt yekis, since the pair he kept for games died but lately. As for the lodge—"

Hasselborg copied down the directions, thinking that to one who had hunted the most dangerous game, man, riding out and spearing some poor animal would seem pretty stupid. However, orders were orders.

At the appointed hour, Hasselborg presented himself at the dasht's hunting lodge, ten hoda outside the city. The rest of the previous day he had spent buying himself a hunting outfit and a saddle and bridle for Faroun, and moving his gear to another and he hoped a more reputable inn within the walls.

The hunting suit he had obtained ready-made from the Rosido. This swank establishment had also tried to sell him a wagonload of other equipment: a short hunting sword, a canteen, and so on, all of which he had refused. The suit was bad enough—an affair of shrieking yellow satiny material with indecently tight breeches, which made Hasselborg feel as if he were made up to play the toreador in *Carmen*.

Hasselborg heard the racket in front of the lodge long before he reached the spot. The gentlemen were sitting on their ayas in the half-light, drinking mugs of kvad and all talking at once. It did Hasselborg little good to listen to them, because he found that hunting enthusiasts used a vocabulary incomprehensible to outsiders.

Other characters ran about afoot in red suits, some struggling with a pack of six-legged *eshuna* the size of large dogs but much uglier. Somebody pressed a mug of kvad upon Hasselborg, who downed half of it before he had to stop to keep from gagging. The dasht, trotting past, shouted:

"I'll watch you, master painter! If you play not the man, I can always feed you to the yeki, ha ha ha!"

Hasselborg smiled dutifully. A group of servitors were wrestling with a great net and a set of poles that went with it; another pair was lugging out a rack in which were stuck a couple of dozen long lances. (They must import timber for their bows and spears, thought Hasselborg; this country seems to have few decent trees.) As the workmen set up the rack in front of the lodge, the hunters began guiding their mounts past it to pick out lances. As Hasselborg snatched his, he heard the dasht shouting behind him:

". . . and if I find some knave's slain our quarry without absolute necessity, I'll do to him what I did to Sir Daviran—"

Somebody blew a horn that sounded full of spit. The mess of men and animals pulled itself into formation and streamed out onto the road—eshuna and their handlers first, then hunters with their lances, then more servants with the net and other equipment like gongs and unlit torches.

The parade stretched itself out over a longer and longer piece of road as the eshuna pulled away from the hunters and they from the slower assistants in the rear. Hasselborg rode silently at a trot, his sword banging against his left leg. It seemed an hour, although the sun had not yet risen.

"A good rally," said a vaguely familiar voice. Ye'man, his smörgasbord acquaintance of the day before, pulled up alongside. "Let's hope the ball scrambles not in the beard."

"Yes, let's," said Hasselborg, not having the faintest notion of what the man meant. The loud voices died away, leaving only the drumming of hoofs, the rattle of equipment, and the occasional mewing of the eshuna up front. Hasselborg, whose riding muscles had never got properly hardened at Novorecife, found the whole thing very tiresome.

As the sun came up in the egregious glory of a Krishnan sunrise, the hunt left the road and headed up a shallow valley. Hasselborg, in his first taste of cross-country riding, found that he had to pay full attention to simply staying in his seat. As the bigger animals of his fellow-hunters were pulling ahead, he spurred his aya to an occasional canter to keep pace.

On they went, up one gentle slope and down another, over cultivated fields—which would not be of much use to their owners thereafter—and through brush. The hunt came to a low stone wall. Eshuna and aya flowed over it in graceful leaps—except Hasselborg's aya, which, having been trained for road work only, refused the jump, almost spilling its rider. As the rest of the party began to leave it behind, the animal galloped in a wide curve around the end of the wall and scurried to catch up. Hasselborg swore under his breath.

Next time he had to detour around a fence which the rest jumped. This was getting more tiresome every minute, though no doubt his aya showed better sense than those that let themselves be forced to jump.

A horn blew raucous notes up front, and the eshuna gave a weird howl. Hasselborg could have sworn they howled in parts. Everybody broke into a run. Now Hasselborg found himself really falling behind. Another detour, around a wall, put him back among the servants.

At the next obstacle, he spurred his mount right at a fence, holding the reins tightly to keep it from turning, and letting go at the last minute as he'd been taught. The aya hesitated, then jumped. While Hasselborg went up with it all right, he kept on rising after the beast had started down, with disastrous results. In his fall, he caromed off its rump into the moss.

For an instant he saw stars. The stars gave place to the bellies of the servants' ayas leaping the wall after him. They looked as though they were coming right down on top of him with all six hoofs. Somehow they all missed him.

Then as the universe stopped whirling, he climbed to his feet. A sharp stone had bruised his fundament; he had bitten his tongue; his pants were burst open at the right knee; his sword belt had somehow got wound around his neck; and altogether he was not feeling his best.

The servants were disappearing over the next rise, and the notes of the horn and the weird howl of the eshuna died in the distance.

"Give me an automobile," he muttered, picking up his lance and limping toward his aya. Faroun, however, wanted a rest and a quiet graze. It stopped eating as he neared it, rolled an indignant eye, and trotted off.

"Come here, Faroun!" he said sternly. Faroun walked a little farther away.

"Come here!" he yelled, thinking: *I said it very loud and clear; I went and shouted in his ear.* . . . but no heed did the beast pay. Hasselborg was tempted to throw a stone at the perverse creature but refrained for fear of driving it farther away.

He tried stalking. That did no good either, for the aya looked up between mouthfuls of moss and kept a safe distance between itself and its owner. Perhaps he would just have to walk the animal until it tired. He grimly plodded toward it.

A Krishnan hour later, he was still at this forlorn pursuit, when something erupted out of a little bushy hollow with a frightful roar and charged. Hasselborg had just time to swing the point of his lance toward this menace before it swerved and leaped upon the truant Faroun. There was a crunch of neck bones, and the aya was down with the newcomer standing over it. Hasselborg recognized the animal from descriptions as a yeki, the very beast they were after—a brown furry carnivore about the size of a tiger, but resembling an overgrown mink with an extra pair of legs to hold up its middle.

For a few seconds, it stood watching Hasselborg and making guttural noises, as if wondering whether to drag off the dead aya or to try to dispose of this other prey, too. Then it slithered forward towards the man.

Hasselborg resisted the impulse to run, knowing that such a move would bring it on his back in a matter of seconds. He wished harder than ever for a gun. Since wishing failed to produce one, he gripped his lance in both hands and stepped towards the beast, shouting:

"Get out of here!"

The yeki advanced another step, growling more loudly. Presently Hasselborg, still shouting, had the lance point in the creature's face. As he thought of trying for an eye, the yeki reared up on its four hind legs and batted at the point with its forepaws. Hasselborg sent a jab into one paw, whereat the beast jumped back a step, roaring furiously.

Hasselborg followed it, keeping his spear ready. How long could he keep this up? There was little chance of his killing it singlehanded. . . .

Then the howl of the eshuna came across the downs. The hunt was flowing past behind a nearby rise. Hasselborg shouted:

"Hey! I've got him!"

This was perhaps a debatable point, and in any case he did not seem to have been heard. He screamed:

"Over here! Yoicks, tally-ho, and all that sort of thing!"

Somebody swerved over the crest of the rise, and then in no time they were all pounding towards him. The yeki began to slink off, snarling right and left. The eshuna swarmed around the yeki, howling like banshees but not closing, while their quarry roared and foamed and made little dashes at them.

Then the servants unfolded the net, and four of them, still mounted, hoisted it by the corners on poles as if it were a canopy. They dashed forward and dropped the net over the yeki, who in another second was rolled up in it, chewing and clawing at the meshes in a frenzy of rage.

"Good work!" roared the dasht, clapping Hasselborg on the back so hard as almost to knock him down. "We'll have our game now after all. Your mount dead? Take mine. *Ao,* you!" he shouted at a servitor. "Give Master Kavir your aya. You, Kavir, keep the beast with my compliments, for the manful part you've played."

Hasselborg was too conscious of his bruises to worry about how the servitor should get back to Rosid. He salvaged his saddle, mounted, and rode home with the rest, acknowledging their praises with smiles but saying little. When they got back to the road, they passed a big bishtar wagon driven by men in Jám's livery, evidently to bring home the captive.

The dasht told him: "We're having an intimate supper this night; third hour after sunset. But a few friends—you know, people like Namaksari the actress and Chinishk the astrologist. Come and we'll talk of that portrait, will you?"

"I thank Your Altitude," said Hasselborg.

Back in Rosid, he spent some time window shopping. Although he knew better than to load himself down with more chattels than he absolutely needed, the temptations of Batruni's unlimited expense account proved too great. He arrived back at his hotel bearing an umbrella with a curiously wrought handle, a small telescope, a map of the Gozashtando Empire, and an ugly little ivory god from some backward part of the planet. When he got home—after wasting another hour by getting lost in the crooked streets—he felt sticky and suspected himself of being stinky as well, not have had a bath since leaving Novorecife.

When he asked the landlord about baths, the latter referred him to a public bathhouse down the street. He went down to have a look at the place, identified by a sea shell big enough for a bathtub over the door. He paid his way in, then found to his dismay that the bath customs of Rúz were much like those of Japan. While as an ex-married man he had no strong inhibitions along that line, a look at the male Krishnans convinced him that he'd never pass as one under those circumstances. For one thing, Krishnans had no navels.

He returned to his inn and told the landlord: "Sorry, chum, but I just remembered—I'm under a religious penance not to bathe in public. Could you furnish me with a tub and some hot water in my room?"

The landlord scratched the roots of his antennae and reckoned he could.

Hasselborg added: "Also I should like some—uh—" What was the word for "soap"? "Never mind; I'll tell you later." He climbed the stairs on aching feet to consult his dictionary in private, learning that there was no such word in Gozashtandou. Evidently the stuff had not yet been invented. No wonder the Krishnans used perfume!

The scullery maids who arrived in a few minutes with tub, brush, and buckets of hot water showed an embarrassing interest in their guest's eccentricity, wanted to scrub his back, and had to be curtly dismissed. He'd have to depend upon a prolonged soak and a vigorous scrub to dislodge dirt and deadly germs. No more soapless expeditions to strange planets for him, even if he had to smuggle the stuff past the Viagens' vigilance!

As soon as the water had cooled to a bearable temperature, he lowered himself into it as far as he could go and settled the back of his head against one of the handles with a sigh of relief. Boy, that felt good on his poor beat-up feet! With a glance at the door to make sure the bolt was home, he burst into song. He had just gotten to:

"He knew the world was round-o,
  He knew it could be found-o—"

when a loud knock interrupted him.

"Who's there?" he said.

"The Law! Open up!"

"Just a minute," he grumbled, getting out of his tub and trying to dry himself all over at once. What was he getting into now, in the name of Ahuramazda?

"Open right away or we'll break the door!"

Hasselborg groaned internally, wrapped the towel around himself, and slid back the bolt. A man in black entered, followed by two others in official-looking armor.

The first said: "You're arrested. Come."

VI.

"What for?" said Victor Hasselborg, looking as innocent as a plush teddy bear.

"You shall learn. Here, drop that sword! You think not that we let prisoners go armed, do you?"

"But somebody might steal—"

"Fear not; we'll set the seal of the dasht upon your door, so that if acquitted you'll find your gear intact. Not that you will be. Hasten, now."

The dasht, thought Hasselborg, must somehow have found out about his alteration of that letter from Góis. He was given little time for reflection, though, for they bundled him out of the hotel and onto a led aya. Then they set off at breakneck speed through the city, yelling *"Byant-hao!"* to clear their way.

The jail, about a block from the ducal palace, looked like—a jail. The jailer proved a wrinkled individual with one antenna missing.

"How now?" cried this one. "The gentleman from Novorecife, I'll be bound! Ye'll wish one of our better chambers, won't ye? A fine view of Master Raú's countinghouse, and the rates no higher than in some of the more genteel inns, heh heh. What say ye, my fine lad?"

Hasselborg understood that he was being offered a cell to himself if he could pay for it, instead of being

58

tossed in the general tank. He took the jailer up on his offer with only a slight haggle. While the jailer and the black-clad one fussed with papers, an assistant jailer led Hasselborg to his cell. This contained a chair, which was something, and being on the second story had fair lighting despite the smallness of the barred window. More importantly from Hasselborg's viewpoint, it seemed fairly clean, though he would still have given a lot to know whether the previous tenant had anything contagious.

He asked: "What's the head jailer's name?"

"Yeshram bad-Yeshram," replied the assistant jailer.

"Will you please tell him I should like to see him at his convenience?"

The jailer arrived with disconcerting promptness, saying: "Look ye, Master Kavir, I'm no monster joying in the sufferings of my wards, like the giant Damghan in the legend, nor yet a saintly philanthropist putting their welfare ahead of my own. If they can pay for extras to lighten their last hours, why, say I, why not let 'em have 'em? I had Lord Hardiqásp in my personal charge for thirty ten-nights ere they headed him, and before they took him away he said: 'Yeshram, ye've made my captivity almost a pleasure!' Think of it! So fear not that if ye treat Yeshram right, obey the rules, not try to escape, not form seditions with the other prisoners, and pay your way, ye'll have little to complain of, heh heh."

"I understand," said Hasselborg. "Right now I most want information. Why am I here at all?"

"That I know not precisely, save that your indictment reads 'treason'."

"When am I to have a hearing? Do they let you have lawyers?"

"Why, as for your hearing, know ye not that ye're to be tried this afternoon?"

"When? Where?"

"The trial will take place in the chambers of justice, as of always. As to the precise time, I can't tell you; perchance the trial's beginning even now."

"You mean one doesn't attend one's own trial in Rúz?"

"Of course not, for what good would that do? Anything the prisoner said in his defense would be a lie, so why ask him?"

"Well then, when the trial's over, can you find out what happened?"

"For a consideration I can."

Left alone, Hasselborg wondered whether to unmask himself as an Earthman. They would be at least a little more careful how they treated him. Or would they? At Novorecife they had specifically warned him not to count on any interplanetary prestige. Since the Interplanetary Council had ordered a policy of strict nonimperialism and noninterference in Krishnan affairs, the native states did pretty much as they pleased to the *Ertsuma* in their midst. Sometimes they pleased to treat them with honor, and at other times they looked upon them as legitimate prey. When people protested some particularly atrocious outrage upon a visiting Earthman, the I.C. blandly replied that nobody compelled Earthmen to go there, did they?

Moreover, such a revelation might jeopardize the success of Hasselborg's mission. Altogether he decided to stick to his rôle of Krishnan artist for the time being, at least until all its possibilities had been exhausted.

The jailer reported back: "It seems ye came hither with some letter from an *Ertsu* at Novorecife, saying ye be an artist or something. Well, now, that would have been all right, only this morning, while ye were out hunting with the dasht, who comes in but a messenger from this same *Ertsu,* with another letter. This letter would be about some other matter, some different thing entirely, ye see, but at the end of't the *Ertsu* puts in one little sentence, something like: 'Has that Mikardando spy I sent on to you with a letter of introduction arrived yet, and if so what have ye done with him?' That makes the dasht suspicious, the gods blind me if it don't, and he takes the original letter—the one ye brought—and looks it over carefully, and sees where it looks like as some knave's rubbed out part of the writing and put in some new words over the old. Tsk, tsk, ye spies must think our dasht a true simpleton."

"What happened at the trial?" asked Hasselborg.

"Oh, now, the dasht presented his evidence, and the lawyer for the defense said he could find nought to be said in your favor, no indeed he couldn't, so the court sentenced you to be eaten in the game, day after tomorrow."

"You mean they're going to stick me in an arena with that yeki I helped catch?"

"Surely, surely, and great joke the dasht thought it, heh, heh. Not that I have aught against you, Master Kavir, but it do seem like the gods taking a hand to blow up a man with his own firework, now don't it? But take it not too hard, lad, all must go when their candle's burnt down. Truly sorry am I to lose so fine a guest so soon, however; truly sorry."

I weep for you, the Walrus said; I deeply sympathize, thought Hasselborg. He said: "Never mind that. What happens at this game?"

"A parade, and fireworks, and a show at the stadium —races afoot and mounted, boxing and wrestling, you being eaten, and finally a battle between some tailed Koloftuma and some of our own condemned criminals with real weapons. That'll be an event worth waiting for; too bad ye'll not be there to see it!"

Although not a vain man, Hasselborg felt a slight pique at not being deemed good enough for the main attraction. "What's this game in celebration of?"

"Oh, now, some astrological conjunction; I misremember which. They come along every few ten-nights, that is the well-omened ones do, if ye believe in that stargazing foolishness, and the apprentices quit work to riot in the streets and the dasht stages a big party for his court with a circus for the common folk."

"Do I fight this critter with weapons?"

"Oh, my honor, no! Ye might hurt the beast or even slay it. Time was when the victim was given a wooden pretend sword for the amusement of the people, but one of them—an *Ertsu* 'twas, too—hurt the eye of the favorite yeki of the dasht, so he ordered that thereafter they should be sent in with nought in their hands, heh heh. 'Tis quite a sight; blood all over the place.''

Hasselborg leaned forward intently. "Did you say an earthman was eaten at one of these celebrations?''

"Aye, to be sure he was. What's so singular about that? 'Tis true it's been said in Rúz that the dasht ought to give special consideration to the *Ertsuma,* because, forsooth, 'tis rumored that they have weapons of such might that one of their fireworks would blot Rosid off the face of the planet. But the dasht will have nought of't, saying, so long as he's Dasht of Rúz he'll see that justice is administered in the good old Rúzo way—nobles to have precedence over commoners, commoners over foreigners, and all over slaves. That way every wight knows where he stands and what he faces; start making exceptions, and where's justice? For isn't consistency the essence of justice? Though I be no doctor of laws, meseems he has the right of it, now don't he?''

Hasselborg looked at the ceiling in thought. Evidently the fact of his being an Earthman, if made known, might prove more a liability than an asset. "Yeshram, what would you do if you had . . . let's say a half-million karda?''

"*Ohé!* Think ye to befool me, Master Kavir? Ye've no such sum on your person, for we looked into that when ye came hither. That's a dasht's ransom. Let's talk sense, lad, in the little time ye have left.''

"I'm serious. What would you do?''

"Truly I know not. Quit this dirty post, surely. Buy up some estates and have a try at being a gentleman. Perhaps even get my eldest male-chick knighted in time. I know not. There's hardly a limit to what one could do with so vast a sum. But tantalize me not or I'll take it ill.''

"Even if I don't have that much on me, I might be able to get hold of it."

"So? Tell me not that besides being a spy and a picture painter, ye're a spinner of fine tales of fire-breathing dragons and invisible castles to boot?"

"No, this is no romance. I've got a letter of credit on deposit at Novorecife that's worth that amount, and if somebody could get me out of here I'd naturally be willing to pay liberally."

Now the jailer was thoughtful. "But how could I get this money? How can I be sure 'tis there to be had?"

"You'd have to send somebody to fetch it. Let me see —I know who'd be glad to go—a trooper of the highway patrol named Garmsel bad-Manyao. If you can get word to him, he'll ride day and night to Novorecife with a draft from me on that letter."

The jailer made the negative head-motion. "I see difficulties, lad. We'd have to fake a delivery, ye see, and that means letting more people into the scheme and paying them off. Then, too, no matter how fast this soldier friend of yours rode, he couldn't make Novorecife and back by the time you were down the yeki's gullet. Moreover, if ye didn't appear for the games, the dasht would have my head for it, or at least my post. No, I couldn't chance it, especially I couldn't chance it before I had the money in hand. Once I had it in hand, of course, I'd defy any wight but the dasht himself."

After they had brooded in silence a while, the jailer resumed: "Perhaps I can get you through the games alive, despite all. Yeshram has a scheme. If ye'll give me the draft now, I'll do my best, and if I fail, ye'll have no use for gold anyway, will ye now?"

Hasselborg, disinclined to trust the jailer so far, countered: "Tell you what. I'll write you a draft for a quarter-million karda now, and another other quarter-million when I get out."

"But how know I ye'll pay me the second half, once ye're free and fleeing with the eshuna baying on your track?"

"How do I know you'll get me out once you get your hands on the first instalment? Wouldn't you be happier with me inside the yeki and so unable to expose our little deal? Not that I distrust you, Master Yeshram, but you see how it is. You trust me, I trust you. Whereas if we fail to agree and I get eaten, you'll have nothing but what I've got on me, which won't set you up in any baronial splendor."

They haggled for an hour before Hasselborg won his points. Yeshram, for instance, wanted a half-million net, while Hasselborg insisted on a half-million gross, out of which Yeshram would have to pay such other bribes as proved necessary.

Finally Hasselborg wrote his draft, saying: "What's this scheme of yours?"

"I mislike to tell you, since a secret known to many is no secret at all, as it says in the Proverbs of Nehavend. Howsomever, do but face the beast boldly and ye'll find him perchance less inclined to devour you than is his wont."

Then Hasselborg had the excruciating experience of waiting for two Krishnan days and nights until the time neared for his execution. He tried to read a textbook on Gozashtando law, which Yeshram furnished him, but found it tough going—the law here was mostly precedent, and Hasselborg was not fluent enough in the written language yet to read it with any ease. He paced, smoked, ate little, and spent half-hours gazing sentimentally at Alexandra's tiny handkerchief.

He also kept sending the assistant jailer out to ask if there were any news from Trooper Garmsel yet. He knew there would not be but could not help hoping for a miracle. He got some small comfort out of the fact that he had exercised enough self-control to strike this bargain with Yeshram for less than half the total amount his letter of credit had been good for; there had been a time, when Yeshram was hesitating, when he'd been strongly tempted to throw the entire amount at the jailer, although he knew that would be money wasted.

The second afternoon after his arrival, Yeshram came in, saying: "Be ye ready? Courage, my master. No, no, for the hundredth time, no news. Garmsel would need a glider towed by trained aqebats, like Prince Bourudjird in the legend, to have got back by now. Why shake ye so? I run a risk like unto yours, don't I?"

They loaded Hasselborg into a kind of cage on wheels and drove it across the city to the stadium. Armed men let him out and led him to a room under the tiers of seats, where they watched him silently while noises of the entertainments filtered in from outside. One said to the other:

"The crowd's in a bad mood today."

"A dull performance," said the other man: "They do say the dasht has been too much wrapped up in his love-life to put the care he should upon the events."

Then silence again. Hasselborg lit a Krishnan cigar and offered one to each of his guards, who took them with a grunt of thanks.

More waiting.

At last a man stuck his head in the door and said: "Time!"

The guards nodded to Hasselborg, one saying: "Leave your jacket here. Stand up and let us search you." After a last-minute frisk, they led him into one of the tunnels connecting the dressing rooms with the arena.

At the end of the tunnel was a heavy gate of criss-crossed iron bars. A man swung it open with a creak. Hasselborg looked back. The guards had a tight grip on their halberds in case he should get any funny ideas about bolting.

Hasselborg, seeing no alternative, stuck his thumbs into his belt and strolled out into the arena with elaborate unconcern.

The place reminded him of some of the bowls he'd played football in years before as a college undergraduate; he had played fullback. This arena was a bit too small, however, for football; more like a bull ring than a North American athletic theater. The seats pitched down at a steep angle. The floor was sunk a good twenty feet below the lowest tier of seats so that there would be no question of a mighty leap into the audience. In front of the first row of seats, guards paced a catwalk. Could he somehow get one of those halberds and do a pole vault up to the catwalk? Not likely, especially for one who, while something of an athlete in his day, had never practiced pole-vaulting.

The sky was overcast, and a dank wind whipped the pennons on the flagpoles around the upper edge of the stadium. The dasht sat in his box, wrapped in his cloak and too high up for his expression to be seen.

As the gate clanged shut behind Hasselborg, he saw a gate on the far side of the arena open and his friend the yeki issue from another tunnel.

The people in the stands gave a subdued roar. Hasselborg, facing this particular jabberwock without any vorpal sword, stood perfectly still. If Yeshram had had a bright idea, let it work now!

The yeki padded slowly forward, then stopped and looked about it. It looked at Hasselborg; it looked at the people above it in the audience. It grumbled, walked a few paces in a circle, flopped down on the sand, yawned, and closed its eyes.

Hasselborg stood still.

The audience began to make crowd noises, louder and louder. Hasselborg could catch occasional phrases, the rough Gozashtandou equivalent of "Kill dose bums!" Objects began to whizz down into the arena—a jug, a seat cushion.

Here a couple of Gozashtanduma were punching each other; there another was throwing vegetables in the direction of the dasht's box; then some more were pushing one of the guards off the catwalk. The guard landed in the sand with a jangle, got up with an agility astonishing for one burdened with full armor, and ran for the nearest exit, though the yeki merely rolled an eye at him before shutting it again. Another guard was beating a group of enraged citizens over the head with the shaft of his halberd. Other members of the audience were prying up the wooden benches and making a fire.

"Master Kavir," cried a voice over the uproar, "this way!"

Hasselborg turned, saw that the barred gate was open a crack, and walked quickly out without waiting to see how the riot developed. One of the assistant jailers shut the gate behind him.

"Come quickly, sir." He followed the man out of the warren of passages into the street, where they put him back into the cage on wheels. Thunder rumbled overhead as the conveyance rattled on its springless wheels over the cobbles back toward the jail. They were nearly there when the rain began. The driver lashed his ayas and yelled *Byant-hao!"*

"We did it, heh heh," said Yeshram afterward.

"How?" asked Hasselborg, who was rigging a string across his cell to hang his wet clothes on.

"Well, now, then, I suppose 'twill do no great harm to tell you, since the deed's done and if one's betrayed all are lost. 'Twas simple enough; I bribed Rrafun the beast-keeper into keeping the yeki awake all night by squirting water into its cage. Then I prevailed upon him to let it eat an entire boar unha just before the game. So, to make a long story short, 'twas far more interested in sleep, sweet sleep, than in forcing one Mikardando spy into an already overstuffed paunch. Be ye adequately equipped for blankets? I'd not have you perish of the rheum owing me half my reward. Let's hope Garmsel makes a speedy return, ere the dasht thinks to look into his pet's curious lack of appetite."

The rest of that day passed and the night that followed it, however, without word from either the soldier or the dasht. Hasselborg tried to console himself with the thought that another of these games would not be along for some days at least, until the next conjunction — Although no doubt, if sufficiently annoyed, Jám could have Hasselborg executed out of hand.

After dinner there were sounds of voices and movement in the jail. Presently Yeshram came in with Garmsel, the latter wet and worn-looking.

"You still live, Master Kavir?" said the latter. "Thank the stars! I believed it not when this knave, my friend Yeshram, said so, for 'tis notorious that of all slippery liars he's the chief and slipperiest. At least now I'll not have to worry about my death horoscope for a time."

"What's this?" asked Yeshram. "What death horoscope?"

"Just a private understanding between Garmsel and myself," said Hasselborg, who did not want the soldier's faith in the psuedo-science undermined by the jailer's skepticism. "How'd you make out?"

"I got it," said Garmsel. "The ride to Novorecife I made in record time on my good shomal, but coming back I was slowed by having to lead three great stout pack-ayas behind me with the bags of gold. 'Tis in the foyer below, and I trust there'll be no unseemly forgetting my just recompense for this deed."

"When has Yeshram forgotten a faithful friend?" said Yeshram.

"Never, the reason being you've never had one. But come; pay me my due and I'll back to barracks to dry. *Fointsaq,* what weather!"

When Yeshram returned to Hasselborg's cell, the prisoner said: "Since it's still raining, wouldn't this be a good night to get me out of here?"

The jailer hesitated. Hasselborg read into the hesitation a feeling that now that he had the money, it might be safer to hold Hasselborg after all rather than risk his present gain in trying to double it. Careful, Hasselborg told himself; whatever you do, don't show despair or fly into a rage.

Hasselborg said: "Think, my friend. As you've said, the dasht may do some investigating sooner or later. Something seems to have interfered with it so far, and rumor tells me he's having love-life trouble. Now, when he does come around, wouldn't you rather have me far away from here, making arrangements to send you another quarter-million, than here where the dasht can lay his red-hot pincers on me and perhaps wring the truth from me?"

"Certainly, such was my idea, too," said Yeshram readily—a little too readily, Hasselborg thought. "I but pondered how to effect this desired end of ours. Ye'll want your gear, won't ye? 'Twere not prudent to leave bits of it lying about Rosid for the agents of His Altitude to find and perhaps trace you by. What stuff have ye, and where's it stowed?"

Hasselborg gave him the information.

Yeshram said: "Clothe yourself for a speedy departure, lad, and try to snatch some sleep, for the arrangements will take some hours to perfect. By which road would ye wish to flee?"

"The road to Hershid, I think."

"Then leave all to Yeshram. We'll have you out as neat as the Gavehon thief spirited away King Sabzavarr's daughter. And if ye get clean away, when ye're feeling that wonderful relief that'll be yours, think whether Yeshram mayhap deserves not a mite extra for his trouble, heh heh. May the stars guide you."

Next to Earthmen, perhaps the most mercenary race in the galaxy, thought Hasselborg. He found that his physical organism perversely refused to sleep, however. He tossed on his bunk, paced the floor, and tossed some more. His sleeping pills were still in his room at the inn and so out of reach. Over half this interminable night must have gone past when to his delight he at last found himself getting sleepy. He threw himself down on the bed, closed his eyes, and instantly was aroused by the opening of his cell.

"Come," said a figure holding a candle.

Hasselborg jumped up, whipped his cloak around him, and strode out the door. As he got closer to the figure, he saw that it was masked and that it held a cocked crossbow in one hand. As he brushed past, he was sure that he recognized the eyes of one of the assistant jailers. The size and voice were right, too. However, no time for that now.

Below, he found another masked man standing guard with a crossbow over the jailer and his remaining assistant, both thoroughly bound and gagged. Yeshram caught Hasselborg's eye and wiggled his antennae in the Krishnan equivalent of a wink. Then out they went into the rain, where a man held three saddled ayas.

Hasselborg's companions stopped to uncock their bows and remove their masks. They were two of the assistant jailers, sure enough. All three, without a word, mounted and set off at a canter for the east gate.

Hasselborg, practically blind in the rain and darkness, hung on to his saddle, expecting every minute to be thrown out or to have his mount skid and fall on the wet stones. He concentrated so hard on keeping his seat that he did not see his companions pull up at the gate. When his own mount stopped, too, he almost did take a header.

One of his deliverers was shouting at a spearman: "Fool, where is he? Who? Why, the prisoner who escaped from the jail! He came through here! If ye caught him not, that means he's out of Rosid and away! Stand aside, idiots!"

The gate swung open. Hasselborg's escort spurred their animals to a furious run, although how they could see where they were going mystified the investigator. He bounced along behind them as best he could, barely able to make them out in the murk. A glob of soft mud thrown up by one of their hoofs smote him in the face, spreading over his features and for a few minutes cutting him off entirely from the world. By the time he could see again, they were just visible ahead, and the lanterns of the city gate could no longer be seen behind.

After a few minutes more of this torture, one of them held up an arm and they slowed. Before he knew it, Hasselborg came upon his buggy, parked on the edge of the road. A man was holding the head of his new aya, which was already hitched up.

"Here ye are, Master Kavir," said a voice in the dark. "Ye'll find your gear in the back of the carriage; we packed it as best we could. Waste no time on the way, and show no lights, for a pursuit might be sent after you. May the stars watch over you!"

"Good night, chums," said Hasselborg, handing over the reins of the aya he had ridden to the man who was holding the carriage. The man swung into the saddle, and all three splashed off into the dark.

Hasselborg got into the buggy, gathered up reins and whip, released the brake, and started off at the fastest pace he could manage without blundering off the road—a slow walk.

VII.

When the sky began to lighten, Hasselborg had been alternately dozing and then waking up just in time to stop himself from falling out of the vehicle. He had discovered one of the very few advantages that an animal-drawn vehicle has over an automobile—that the animal can be trusted not to run off the road the second the driver takes his mind off his business.

The rain had stopped, although the sky was still overcast. Hasselborg yawned, stretched, and felt monstrously hungry. No, his friends of the Rosid jail, who had thought of so much else, had not thought to provision the buggy with food. Moreover, no villages were in sight. Thank the pantheon they'd packed his pills and disinfectants, without which he felt himself but half a man!

He whipped his new aya, Avvaú by name, to a brisk trot and for some hours rolled steadily over the flat plain. Finally a ranchhouse provided him with a meal. He bought some extra food to take with him, drove on a few miles, and pulled up where the road dipped down to a ford across a shallow stream. He forced the aya to draw the buggy downstream around the first bend, where the walls of the gully hid him and his vehicle from the view of the road. There he caught an uneasy nap in the carriage before going on.

Just before sunset, the clouds began to break. The

road was now bending and weaving around the end of a range of rugged hills: the Kodum Hills if he remembered his map. Here were trees—real trees, even if they did look like overgrown asparagus-ferns with green trunks and rust-red fronds.

The sunset grew more gorgeous by the minute, the undersides of the clouds displaying every hue from purple to gold, and emerald sky showing between. Hasselborg thought: If I'm supposed to be an artist, maybe I should learn to act like one. What would an artist do in a case like this? Why, stop the buggy on the top of a rise and make a color sketch of the sunset, to be turned into a complete painting at leisure.

The aya was trotting toward just such a rise—a long spur that projected out from the dark Kodum Hills into the flat plain. The animal slowed to a walk as it breasted the slope, while Hasselborg fussed with his gear to extract his painting equipment. Just short of the crest, he pulled on the reins and set the brake. The aya began munching moss as Hasselborg got out and dragged his easel up to the top of the rise. As his head came above the crest, so that he could see over the spur into the plain beyond, he stopped short, all thoughts of surpassing Claude Monet driven from his head.

There on the plain ahead, a dozen men on ayas and shomals were attacking a group of vehicles. The attackers were riding up one side and down the other shooting arrows, while several men in the convoy shot back. The first vehicle had been a great bishtar cart, but the bishtar, perhaps stung by an arrow, had demolished the cart with kicks and gone trumpeting off across the plain.

Hasselborg dropped his easel and snatched out the little telescope he had bought in Rosid. With that he could make out details—one of the defenders lying on the wagons; another lighting a Krishnan firework resembling a Roman candle. (Hasselborg knew that the Krishnan pyrotechnic was not gunpowder, but the collected spores of some plant, which, while it did not explode, made a fine sizzle and flare when ignited.) The firework spat several balls of flame, whereupon the movement of the attackers became irregular. One shomal, perhaps singed by a fireball, broke away and ran across the plain towards Hasselborg, who could see its rider kicking and hauling in a vain effort to turn it back.

Shifting his telescope back to the convoy, Hasselborg saw a female Krishnan in the last carriage. Though she was too far to recognize in the fading light, he could see that she wore clothes of good cut and quality. She was also of an attractive size and shape and seemed to be shouting something to somebody up forward.

Although Victor Hasselborg was a seasoned and self-controlled man, who seldom let himself be carried away by emotion, this time his adrenal glands took the bit in their teeth and ran away with him. Even as he told himself sternly that he ought to hide until the fracas was over and then continue quietly to Hershid, he ran back to the carriage, unhitched the aya—he was getting fairly expert with harness—got his saddle out of the buggy, took off the animal's harness, saddled and bridled the beast, buckled on his sword, mounted, spurred the aya, and headed for the fray as fast as the animal's six legs would carry him, as if he were the legendary Krishnan hero Qarar out to slay a slither of dragons.

The robber whose shomal had run away with him had finally got his animal under control and turned it back toward the convoy. Therefore he did not see Hasselborg until the latter was almost upon him, when the sound of hoofs behind him made him turn. He was just reaching for an arrow when Hasselborg took him in the ribs with his sword from behind. Not quite sporting, thought Hasselborg, but this is no time for chivalry. The blade went in clear to the hilt. Unfortunately the aya carried Hasselborg past so fast that the handle was wrenched out of his hand before he had time to withdraw the blade from his victim's body.

And there he was, riding full-tilt and weaponless towards the convoy. Resistance had died down. One man was tearing off across the plain with a couple of robbers after him, while another fenced with three more from aya back. The other robbers were busy with the remaining people of the convoy, binding those who had fallen to their knees and subduing those who had not. The woman was still standing in the rearmost vehicle, as if waiting for the first robber who felt so-minded to ride by and scoop her up.

Hasselborg headed for her, calling: "I'll try to get you away!" As he came nearer he saw that she was young and beautiful, with the light-blue hair of the western races.

She hesitated as he held out an arm, then let herself be lifted down onto the back of the aya behind Hasselborg. He spun his mount and headed back the way he had come as a chorus of shouts told him that the robbers did not intend to let this act go unnoticed.

While Hasselborg wondered how to get out of the predicament into which his impulse had plunged him, his aya carried him past the robber he had run through. This Krishnan had fallen off his shomal and was crawling on all fours with the hilt of the sword sticking out of his back. Hasselborg, feeling that he was likely to need a whole arsenal of weapons in the next few minutes, reached down and retrieved his sword. *I ought to have a movie film of that stunt,* he thought; *anybody'd think I planned it that way.*

"Here comes one," said the woman. Hasselborg looked around to see another robber riding hard at him.

He said: "Hold on!" and put his mount into a sharp curve, leaning inward as he did so. *These six-legged creatures could certainly turn on a dime,* he thought. The robber pulled up a little, as if surprised to see a supposedly unarmed man suddenly whirl and charge him with a sword.

As Hasselborg went by, too excited to remember to thrust, he aimed an overhead cut at the robber's head.

Too late he realized that he'd probably break his blade on the man's iron hat. But Da'vi, the Krishnan goddess of luck, was still with him, for the blow missed by just enough to shear off an ear and come down between neck and shoulder. The man dropped his mace with a howl.

"You'd better hurry," said the girl. A glance showed that at least three other bandits were riding toward them.

Hasselborg turned again and resumed his flight, wishing he had some shrewd plan of escape all figured out, instead of being in a kind of exalted confusion and anxiety. Still, if he could make the hills before they caught him, he would have an advantage on rough ground over those on the long-legged shomals and might give them the slip in the darkness.

Hasselborg's aya loped up the slope of the rise. A glance back showed that the pursuers were gaining. Hasselborg's beast was slowed by its double load, even though it was one of the dasht's big hunting breed. Something went past with a faint whistling screech. Some flying creature of the night? No; as the sound was repeated, Hasselborg realized that they were shooting arrows at him. He pulled Avvaú off the road and headed cross-country up into the wooded crest of the ridge; no use leading them right to his carriage. Another arrow clattered among the branches.

"Are they gaining?" he said.

"I—I think not."

"Hold on tight."

Hasselborg's own heart was in his mouth as the animal leaped fallen logs, dropped out from under him as it took a dip, and swerved to avoid trees. He clamped the beast's barrel with his knees, leaned right and left, and ducked branches that were upon him almost before he could see them. He thanked Providence that the hunt and the flight from Rosid had given him at least a little practice at rough riding. The aya stumbled a couple of times, and Hasselborg blessed its six legs as it recovered each time without dropping its riders.

A crash from behind and a volley of shrill curses. "One of the shomals fell," said the girl.

"Good. Hope the rider broke his fertilizing neck. If it gets dark enough—"

They must have reached the base of the spur, where the land rose and fell irregularly in all directions. Hasselborg pulled to the right down a shallow draw. The animal crashed through a thicket that tore at its riders' legs; then up—down—left—right— The aya almost spilled them as it ran head-on into a sapling in the darkness. To his horror, Hasselborg felt his saddle, put on in such haste, beginning to slip out of place.

"I think we've escaped them," said the girl.

Hasselborg halted the aya and listened for sounds of pursuit over the heavy breathing of the animal. A distant crashing and the sound of voices came faintly, but after several minutes the noise seemed to be dying away altogether.

"Hasselborg dismounted stiffly and helped the girl down, saying: "Haven't I met you somewhere?"

"How know I? Who are you, that goes about rescuing damsels in distress?"

"I'm Kavir bad-Ma'lum, the painter," he said, adjusting the girths. He seemed to have got half the straps buckled together wrong.

"So? I heard of you at the court of the dasht."

"I know where I saw you! Somebody pointed you out to me at the court as Fouri bab-Something."

"I'm Vazid's daughter."

"That's right, bab-Vazid. And you're somebody's niece, aren't you?"

"You must mean my uncle Hasté. Hasté bad-Labbadé. You know, the high priest."

"Sure." He wasn't, but no matter. Trot out the courtly manner. "I'm glad I was of service to Your Ladyship, though I'd rather we'd met under less strenuous circumstances. Were you on your way home from Rosid?"

"Yes; I but came thither to visit my friend the Lady Qéi, and since the dasht made himself unpleasant, I thought it time to go home to uncle. Charrasp the merchant had collected a group to take the new tabid crop to Hershid before the price dropped, and some people of quality had elected to go with him for safety. So, thought I, why not go at once? I hope no ill came to my man and my maid, who were with me. What do we now?"

"Try to find our way back to the road, I suppose."

"What then?"

"If my buggy's still there, we'll hitch it up and ride into Hershid in it. Otherwise we shall have to ride pillion all the way.

"Whither lies the road?"

"Maybe the stars know, but I don't." He listened, hearing nothing but the breathing of three pairs of lungs. While one of the three moons was up, the sky was still partly cloudy, so that the moonlight came through in fitful beams only.

"Seems to me," he mused, "that we came down this little valley after running along that ridge to the left—"

He started up the draw, leading Fouri with one hand and the aya with the other. He proceeded cautiously, watching for obstacles and listening for robbers. He led them along the ridge he thought they had come by, then along another branching off from it—and realized that the terrain was quite unfamiliar.

VIII.

An hour later he said: "I'm afraid we're lost good and proper."

"What do we then? Stay for the dawn?"

"We could, of course, though I don't like the idea with these hijackers hanging around." After further thought he added: "All we need to make things perfect is to be treed by a yeki."

As if in answer, a low roar came across the mountains. Fouri threw her arms around his neck. "I fear!"

"There, there." He patted her back. "It's many hoda away." Although he could have stood in that agreeable position all night, they had more urgent things to think of. "If I could only find that long ridge again, we could walk right down the top of it—I know, you hold Avvaú." No more letting his mount run loose for him!

He took off his sword belt, found a tree with low branches, and climbed. While it was hard going, especially since the trunk was smooth and the branches widely spaced, he nevertheless managed to raise himself eight or ten meters above the ground.

There were still only hills dotted with patches of woods and isolated trees, fitfully moonlit. Was that the missing spur? Couldn't be sure—

Then he snapped his attention to one thing—a little spark of light, far off, like a fifth-magnitude star. He strained his eyes, then remembered to look just to one

79

side of it. Yes, there it was all right, twinkling like a star on a cold Earth night. That meant, probably, a fire. The robbers?

He studied as much as he could see of the terrain, noted the position of the moon, and descended. "If we go over that way, we may run into trouble. On the other hand, if they're sitting around the fire, they probably won't see us if we're careful, and we should be able to find our road at least."

"Whatever my hero says."

Hasselborg's eyebrows went up with a jerk. So, he was a hero now? He set out again briskly, stopping from time to time to verify his direction. At the end of an hour's walk he could see the spot of light from ground level.

"We'll have to be very quiet," he whispered. "At least I know where I am now. Come on."

He began a big circle to the left of the fire, spiraling gradually closer to it. After another quarter-hour he halted at the top of a steep slope.

"Here's the road," he said. "The thing seems to go right towards our friends."

The fire was now out of sight. As they skidded down the slope and started along the road, Hasselborg recognized the place as the slope up which he was walking the aya that afternoon when the idea of painting a sunset came to him. He dropped Fouri's hand and held his sword to keep it from clanking.

"Here's the buggy," he breathed.

He poked about it but found no sign of its having been tampered with. Up ahead, although the fire itself was invisible, he could see the light from it on trees over the crest of the rise.

"Hold the aya a minute," he said.

He left Fouri and walked slowly up the slope, crouching as he neared the top lest he blunder into the gang unawares. For the last few feet he lowered himself to hands and knees, then peered cautiously over.

Seven robbers stood or squatted about the fire, which had been built alongside the road. Two, crudely bandaged, sprawled in the dirt; the others ate in hasty gulps. Hasselborg could hear the snorts of their animals tethered nearby and the words:

"Why in the name of the stars didn't you——"

"Fool, how knew I you'd run off after——"

"You *zeft!* The caravan was no matter; we were being paid for the girl. All should have——"

"A fine thing—four slain, two hurt, one missing, and not a kard to show! The dasht can keep his gold for all——"

"Why slew you not the folk of the caravan? Then they'd not have taken courage and——"

"Ransoms, idiot——"

". . . hasten, lest the soldiery find us——"

". . . the dasht promised——"

"*Ghuvoi* the dasht! I think of the dour. 'Tis nigh his bourne——"

Hasselborg crept back and whispered: "If we hitch up quietly, we can drive right through them. Are you game to try? I don't think they'll follow us very far into the dour's dominions."

"Whatever you say."

They unsaddled the aya, jumping fearfully at every click of a buckle. Then they put its harness back on it, moving snail-slowly to avoid noise.

"Now," said Hasselborg when they had hitched Avvaú to the carriage, "can you drive?"

"Well enough."

"All right, take the reins. To get speed up fast, I'll have to run alongside and then swing aboard. When I say 'go', use the whip for all it's worth. Ready? Go!"

He reached in and snapped off the brakes as the whip whistled and crackled. The carriage shuddered, the wheels crunched, and dirt flew from the six hoofs of the outraged animal. Hasselborg, walking alongside with one hand on the carriage body, broke into a trot, then into a run, and then swung aboard.

"Give him the business!" he said. Hanging onto the dashboard with his left hand, he drew his sword with his right and leaned out.

As they topped the rise into the firelight, they picked up speed until they were hurtling at the group of men by the fire.

The minute they appeared, some of the robbers looked around at the noise. These jumped to their feet and reached for weapons as the vehicle bore down upon them. One held up a hand like a traffic cop and shouted, then leaped for dear life. Another stepped forward with a sword. Hasselborg thrust at him. His stroke was parried with a clang, and then they were through and thundering into the dark.

"They don't seem to be coming after us," said Hasselborg, leaning out of the buggy and looking to the rear. "I guess they were as badly scared as we were and didn't know their chosen victim was in this rig."

"What mean you, chosen victim?"

Hasselborg told her what he had overheard.

"That foul unha!" she cried. "Not satisfied with forcing me to flee his court, Jám hires cutthroats to kidnap me! I'll make him pay for this, the way Queen Nirizi made the jeweler pay for what he did."

Although Hasselborg would like to have known what drastic fate Queen Nirizi inflicted upon the jeweler, he had other things to occupy him at the moment. They passed the place where the caravan had been attacked. Aside from a brief glimpse of the ruins of the bishtar cart and a couple of unburied bodies, nothing remained.

Hasselborg said: "I think I see what happened. The bandits thought they had everything under control, and so they did until a couple of them tore away after that fellow who rode off on his aya, and some more came after us, which left only a couple guarding the prisoners. Seeing which, the prisoners grabbed up the weapons they'd just laid down and smote the robbers hip and thigh. When the others came back after hunting for us, the caravan was miles away, and they didn't dare follow it out of Jám's territory, since they'd bought their protection from him."

"Then my people may still live! We should catch them ere they reach Hershid, think you not?"

"Don't know; I'd have to scale it off on the map, and I don't know how accurate that is."

"Well then, will you take over the driving now?"

"In a minute." Hasselborg gave another look to the rear. The robbers' fire slid out of sight. A couple of miles more and he said: "Let's stop long enough to light the lanterns. This tearing around in the dark *à la* Ben Hur gives me the bleeps."

"Is that an expression in your native tongue? Surely my lord showed courage enough on that ride through the hills. I could have done nought without you, O man of might."

"Oh, I'm not so hot as all that," he said, fumbling with the lanterns and glad that she could not see his look of embarrassment. "In fact, the whole idea—" He was about to say that the whole idea of rescuing her had been a piece of irrational folly, which he would never have undertaken if he had stopped to think, but judged such a remark tactless. "There, now at least we shan't miss a turn and smash up."

He took up the reins again. Since her costume was inadequate protection against the coolth of the long Krishnan night, he wrapped his cloak around both of them. She snuggled up to him, tickled his face with her antennae, and presently kissed the angle of his jaw.

So, sex was raising its beautiful head? How nice that the Krishnans had adopted this Terran practice! And how nice that one could take one's eyes off the road and trust one's steed to find the way! *O quente cachorro!*

The sun was well up before Fouri awoke and

stretched. "Where are we?" she asked.

"Somewhere on the road to Hershid."

"I know that, man of little wit! But where?"

"I can only guess that we'll arrive some time this afternoon."

"Well then, stop at the next farmhouse. I would eat."

This sharp, imperious tone was something new. He thought, some of the hero-worship must have already worn off, and gave her a silent, wooden look.

Thereupon she was all contrition: "Oh, did I wound my hero? I crawl! I abase myself! A foul-tempered and selfish witch am I!" She seized his hand and began kissing it. "You break my liver! Bear unkindness from you I cannot! Say I'm forgiven, or I throw myself from your carriage to my doom!"

"That's okay, Lady Fouri," he said, wishing she would not be so theatrical about it. Life was complicated enough without superfluous histrionics. He patted her and kissed her and cheered her up, while his mind ran far ahead, thinking of plans for his arrival in Hershid.

Presently she said: "We must be well into the dour's territory. Passed we not his bourne in the night?"

"You mean that place with a gate across the road and a sentry house? You were asleep."

"How about the sentries? Did they admit you?"

"Matter of fact, they were asleep too, so I just got out and opened the gate myself. Seemed a shame to wake the poor guys."

They stopped at a hamlet for a meal, during which Hasselborg asked: "What's a good respectable inn in Hershid? I landed in some Thieves' Rest in Rosid and don't care to repeat the mistake."

"Oh, but Kavir, you shall stay at no inn! What think you of me? Chambers of the best in my uncle's palace shall be yours, where I can see you every day!"

Although the last item made it plain that more than simple gratitude was involved in this offer, Hasselborg suppressed a smile as he protested: "I couldn't accept such unearned hospitality! After all, I'm a mere nobody, not even a knight, and your uncle doesn't know me from Ad—from Qarar."

"Who Ad may be I know not, but accept you he shall; he'd welcome his niece's rescuer in any event; and should he not, I'd make him wish he'd never been hatched."

He did not doubt that she could, too. "Well . . . if you insist—"

She did, of course, which fact pleased Hasselborg mightily, despite its threat of future complications, because it gave him a free and perhaps luxurious lodging right in the midst of things. While, despite his fear of germs, he could cheerfully put up with the worst in the way of accommodations when he had to, he still enjoyed the best when he could get it.

The rest of the journey proved uneventful. They failed to overhaul the caravan, which must have been making good time to get away from the perils of the Kodum Hills.

Hershid, as befitted the capital of an empire, was a larger and more splendid city than Rosid. As expected, they were halted at the gate. The guards recognized Fouri before she had said two words, jumped to present arms with their halberds, and waved the carriage through.

Fouri guided Hasselborg through the city until they stopped at the gates of a palace. The gates were adorned with geometrical gimmicks, which Hasselborg recognized as Krishnan astrological symbols.

The inevitable gatekeeper stepped out, cried: "Mistress Fouri!" and ran across the court shouting. A whole swarm of people thereupon erupted out of the palace and crowded around the carriage, all trying to kiss Fouri's hands at once.

Then a tall Krishnan in a long blue robe appeared and the crowd opened to let him through. He and Fouri embraced. The latter said: "Uncle, this is my rescuer, the gallant Master Kavir—"

Hasselborg had his hand shaken—another borrowed Earth custom—and tried to follow the conversation with everybody talking at once:

"What happened?" "Sandú, run to the barracks and tell the commander not to send out that squadron—" "Aye, the caravan arrived but a few minutes past their tale of woe—" "Whatever befell your ladyship? You look as if you'd been trampled by wild ayas!"

An exaggeration, even though Fouri's flimsy costume did look beat-up as a result of her ride and hike through the Kodum Hills in the dark. As he was led to his room, it occurred to Hasselborg that if anyone needed valet service, it was himself. He could see that his suit was torn and mud-splattered, and could feel the whiskers sprouting on his chin and the weal where a branch had lashed him across the face on that wild ride into the hills. He'd have to shave soon, or it would be obvious that his bristly beard was reddish-brown instead of Krishnan green, unless he emulated the gent who

> ". . . was thinking of a plan
> To dye one's whiskers green,
> And always use so large a fan
> That they could not be seen."

and was, moreover, of Terran luxuriance.

All that was taken care of by Hasté's household, which ran with un-Krishnan efficiency.

An hour later he was shaved, bathed, perfumed—something he had to endure for the sake of sweet verisimilitude—and his clean suit had been laid out for him. After a short nap, he dressed and went down to meet his host, whom he found awaiting him with what appeared to be a cocktail shaker.

Hasté bad-Labbadé was unusual among Krishnans in having lost most of his hair and all the color from the rest, which was silky white. His wrinkled, parchmentlike features were also sharper than those of most of the race. In fact, had it not been for the organs of smell sprouting from between his brows, he might have passed for an Earthman.

"My son," said Hasté, pouring, "there's little I can say to impress upon you my gratitude, save this: Feel free to call upon me at any time for aught I can do for you."

"Thank you, Your Reverence," said Hasselborg, warily eyeing his drink. However, so skillfully had it been mixed that the taste of alcohol could hardly be detected, and he got it down without gagging. He reminded himself that, as a habitual nondrinker, he would have to be careful and count his drinks, stretching them out as long as possible.

When Fouri joined them, Hasté said: "Tell me all about this extraordinary feat of rescue."

When they had told, Fouri asked her uncle: "Think you the dour will finally take action against Jám on your representation?"

Hasté smiled thinly. "I know not. You know how little weight I have with the dour these days."

" 'Tis only because you lack courage to face down the old aqebat!" she snapped. "I could do better with him myself."

"Why, so you could, the reason being he likes you, looking upon you as a sort of daughter, while he holds me in despite."

"No matter of liking at all; but that he's a hard man and a clever one, who's gained his ends by struggle and expects those about him to be equally hard and clever. Best him and he'll respect you; yield to him, as you've done, and he'll trample you into the mire. Would that I were a man!"

Hasselborg felt a suppressed tension between these two, too strong to be accounted for by a simple difference of opinion on how to manage the king. This might bear looking into. He said: "I—uh—perhaps you could explain this to me, Your Reverence? I've never been in Hershid and so don't know the local situation."

Hasté gave him a keen look. "My niece is no dissembler. Were she on trial for her life, she'd even so tell the judge what she thought of him, be it never so libelous."

"How about the differences between you and the dour?"

" 'Tis a long tale, my son, going back many years and touching upon the very wellsprings of men's actions. I know not how they think in your land, but here in Gozashtand men have been of several minds as to why events follow the course they do.

"The old belief had it, you see, that all was due to the will of the gods. However, with the growth of knowledge, that belief seemed insufficient for divers causes, such as the question of why the gods seemed to make such a mess of human affairs, or why they should interest themselves in us mortals at all. In fact some blasphemers were heard to say that the gods existed not, though these were soon suppressed.

"Then about three hundred years past, our theologians proved to their satisfaction that the gods were neither a crew of lustful brawling barbarians reveling on the heights of Mount Meshaq, as thought our simple ancestors, nor yet a set of impalpable abstractions, the 'spirit of love' and the like, which none ever understood. Instead, they were in truth the luminaries of heaven: the sun, the moons, the planets, and the stars, which as they spun about our world sent down their occult influences singly and in combination and so controlled the fortunes of men. You'll recall 'twas about this time that the roundness of the world was discovered.

"So, thought we, we had at last the true scientific religion which should perform the proper offices of religion—to explain man and the universe, to predict the future, to comfort men in affliction, and to inculcate sound morals in the minds of the young. And so it seemed; the faith was made official in Gozashtand and its neighboring nations, and any deviation therefrom was condignly punished. Later, if you like, I'll show you one of the old cells in my own cellar, where heretics were kept for questioning. Now we can do nothing of the kind, though the dour betimes uses the accusation of heresy to dispose of politically inconvenient persons.

"Then what happened? The *Ertsuma* landed in their spaceships at the place that is now Novorecife, bringing news of other suns and other worlds revolving about them, for they told us for the first time that our world went around the sun and not vice versa. The planet Qondyor"—he meant Vishnu—"for instance, far from being the god of war, was but another world like our own, save warmer, with creatures on it not wholly unlike those of this world.

"So you see, good Master Kavir, the result has been a falling-away from the true faith. The Church may no longer punish her foes directly but must sit in silence while a host of minor cults, even some brought in by the *Ertsuma,* spreads over the land like a murrain, sapping our spiritual strength and preëmpting our income. And as our power declines, that of the dour waxes, wherefore relations are less cordial than once they were."

A little astonished by such frankness, Hasselborg asked: "your Reverence, what's your opinion about the gods, the planets, and so on?"

Hasté smiled faintly again. "As head of the Church, my official views are, of course, in accord with those adopted at the Council of Mishé forty-six years past. Privately, though I prefer that this be not repeated, I'm somewhat puzzled myself. Let's to dinner."

Fouri had put on another of her dazzling variety of personalities—grave and formal. She said: "Kavir's in Hershid to get commissions for painting portraits. Could we not put him in the way of some business? 'Twere the least recompense for his heroism."

"To be sure we could. Let me think—I'd order one

myself, had I not had one done within the year; I'll still do so if all else fails. As for the court, I know not quite how . . . my star is not in its dominant sector at the moment, but—"

"Oh, come, uncle! Why try you not the dour himself?"

"The dour, Fouri? But you know how blows the wind in that quarter—"

"Rouse yourself, you old man of jelly!" she cried suddenly, the grave manner gone. "Always excuses. The privy council meets on the morrow, does it not?"

"To be sure, my child, but—"

"No buts! Take Master Kavir with you and present him to His Awesomeness as the world's greatest portraitist. Unless," she added ominously, "you prefer to try contentions with your loving niece?"

"Dear stars, no; I'll take him! Assuming he'll come, that is. You're for this scheme, my son?"

"Sure," said Hasselborg, adding a murmur of inexpressible thanks.

"I feared as much," said Hasté.

Later, over the cigars, Hasselborg brought up another matter: "Your reverence, I'm on the lookout for a certain young man who bought a portrait from me and then decamped without paying. He had a girl with him."

"Yes?"

"I wondered if there were any place in Hershid where they'd know whether he passed through here?"

"Why, let me think—the dour has a good spy service, though I doubt they'd keep track of every traveler who passes this way, since Hershid is after all the crossroads of the empire. What were these runaways like?"

"Like this," said Hasselborg, producing the sketches.

Hasté frowned at them, then began to laugh. "How much did he owe you?"

"Five hundred karda."

Hasté rang a bell, and when a silent young man in a

plain blue priestly robe answered, he said: "Draw five hundred karda from my privy hoard and give them to Master Kavir."

"Stars preserve me!" said Hasselborg. "I didn't mean to collect it from Your Reverence—"

"All's well, my son, and count not the teeth of a gift shomal, as Qarar did in his dealings with the Witch of the Va-andao Sea. First, 'tis but a mean recompense for your rescue of my niece; and second, time, which brings all things, will bring me the chance to collect the debt from this your debtor."

"You know him?"

"But slightly."

"Who is he?"

"Can it be that you're yet so new in these parts? Why, unless I'm vastly mistaken, this is the true ten days' wonder, the paragon of the political virtues, the new Dour of Zamba, and the other's his douri."

"The King of Zamba?" said Hasselborg. "Since when? And what's Zamba?"

At this point the young priest glided back into the room with a heavy canvas sack, which he set down with a clink beside Hasselborg.

Hasté said: "Fetch a map of Gozashtand and adjacent lands, Ghaddal. Master Kavir, for a traveled man, your knowledge is most—shall I say—spotty? Whence came you originally?"

"Malayer in the far South," said Hasselborg.

"That may be. Know, then, that Zamba is an island in the Sadabao Sea, lying just off the end of the Harqain peninsula, which forms the eastern extremity of Gozashtand. For years have the Zambava been plagued with seditions and uprisings, party against party and class against class. Finally the commons overthrew the aristocracy altogether and slew all those who did not escape. Thereupon, having no more common foe, the commons fell into factions with battles and murders, leader against leader.

"The upshot was that a few ten-nights ago, your friend Antané—his name, is it not?—landed upon the isle with a gang of bullies whom he'd collected from the stars know whence, and in a few days had made himself master of all. Oh, 'twas neatly done, and he's gone on to effect many changes. For instance, you see, he's built a new aristocracy of leaders of the commons—those who came over to his side, that is—with all the titles and trappings of the old. However, the titles but cover the official posts of his little kingdom, are not hereditary, and are withdrawn the instant the incumbent fails to give satisfaction. No more young noblemen wallowing in the sin of idleness on Zamba!"

Maybe Fallon had been reading a life of Napoleon, thought Hasselborg, or maybe in that social situation things just broke that way. Although he would have liked to hear more about King Anthony, Hasté seemed disinclined to discuss the subject further. The priest preferred to talk about large generalities like progress versus stability, or free will versus predestination.

"For look you," he said, "there be those who pass rumors to the effect that King Antané's no true man at all, but an *Ertsu* in disguise. Not that it would matter greatly to me, since for years I've been telling my flock that 'tis wrong to judge people on a basis of their race rather than of their individual merits. I'm sure, however, that Antané's no earthman; for they believe, most of them, in the curious doctrine of equality for all men, while our young paragon has set up no such system in his island kingdom. Now, you were among the *Ertsuma* during your stay at Novorecife, my son. Enlighten an old man on these matters. What is this doctrine of equality, and do all Earthmen indeed adhere to it?"

"As a matter of fact," Hasselborg began, and would have launched into a brilliant ten-minute speech on the subject when it occurred to him that a Krishnan painter would hardly know that much about Earth's political theory. Was the old boy trying to trap him? He cautiously qualified his reply: "I don't know about these things from first-hand knowledge, Your Reverence; all I know is what I heard my *Ertso* friends saying in the course of conversation. As I get it, this theory is now the dominant one among Earthmen, although it has not always been and may not always be. Moreover it doesn't mean literal equality of individuals, but a legal equality, or equality in matters of law—rights, obligations, and so on.

"They told me there were two great difficulties in building a political system on such a basis—first that people aren't biologically equal, but individuals differe widely in ability; second, that you have to have some sort of political organization to run the society except among the most primitive groups, and those in power have a natural tendency to try to alter the setup to make themselves legally superior to the governed. They all do it, whether they call themselves counts, capitalists, or commissars—"

As they fenced with ideas, Hasselborg thought that Hasté showed flashes of a rather surprising knowledge of Terran institutions.

Fouri maintained her gravity all evening, through supper, until they were saying good night. She gave Hasselborg her hand to kiss, glanced at Hasté's retreating back, leaned forward, and whispered: "Are you married, my hero?"

Hasselborg raised his eyebrows. "No."

"Excellent!" She gave him a swift kiss and went.

Oh-oh, thought Hasselborg, you don't need X-ray eyes to see what she's leading up to! Now that he knew where Fallon was, he had better get away from Hershid quickly. Could he sneak out that very night on the pretext that he liked to take buggy rides in the moonlight? No. In the first place, that wouldn't get him to Zamba; the map showed the rocky Harqain peninsula as roadless. You had to take ship from Majbur.

Moreover, did he want to go to Zamba so precipitately? If he simply walked in on Julnar to argue that she should return to her papa, Fallon might have him liquidated out of hand. Maybe he had better hang around Hershid for a few days despite the matrimonial menace of the fair Fouri, and try to work out an angle.

Hasselborg was surprised when Hasté presented him to the dour. From Fouri's remarks, had been led to expect something physically impressive, like the Dasht of Rúz. Instead, King Eqrar bad-Qavitar reminded Hasselborg of nothing so much as a terran mouse.

"Yes, yes, yes," squeaked the mighty monarch quickly, offering his small hand to be kissed. "I've often thought of the same thing. A portrait. Hm-m-m. Hm-m-m. A fine idea. An excellent suggestion. Glad am I that you brought this wight around, Hasté. I'll wager that niece of yours put you up to it; she knows how to get around the old man, ha. Knew you as much, you'd be a power in the land. Master Kavir, how many sittings would you require?"

"Perhaps a dozen, Your Awesomeness."

"Right, right, right. We'll have the first this afternoon. An hour before dinner. West wing of the palace. The flunkies will pass you in and show you where. Bring all your gear. All of it. Nought vexes me more than an expert who comes to perform some office for one and then has to return home for more tools. Mind you, now."

"Yessir," said Hasselborg. Eqrar was evidently one of those who believed that "What I tell you three times is true."

"Good, good. And it is my command that you leave not the city of Hershid until the portrait be completed. A busy king am I, and I shall have to fit the sittings into my schedules as best I can. You have my leave to go."

Hasselborg, outwardly obsequious, swore under his breath. Now he was stuck in Hershid for the gods knew how long, especially if the dour was given to canceling appointments. While he might run away in defiance of the dour, he might also be caught and dragged back before he reached the border. At best, he would land in this nervous but powerful king's black book.

When he got back to Hasté's palace, he asked Fouri: "How do you get to Majbur?"

"Depart you so soon?" she cried, her voice rising in alarm.

"Not yet; the king says no. Still, I should like to know."

"Then you might drive your carriage—there's a good road from the south gate—or you might take the railroad."

"Railroad?"

"Of course! Knew you not that Hershid's on the end of the line to Majbur and on down the coast to Jazmurian?"

This I must see, thought Hasselborg, forbearing to ask more questions for fear of revealing ignorance. "Like a ride before lunch?"

She would, of course, and showed him the way to the terminal outside the wall on the south side of the city. The rails were about a meter apart, the cars little four-wheeled affairs with bodies like those of carriages, and the locomotives bishtars. A couple of the beasts were pushing and pulling cars around the yard under the guidance of mahouts, who sat on their necks and blew little trumpets to warn of their approach. Fouri said:

"Alack, my hero, you're too late to see the daily train for Qadr pull out, and that from Qadr comes not in till around sunset."

"Where's Qadr?"

"A suburb of Majbur, on this side of the Pichidé. No through train to Jazmurian, you see, because the river's too wide to be bridged; one must detrain at Qadr and cross the river by boat ere continuing on."

"Thanks."

After they had watched for a while she continued: "I

can see we're truly soul mates, Kavir, for I, too, have always loved to hang on the fence of the railroad yard and watch the trains made up."

Hasselborg shuddered a little mentally, as though he had cut himself on a dirty knife with no disinfectant available.

She went on: "If you're really set on going to Majbur —I can wheedle aught I wish from the dour. Should I, for example, tell him that my affianced husband wished to travel, I know I could persuade him—"

Hasselborg changed the subject by asking about Zamba and its new ruler, although Fouri could add but little to what he already knew.

The king proved a difficult portrait subject, always fidgeting and scratching and wiping his pointed nose on his sleeve. To make matters worse, characters kept coming in to whisper in his ear or to present papers for him to sign. All this distraction reduced Hasselborg, who had little enough confidence in his ability as a painter, to a state bordering on frantic despair. He complained:

"If Your Awesomeness would only hold that pose for five minutes on end—"

"What mean you, painter?" yelped the king. "You scoundrel, you criticize me? I've held this pose without moving the breadth of a hair for the better part of an hour, and you dare say I've not? Get out! Why did I ever let you begin this thing? Begone! No, no, no, I meant it not. Come back and fall to work. Only let it be understood, no more irreverent criticisms! I'm a very busy man, and if I work not on my royal business every minute, I never get it fulfilled. You're a good and faithful fellow. Fall to, waste no time, stand not gaping, get to work!"

Hasselborg sighed and stoically resumed his sketching. Then another man came in, this time omitting to whisper. The newcomer cried:

"May it please Your Awesomeness, the Dasht of Rúz

has arrived unannounced, with fifty men-at-arms! He seeks an escaped prisoner who he thinks has fled to your court!''

IX.

After sitting with his mouth open for a few seconds, the king jumped up with a yell. "That blundering fool! 'Tis just like him to descend upon me without an hour's warning! No permission, no invitation, no request, no nought—*Ohé!*" He looked keenly at Hasselborg, who had given up trying to make a sketch for the time being. "You, master painter, arrive one morning with a fine story of rescuing Hasté's niece from robbers in Jám's demesne. Then at the close of that selfsame day comes Jám himself hot on the trail of an alleged fugitive. A singular coincidence, would you not say?"

"Yes, Your Awesomeness."

"Well, show him in, show him in! We'll soon get to the bottom of this coil." The king paced up and down. "I doubt not that the rescue took place even as stated, for my men questioned the survivors of that unlucky caravan at length. Still there's a mystery here; there's a mystery; there's a myst— Ah, my good vassal Jám!"

The Dasht of Rúz strode into the room, made the barest pretense of dropping to one knee in front of the king, and then went for Hasselborg with a roar, pulling at his sword. "You *zeft!* I'll show you to bribe your way out of my jail!"

Hasselborg, who was getting a little tired of hair-breadth escapes, looked around frantically for a weapon, since he had been required to check his sword before

98

being closeted with the king.

Eqrar, however, took care of that. Placing one of the big rings on his fingers in his mouth, he blew a high, piercing whistle. Instantly a pair of inconspicuous little doors in the wall flew open, and out of each sprang a couple of guards with cocked crossbows.

"Stand, or you're a dead vassal!" squeaked the king.

Jám sheathed his sword reluctantly. "Your Awesomeness, my humble apologies for an irreverent intrusion. But by Qondyor and Hoi, 'tis not to be borne that this heap of foulness who calls himself a painter shall be allowed to encumber the earth with his loathsome presence any longer!"

"What's he done?"

"I'll tell you straight. He comes to me, pretending to paint portraits, and is welcomed as an old friend. What happens? Within the day I learn that he's no painter at all, but a spy from Mikardand sent to assassinate me. So, naturally, I fling him in pokey to be expended at the holy games. Then by some witchcraft he magicks the yeki so the beast won't eat him, and subsequently is spirited out of jail by a pair of fellow-desperadoes and disappears. Belike he corrupted someone in my service, or 'twould not have passed off so smoothly, though the villains all swear innocence and I can't hang 'em all in the hope of getting the right one."

"How know you he's a spy?" asked the king.

"My friend at Novorecife, Julio Góis, sent word. Here's his letter, see you, and here's another he sent with yon *baghan* who altered it."

Hasselborg broke in: "May it please Your Awesomeness, I'm not a Mikardandu, as you'll find out if you inquire there. I only stopped a night at Mishé on my way to Novorecife, since Mikardand is no place for an artist. At Novorecife I made Góis's acquaintance and asked for an introduction to somebody in Rosid; that's all I know about it. The reason the dasht is so sore is that I busted up his attempt to have the Lady Fouri kidnaped by his gang of tame bandits."

"What's this? What's this?" said Eqrar.

"Sure, he did it. She told me herself she left Rosid because he wouldn't let her alone, so he had her snatched, and I don't think because he wanted a partner to play checkers with, either."

"What about this, my lord Jám?" said the king.

"Lies, all lies," said the dasht. "Where's his proof?"

Hasselborg said: "I heard the robbers discussing the matter around their campfire. Bring some of them in and they'll tell you."

The king asked: "Where be these robbers now?"

"Hanged, every one of 'em," shouted Jám. "I chanced upon 'em whilst in pursuit of this wretch, and applied the high justice on the spot."

Hasselborg thought, I passed by his garden, and marked with one eye, how the Owl and the Panther were sharing a pie— "Because they'd failed to get her as he ordered, or else to shut their mouths for good."

The dasht started to bellow obscenities, when the king said: "Peace, peace, peace, both of you. Now, here's a veritable puzzle. You, Jám, say that Master Kavir's a spy, though your only evidence is the word of the *Ertsu* Julio, which is inadmissible in Gozashtando law and worthless as a matter of general experience. Then you, sir painter, accuse my faithful vassal of suborning the abduction of the niece of the high priest of the Established Church for fell purposes—though the fellness of these purposes might be mitigated by the damsel's excessive beauty, which would rouse thoughts of love in the liver of the holiest eremite. Still, the chick's a favorite of mine, since I have no girl-children of my own, and therefore I'd take a grave view of the matter were it substantially proved. Yet your only proof is the word of men whose word would carry little weight were they alive and none at all since they're deceased.

"I could, of course, have both of you interrogated with hot pincers"—he smiled unpleasantly, whereupon

both Hasselborg and Jám looked gravely respectful—
"save that in my experience that treatment, while oft
beneficial to the victim as well as edifying to the spec-
tator, fails to elicit that for which we're most eager—to
wit, the truth. What would you with this man, Lord
Jám?"

"I would snatch him back to Rúz, Your Awesomeness, to commute his sentence from death-by-beast to
death-by-beheading, thereby showing my merciful nature, though I doubt he'll appreciate the change. If his
magic'll glue him back together after his head's been
separated from the rest of him, I'd say he'd earned his
worthless life."

"But," cried the king, "how then shall my portrait be
finished? From his sketch I can see that 'twill be the best
ever made of me, which implies that, spy or no, he's a
true artist even as he claims. No, no, no, Jám, you shall
not take him away ere he's finished the great work; we
owe that to the empire and to posterity!"

Jám chewed his lip, then said: "Could we not leave
him here under guard long enough to complete the picture, and then slay him as he deserves?"

Hasselborg said: "Your Supremacy, d'you really
think a man with my artistic temperament could give his
best to his art with a death sentence hanging over him?"

"No, no, I see your point, Master Kavir, and moreover there's the matter of your charge against Jám—"

"You're not crediting these fantastic lies?" said the
dasht.

"You will kindly not interrupt your sovereign. 'Tis a
serious matter, Master Kavir, to level such a charge
against an anointed dasht. But withal, your charge is as
well-attested as his, which is to say not at all. Now, hear
my judgment, both of you: You, Kavir bad-Ma'lum,
shall remain inviolate at Hershid until the work be done.
After that you may remain in this city, taking the hazard
that Jám will return with evidence that would force me
to give you to him; or you may leave, and in that case he

may have you if he can catch you. You, Jám bad-Koné, abide by these conditions, and no sending of one of your ruffians to extinguish Master Kavir by stealth while he's in my territory. Should aught of that nature befall him, I'll know where to look. Seems that not fair?"

"Then," roared Jám, "there remains but one course. Kavir bad-Matlum or whatever your name is, I declare you a knave, pervert, scoundrel, spy, coward, liar, and thief, and challenge you to disprove these assertions with weapons of war upon my person." With which the dasht pulled off his glove and threw it at Hasselborg.

The king sighed. "I thought I had everything arranged, and you do *that*. 'Tis true there's some question as to whether a person in Master Kavir's station be compelled to accept a challenge from a gentleman, especially one of your not inconsiderable rank—"

"See the case of Yezdan versus Qishtaspandú, only last year," retorted Jám. "A professional artist is considered constructively a gentleman, and so may be challenged."

"Here, here," said Hasselborg. "We do things a little differently in Malayer. Somebody explain. Jám wants to fight me, is that right?"

"And how I do!"

"What happens if I don't feel like fighting?"

"Ha hah!" said Jám. "A thin-livered wretch, said I not? Already he seeks to crawl out. Well sir, in that case we inflict upon you, as stigmata of your cowardice, the five mutilations, beginning with your ears—"

"Never mind the rest. Do I get a choice of weapons?"

"Surely. Any weapon in the approved list—lance, pike, sword, dagger, battle-ax, mace, halberd, gisarme, flail, javelin, longbow, crossbow, sling, or throwing-knife; with or without shield, armored or bare, afoot or mounted. I'll take you on with any combination you care to mention, for you'll be the twelfth to try to stand against me. Twelve's my lucky number, you know."

Hasselborg, not thinking it necessary to ask what had become of the other eleven, got out his knuckle-duster and showed it to the king. "Would this be allowed?"

"No, no, no!" said the latter. "What think you, that we're savages from the Koloft Swamps, to pummel each other with fists?"

"Then make it crossbows, unarmored, and afoot," said Hasselborg, who as an expert rifle shot figured that this weapon would give him the best chance. "You'll have to give me a couple of days to practice up."

"Accepted," said Jám. "A fine brabble 'twill be, with me the best crossbow-hunter in Rúz. Saw you my collection of heads?"

"You mean the ones on spikes over the city gate? Vulgar ostentation, I thought."

"No, fool, the heads of the beasts I've slain. Your Supremacy, let me urge that you set a guard over this scum, lest he steal away in the night."

"Fair enough," said the king. "Master Kavir, hear my royal command: That you move your gear forthwith to this the royal palace. I'll send men to help you move."

Hasselborg mentally added: To keep him from making a break for liberty.

Fouri's eyes widened with horror when Hasselborg told her what was up, and Hasté seemed mildly distressed.

"A foolish business, dueling," said the priest. "The Council of Mishé condemned it in unequivocal terms. Although we of the cloth have long striven to convince the nobility of its sinful folly, they throw our own astrology back in our teeth, saying: won't the stars grant victory to him whose triumph is foreordained? Discouraging."

When he went to his room to pack, Fouri followed him, imperiously telling his pair of guards: "Stand you outside the door, churls! I command!"

Either the guards thought better of picking an argument with so domineering a young lady, or they knew her as a privileged character. She threw herself on Hasselborg's neck, crying:

"My hero! My love! Can I do aught to save you?"

"Yes, as a matter of fact you can," he said. "Could you sew a pair of pads into the elbows of the jacket of my old suit?"

"Pads? Sew? What mean you?"

Hasselborg patiently turned the coat inside out and explained what he wanted.

"Oh, I understand now," she said. "A wretched seamstress I, but still I'll let none other do it, for then when you wear this jacket, the occult force of my love will flow through your veins and nerve you to deeds of might."

"That'll be nice," he said, folding his clothes on the bed.

"Oh, it will. And then at last shall I be avanged upon this filthy fellow." She stitched away clumsily for a while, then said: "Kavir, why hold you yourself aloof from me? You're colder than the great statue of Qarar in Mishé!"

"Really?"

"Yes, really. Have I not given you all the encouragement a decent maiden can, and more? Look you, Uncle Hasté could join us tonight in a few words, and the king wouldn't boggle at my accompanying you to your new chamber in his palace. Then whatever ensued, we'd have a sweet memory to carry with us to our graves, be they early or late."

Hasselborg began to worry lest he say "yes" against his better judgment simply to end the argument. When he looked at her it took all his will power not to take her up on her offer. He would have done so had he been willing to discard his disguise. Of course there was Alexandra, but she was light-years away.

He pulled himself together. "I'm grateful for your regard, Fouri, but I don't anticipate an early grave; not this time anyway. Marriage is a serious matter, not to be entered into as a preliminary to a duel—"

"Then finish your sewing yourself, and I hope you prick your finger!" She threw the coat, needle and all, at his head, and stamped out, slamming the door.

Smiling wryly with a mixture of amusement, pity, and annoyance at the position in which circumstances had placed him, Victor Hasselborg picked up the jacket, donned his glasses, and began complying with her order. Between Hasté's mercurial and amorous niece and the Lord of Rúz, he knew just how Odysseus felt in trying to steer between Scylla and Charybdis.

His move completed, Hasselborg spent a dismal evening. The guards whom the king had assigned to him had evidently received orders to stick like leeches. Although he would like to have mingled with the court and found out more about Zamba and its new rulers, the people proved unexpectedly impervious to the charm he turned on. He wondered if the presence of the guards at his elbow might not dampen conversation, until one of his victims set him right:

"Not that we esteem you not, Master Kavir, but that, should you succumb in the forthcoming contest, we'd have likely contracted some of your ill luck by fraternizing with a doomed man."

He retired morosely to his new room. Hasté and Fouri—who had become the courteous hostess again— kept him company for a while, the former seeming distressed in his long-winded and ineffectual way.

"Officially, you understand," said Hasté, "the Established Church discountenances magic. Still in such a case I might get in touch with one of the local witches, who'll put a spell on the dasht's bow—"

"Go right ahead," said Hasselborg.

"Not that I really believe in witchcraft," continued Hasté, "but one can't deny that strange things do happen, not to be explained by ordinary philosophy, as the prince says in Harian's play—"

Finally Hasté had to leave to check some astronomical observations, and took Fouri none too willingly along.

Left alone except for his ubiquitous guards, Hasselborg tried to read a Gozashtando book but soon gave it up. The curlicues were just too hard to puzzle out, especially since he did not want to betray his ignorance of the written language in front of the guards by using his dictionary. Moreover, the work itself seemed to be an interminable metrical romance, perhaps best comparable to the Terran epics of Ariosto and Vega Carpio.

He tried engaging the guards in conversation, finding them agreeable enough, but also that he had to do most of the talking. He dropped a few broad hints about his escape from the Rosid clink:

". . . you know, I've been lucky in making friends in fixes like that, and happily I've been able to pay them back handsomely. The friend who helped me in Rosid will never want for anything again—"

One of the guards said: "Very interesting, sir, but that could never happen here."

"No?"

"No. Our dour be a shrewd judge of men, most careful to pick those for his personal guard who can't be bribed or corrupted."

He asked the other guard:

"Would you agree with that, chum?"

"Absolutely, sir."

Either he's equally honest, thought Hasselborg, or he's afraid to admit otherwise in front of his pal. If one could get him alone, then maybe—

But as time wore on, Hasselborg realized that he could not get either one of them alone, for they were under orders to watch each other as closely as they watched him.

Disgustedly he went to bed, revolving impractical

schemes for talking Fouri, on a promise of marriage, into ordering these guards to look the other way while he bolted. He was still thinking thus when he fell asleep.

The next morning, Hasselborg went down to the royal armory to borrow a crossbow. He chose one that fitted his length of arm and whose steel bow was as strong as he could cock with a quick heave of both hands on the string. Then he went out to the exercise ground, where he understood the duel would be held the following morning.

The minute he appeared, an official-looking person rushed up. "Master Kavir, you may not bring that weapon hither now!"

"Huh? Why not?" A crowd with their backs to Hasselborg was watching something. Being taller than most of them, he soon made out that they were looking at Jám bad-Koné at target practice.

"Why, the rule! Ever since Sir Gvastén 'accidentally' skewered the Pandr of Lúsht with a longbow shaft while they were at friendly practice for their duel, the dour has forbidden that two gentlemen under challenge should practice here at the same time."

"Okay; suppose you hold the bow until he's finished," said Hasselborg, handing over the weapon.

"Yes, yes, but I dare not let *you* promenade around here while *he's* armed; comprehend you not?"

"Oh, I'll be careful and not get close to him." Followed by his guards, Hasselborg strolled over to the crowd and watched quietly for some time before the other spectators became aware of his presence. Thereupon they turned heads to look at him. The dasht, seeing him also, flashed him a rousing sneer over his shoulder and addressed himself again to the target.

The system appeared to be that the duelist had to stand with an uncocked crossbow in his hands and his back to the target. On a signal given by a whistle, he snatched a bolt from his belt, cocked his weapon,

whirled, and shot. The dasht's next bolt went through
the man-shaped target in the heart region—that is, the
Krishnan heart region, which was more centered than
that of Earthmen—adding one more to a sinister con-
stellation of holes in the cloth. Jám was obviously no
tyro.

Hasselborg watched the dasht closely for hints on
how to beat this game. He remembered reading a case
years before at Harvard Law School on the subject of
obsolete laws—about the Englishman who around 1817,
losing a lawsuit, challenged his opponent to trial by battle and appeared in the lists on the appointed day with
lance and sword, armed *cap-à-pie* and then claimed to
have won his suit because the other litigant had not
shown up. The lawyers scurried about frantically and
found that the man *had* won his suit, and the next ses-
sion of Parliament had to abolish trial by battle.

After an hour or so, the dasht quit and marched off,
followed by the men-at-arms he had brought from
Rosid. Several of the local gentry hung around, waiting
to see Hasselborg perform.

Hasselborg, however, had no intention of making a
fool of himself in front of company. He sat lazily on a
bench and engaged his guards in conversation on the
technical points of crossbowmanship, on the pretext
that: "We do things differently in Malayer, but perhaps
you local men have better ideas—"

Since the incorruptible whom he had approached
without success the previous night proved an enthusiast,
Hasselborb had merely to feed him occasional questions
until the spectators, becoming bored, drifted off.

"Now I'll try a few," said Hasselborg, to whom the
marshal had given back his bow after Jám had departed. "Remember that they use a different kind of
bow in my country, so I shall make a few misses at
first."

And a few clean misses he did make. The trouble with
this thing was that it had no sights, but perhaps that
could be remedied.

He asked: "Where can I get a couple of pins about so long, with round heads like so?" He indicated something on the order of a corsage pin.

"I can get you such," said the enthusiast, "for my sweetheart is maid to the Lady Mandai. Since I may not leave you, 'twill take some little time—"

Half an hour later, Hasselborg had his pins. He firmly pressed one into the wooden stock of the crossbow near the muzzle end, to one side of the bolt groove, and the other into a corresponding position to the rear. Then he made a few more shots, adjusting the pins until, from the official distance, he could make a clean hit by shooting with the heads of the two pins in line with the target.

"By all the gods," said the enthusiast, "what's this our good Master Kavir has done? By the nose of Tyazan, 'tis surely a new and deadly idea!"

"Oh, that's old stuff where I come from," said Hasselborg.

He was now confident that he could hit the target all right; the problem remained to keep the target from hitting him. Jám had done all his shooting from an erect position. "Do the rules require you to shoot standing?"

"What other position is there?" said the enthusiast.

The other guard said: "I've seen men shoot kneeling. In truth, the drillmaster the dour had before the present one taught sinking to one knee to shoot from behind a wall or other obstacle. That was before your time, Ardebil."

Hasselborg asked: "How about the rules?"

"I know of nought to prevent one from shooting from any position he likes," said the enthusiast. "For aught I know, 'tis legal to charge your foe and smite him on the pate with the stock of the bow."

Hasselborg cocked the bow and lay down prone, thankful for the pads in his jacket but also wishing the flagstones of the exercise court were cleaner. His shooting, however, became so good that the guards whistled their appreciation.

The enthusiast said: " 'Twere a chivalrous thing to

warn the dasht of that which he faces."

"You wouldn't want to spoil his surprise, would you?" said Hasselborg.

Next morning, Hasselborg stood on the same flagstones, listening to the marshal intone the rules of the contest: ". . . and at the ends of the court your bows will be handed unto you. You shall stand facing the wall and making no move until the whistle. Then may you fight howsoever you will, and may the stars grant victory to the right."

The marshal was standing in back of a little wooden wall about a meter long and breast-high, behind which he could duck if things got too hot. He and the duelists were the only people in the court, although the palace windows, which surrounded the court on three sides, were full of faces. King Eqrar, High Priest Hasté, Fouri—

"Stand back to back," said the marshal. "Now walk to the ends of the court: one—two—one—two—"

"Are you ready?"

Hasselborg stood facing the stone wall, gooseflesh on his back, into which back he more than half expected Jam to send an iron bolt any second. He was finding a formal duel harder on his nerve than he expected. A fight was one thing; he'd been in several on Earth that had resulted fatally for his antagonist. The first time it had given him the bleeps, but after that he'd taken it as a matter of course. Now the shivery feeling of his first lethal fight had come back. This standing up like a fool and deliberately risking—

The whistle blew piercingly. Hasselborg, tensed for action, dropped the nose of his crossbow to the ground, stuck his toe into the stirrup on the end, and heaved on the string. It came back with a faint sound into the notch. He snatched a bolt from his felt, whirled, and

threw himself prone on his elbow pads, placed the bolt in its groove, and sighted on his target.

Jám bad-Koné was just sighting along his cocked crossbow as Hasselborg brought the heads of the pins into line with the shiniest of the medals on the chest of the dasht. Jám seemed to hesitate; raised his head for a second to look at the antagonist who had fallen down without waiting to be hit, then squinted down the stock of his weapon again.

Hasselborg squeezed the trigger. The stock kicked sharply and the bolt flashed away with a hum, rising and falling a few centimeters in its flat trajectory.

Then something exploded in Hasselborg's head, and the light went out.

X.

Feeling hands trying to turn him over, Victor Hasselborg opened his eyes. His head ached frightfully.

"He lives yet," said one.

"Which can't be said for the other," said somebody else. Their general chatter made a dull roar in Hasselborg's head.

With great effort he pulled himself into a sitting position and felt of his pate. At least there did not seem to be any fragments of skull grinding together like ice floes in an Arctic storm, though his hand came away bloody. The dasht's bolt must have grazed his scalp and carried away his hat, which lay on the stones between him and the wall.

"I'm okay," he said. "Just let me alone a minute." He wanted no Krishnan fingers exploring around the roots of his dyed hair or his glued-on antennae.

"Look!" said a voice, "a new method of sighting a bow, by the stars! Had we such at the battle of Meozid—"

". . . by Qondyor, not knightly; he should have warned Jám, so that—"

". . . has the new dasht reached his majority?"

Hasselborg realized that the king was looking down at him. He got up, staggered a little, and finally found his balance.

"Yes, sire?" he said.

The king replied: "Master painter, you've riven me of a good vassal, a good stout fellow. Though since it had to be one or the other of you, I'm not altogether displeased 'twas he. While a strong and loyal right arm, there's no denying he was difficult. Yes, difficult. Kidnaping gentlewomen. Get you to the surgeon and have your crown patched, and then let's to the painting again. It had better be good, now. I suppose I shall have to attend his funeral; barbaric things, funerals."

"I thank Your Awesomeness, but with my head feeling the way it does, I'm afraid the picture would look pretty gruesome. Can't we put off the next sitting for a day at least?"

"No, varlet! When I say I wish it today—but then, perhaps you're right. I shouldn't wish my nose in the picture to wander over my face like the Pichidé River over the Gozashtando Plain, merely because my artist can't see straight. Get you patched and rested, and resume your work as soon as may be thereafter: Stray you not from the city, however."

"I don't suppose I need these guards any more, do I?"

"No, no, they're dismissed."

"And d'you mind if—"

"If what? If what?"

"Nothing, Your Supremacy. You've done me enough favors already."

He managed a teetery bow, and the king minced off. Hasselborg had been about to ask to be allowed to move back to Hasté's palace, where the service was better organized, when it occurred to him that he would be encouraging Fouri to think up some scheme to lure or coerce him into marrying her.

Fouri was gushing over his survival and Hasté was congratulating him in more restrained style, when a rough-looking individual said: "Master Kavir, may I have a word? I'm Ferzao bad-Qé, captain of the late dasht's personal guard."

When he got Hasselborg aside, the man continued:

"Now that the death of the dasht has canceled our oaths to him, the lads and I wonder what next, d'ye see? The late dasht was a good fellow, albeit careless with his coin, so that our pay came somewhat irregularly. Now he's gone, his eldest inherits, but is not yet of age, wherefore his widow's regent. A sour wench, as thrifty as the dasht was liberal, and will no doubt start by letting half of us go and cutting the pay of the rest.

"So we wondered if, in accordance with the old custom, ye'd like to take us on as your men. We're stout fighters, none fiercer, and if ye but give us the word we'll seize an isle in the Sadabao Sea and make you a sea king, like that fellow on Zamba. What say ye?"

This was a new problem. "How much did the dasht pay you?" asked Hasselborg.

"Oh, as to that, the amount varied with rank, length of service, and the like. The total came to mayhap forty karda a ten-night."

Not bad for an armed gang, thought Hasselborg, though no doubt he'd find he'd let himself in for a lot of extras as well. Maybe these birds would come in handy, and the money Hasté had given him would pay them for some time even without his sending to Novorecife.

"I'll do it," he said.

As things turned out, not all of Jám's men wanted service under Hasselborg; only twenty-nine of them did when all were counted. Some of the others said they might consider it after they'd returned to Rosid for their former master's funeral. *Tant mieux;* the money would last even longer.

Hasselborg shut himself up in his room, applied his pills to his headache, and tried to examine his wound. Unfortunately the latter was on the extreme top of his head where he could not see it with a single mirror. After half an hour's experimenting, he rigged up a second mirror so that he could look down on himself.

The gash had stopped bleeding, and the hair around it was thick with dried blood. He washed some of the blood out, cut off some of the hair next to the scalp with the little scissors from his sewing kit, applied disinfectant, and closed the wound with a small piece of adhesive tape. Not a professional job, but it would have to do.

In the process he noticed that his hair was beginning to show brown at the roots. Therefore, with a small brush, he applied the dye that the barber at Novorecife had sold him, around the edges where it showed. The antennae seemed still secure; however, one of the pointed tips of his ears was coming adrift and had to be re-glued.

He spent most of the day napping. Then he set out for dinner at Hasté's palace, having promised the high priest with some misgivings that he would eat with them that night to celebrate his survival. This time, however, he had a legitimate excuse to turn down Hasté's cocktails, saying his head ached still. He had noticed with alarm that he was actually getting to like these drinks.

"Tell me about Zamba and its new dour," he asked Hasté.

The priest raised his antennae. "Why are you interested, my son? I should think that, having received your fee for Antané's portrait, your curiosity would be satisfied."

"Oh, well—I just wondered how Antané got so far in such a short time. He never impressed me that much when I knew him. And what's he going to do next, now that he has his kingdom?"

"As to that, that's as the stars—yes?"

A younger priest, the one Hasselborg had seen on previous occasions, had just come in to whisper in Hasté's ear. The high priest said: " 'Tis as bad as being a physician. I must go to check the heliacal setting of Rayord. Tell the cook to hold dinner a few moments, will you, Fouri?"

When her uncle had gone, Fouri leaned towards

Hasselborg and looked at him out of her fathomless green slanting eyes. "I could tell you news of Zamba. My gossips at the dour's palace fill my ears with it."

"What is it?"

She smiled. "I but said I could tell, not that I would."

"What d'you mean?" Of course he knew well enough. Oh boy, here we go again!

"I could be a valuable helpmeet to one like yourself but see no point in throwing away my favor to one who'll merely say 'thank you' and ride off and think no more of Fouri."

"How do I know your gossip's as valuable as all that?" he said.

"Trust my word. I have news of import about King Antané."

Hasselborg shook his head. "I'm afraid I can't make a trade for any secret sight unseen." Seeing her look of pain, he added: "Of course I am fond of you in a way, and if your news were important it might help me to make up my mind about other things."

"*Chá!* Let's not spar with wooden swords any longer. Will you promise, if it does in truth prove important, to wed me instanter, by the rites of the Established Church?"

"No."

"Oh, you wretched man! So I'm to give you all I know and mayhap you'll consider what to do next, as if that were a great kindness! Am I so ugly? Am I so cold?"

"No."

"What then?"

"Matter of principle."

"Principle! Curse your principles!" She strode up and down in agitation, storming: "I should hire a bravo to put steel through your gullet, to see if you'd bleed or merely run ink from the wound! Never have I known such a man! One would think you—"

Hasselborg found himself disliking this scene more and more. He fought down a temptation either to break off their equivocal relationship finally, or else to accept her offer.

"Well?" she said.

"What I've told you. I'd love to hear your news, and the more you help me the more grateful I'll be. But I absolutely won't promise to marry you. Not at this stage, anyway."

She stood breathing hard. "Look you. I'll tell you what I hear. Then do as you like—go where you will, cast me aside, revile and beat me if you will. I'll ask nought of you, save that you believe that I truly love you and wish you well."

"Okay, I'll believe that. And I won't say I mightn't feel the same—some day. But what's the news?"

"This—King Antané and his queen sail from Zamba for Majbur any day."

Hasselborg sat up sharply. "What for?"

"That I know not, nor my informant. Antané comes betimes to Majbur to buy, both for himself and for his kingdom, or to talk trade with the syndics of the Free City. For aught I know, his present visit's of that kind. But see you not the true weight of what I've told you?"

"How?"

"Why, if you'd accost this sea king with whatever mysterious business you have with him, and him unwilling, you'd have to pick a time when he's ashore. On his island you could never draw nigh without his leave, for his galleys command the seas thereabouts. Now see you?"

"I do, and thanks a lot. The next problem is, how am I to get away from Hershid without having King Eqrar get sore and send his army after me?"

Fouri thought an instant and said: "Perhaps I could persuade him. The old *baghan* likes me well, though he cares not overmuch for my uncle. I know not if he'd listen or no. Could I prevail upon him, would you change your mind?"

Hasselborg grinned. "No, darling. You're a most

persistent young person, aren't you?"

"No joking matter! See you no⁻ ʰhat you're tearing my liver in shreds? Oh, Kavir, I always dreamed of a man like you—" And she began to weep.

Hasselborg comforted her as best he could, then said: "Pull yourself together. I think I hear your uncle coming back."

In an instant she was the solemnly courteous hostess again. Hasselborg thought, whatever Krishnan finally joins his lot with hers will certainly never have a dull moment.

Next morning, Hasselborg went to the king saying: "May it please Your Awesomeness, my headache's gone—"

"So? Good! Excellent! Then we'll resume the sittings at once. I have an hour this afternoon—"

"Just a minute, sire! I was about to say that, while my headache's gone, I find that my artistic temperament has been so shaken by this duel that I couldn't possibly do good work until my nerves quiet down."

"And when will that be?"

"I don't know for sure; it was my first duel, you know."

"Forsooth? You handled yourself well."

"Thanks. But as I was saying, I'd guess I'll be ready to paint again in less than a ten-night."

"Hm-m-m. Well, well, if that's the way of it, I suppose I shall have to let you hang around ogling the ladies until you make up your mind, or whatever an artist has in lieu of a mind. Most unsatisfactory people, artists. Most unsatisfactory. Can't depend on them. You're like old Hasté, always promising but never delivering."

"I'm sorry if I make Your Awesomeness impatient, but we're dealing with one of those divine gifts that can't be forced. Anyway, aren't you leaving soon for Jám's funeral?"

"That is true; I shall be out of Hershid for some days."

"All right then. In the meantime I'd like permission to take a little vacation away from Hershid, too."

"Where away from Hershid?" said Eqrar with a suspicious look.

"Well—I was thinking of running down to Majbur for a day or two. Change of scene, you know."

"No, I know not! You painters are really intolerable! Here I give you a good fat commission, and anybody would agree that a good subject am I, and the prestige of having painted me alone would be worth your time. I don't even bring a charge of homicide against you when you slay one of my retainers in a fight. And what do you? Excuses, procrastinations, evasions! I'll not have it! Sirrah, consider yourself . . . no, wait. Why come you not to Rosid with me? We might get some painting done on the route."

"Oh, sir! In the first place, Jám's funeral would shatter my nerves utterly; and in the second, I hardly think his people would consider me a welcome guest."

"True, true. Well, if I let you go to Majbur, how know I 'tis not an excuse to get out of my jurisdiction and flee, leaving me with nought but a charcoal sketch for my trouble?"

"That's easy, sir. I'm leaving a good-sized sum of money here, and also that gang of Jám's men who signed up to work for me. There's also the little matter of my bill for this painting I'm working on now. You don't think I'd abandon valuable assets like that, do you?"

"I suppose not. Go on your silly trip, then, and may the gods help you if you come not back as promised!"

"Could you give me an introduction to somebody there? Your ambassador, say?"

"I have a resident commissioner in the Free City. Naén, write this worthless artist a note to Gorbovast, will you? I'll sign it here and now."

This time Hasselborg took pains to stand in front of the secretary's desk as the latter wrote, and to try to read the letter upside down. If written Gozashtandou was hard to read right side up, it was worse inverted. Still, the message seemed straightforward enough, with no deadly words like "spy."

The Krishnan noon therefore found Victor Hasselborg trotting his buggy briskly down the road towards the Free City of Majbur. He had not even said good-by to Fouri; had sent one of his men to Hasté's palace with a message instead, not wanting another scene or demand that he take her along.

He had also been strongly tempted to take one of these burly ruffians with him but had given up the idea. Traveling with a Krishnan would almost certainly result in the native's learning that Hasselborg was an Earthman.

He passed the usual road traffic; overtook and passed the daily train from Hershid to Qadr. It comprised five little cars, three passenger and two freight, pulled along by a bishtar shuffling between the rails. A couple of young Krishnans in one of the passenger cars waved at him, just as children did on Earth. He waved back, feeling, for the first time since his arrival, homesick. Dearest Alexandra— He got out her handkerchief for a quick look at it.

He arrived at the village of Qadr the evening of his second day on the road. As the last ferryboat for Majbur had already left, he spent the night without incident in Qadr and took the first boat across next morning. It was a big barge, rowed by a dozen oarsmen manning long sweeps and helped along by two triangular lateen sails bellying in the westerly breeze that came down the river on their starboard beam. To port, the low shores of the mouth of the Pichidé fell away to nothing, leaving the Sadabao Sea sparkling in the rising sun.

A war galley with catapults in its bows went past, oars thumping in their oarlocks, and off to port a fat merchantman was trying to beat into the harbor against the wind. The latter was having a hard time because at the end of reach the ship wore round like a square-rigger instead of tacking, meanwhile dipping the high ends of the lateen yards and raising the low ends to reverse the set of the yellow sails. During this complicated process, the ship lost almost as much distance drifting downwind as she had previously gained by running closehauled. Hasselborg thought: Why doesn't one of our people show them how to rig a proper fore-and-aft sail? . . and then remembered the Interplanetary Council rule.

A Krishnan objected loudly when Hasselborg's aya snaffled one of the fruits he was bringing into Majbur. Hasselborg had to buy a whole basketful to pacify the man.

Gorbovast, the resident commissioner, was helpful in such essentials as recommending places for Hasselborg to stay and to amuse himself. While the commissioner did not actually say so, Hasselborg got the impression that some of the amusements of this famous seaport were distinctly on the rugged side, like those of Shanghai and Marseilles on Earth.

Unfortunately, Hasselborg could not very well ask the fellow outright about the expected visit of the King of Zamba. He was no longer supposed to be interested in such matters, and the commissioner would report any unseemly curiosity back to his boss.

Since the Krishnans, unlike most intelligent extraterrestrials, had a highly developed system of public eating and drinking houses, there was nothing for it but to brace himself for the ordeal of a waterfront pub-crawl. He'd done it before—you go into the first grog-shop, order one, strike up a conversation with the first fellowcustomer who looks as if he had one brain cell to rub against another, and get him talking. If he proves an empty sack, you go on to the next. Hasselborg had nearly always, at least in the smaller cities, been able to get a line on what he wanted to know by this method, though it sometimes took days and was hard on his delicately conditioned stomach. Furthermore, it always filled him with morbid fears of picking up an infection.

Thus evening found him halfway down Majbur's waterfront, feeling poorly both in the head and in the digestive system, about to pump his twenty-second sucker. Some of the tougher characters had looked at him speculatively, but so far the combination of his powerful build and conspicuous sword had discouraged hostilities.

His present victim, a sailor from the far island of Sotaspé with the quaint name of Morbid, bade fair to prove an empty sack. The man was one who could take but little liquor, and he had already had that and wanted to sing the songs of his childhood. He sang in a dialect that Hasselborg could follow only half the time and remembered these songs in quantity and detail that would have done credit to a psychoanalytical treatment. Hasselborg began to cast about for means of escape.

The other end of the bench held another pair in close converse. One, facing Hasselborg, was a rustic-looking character talking slowly and with great emphasis to a bulky fellow with his back to Hasselborg.

The bulky fellow looked around to see what had become of the servitor, and Hasselborg spilled a drop of his kvad with surprise. It was Chuen Liao-dz.

XI.

"Excuse me, chum," said Hasselborg to his companion. "I see an old friend."

He walked down the length of the bench and placed a hand gently on Chuen's shoulder, saying: *"Ni hau bu hau?"*

Chuen turned his head with a slight smile and no sign of surprise. *"Wo hau,"* he replied in Chinese, then switched back to Gozashtandou: "Fancy meeting you here! Sanándaj, this is my old friend—ah—my old friend—"

"Kavir bad-Ma'lum," said Hasselborg.

"Of course. Sanándaj has been telling me about almanacs. Most fascinating business." He tipped a wink at Hasselborg. "I wondered how long it would take you to notice me. How about your friend, the sailor?"

"He sings."

"Indeed? Then we must introduce them. Master Sanándaj can tell the mariner about almanacs while latter sings. Most jolly arrangement."

"Okay. Ahoy, there, Morbid!" Hasselborg dragged the more or less unwilling sailor down and set him to singing to Chuen's friend, who kept right on talking almanacs, trying to shout down his new acquaintance. Under cover of the resulting racket, Hasselborg asked Chuen: "What name are you going by?"

"Li-yau, which is the nearest they can come to first

part of my name. The surname they cannot manage at all; it comes out Chuvon or something like that. Now, tell me of your adventures."

"Not just yet. Suppose you tell me yours. This is a funny way to investigate economic conditions with a view to arranging high-grade imports and exports, isn't it?"

"A little unusual, perhaps."

"Chum, you're no more an economic official than I am; you're a cop."

Chuen smiled. *"Shi bu shi?"*

"Perfeitamente. Now, I think we can do each other more good by working together than separately."

"So? What do you propose?"

"A general laying of cards on the table. D'you follow me?"

"Very interesting idea."

"Oh, I know, you're wondering how you can be sure I'm honest, and how can I be sure you are, and so on. Do you know my mission?"

"No. You never told me."

"Well then, I'll tell you, and you can decide whether it's worth your while to be equally frank. I don't think you'll have any motive for putting a spoke in my wheel, and I trust I'll feel the same way about you." Hasselborg went on to tell of the pursuit of the truant Julnar Batruni.

Chuen looked really surprised when he had finished, saying: "You mean this man sends you off on this great expensive dangerous trip merely for petty personal motives?"

"If you call wanting to get his daughter back a petty personal motive, yes."

"But—but that is sheer romanticism! And I thought all the time you were involved in some profound matter of interplanetary intrigue; something to do with government policies and interstellar relations! Now turns out nothing but pursuit of runaway young woman!" He shook his head.

"Okay, but how about your opening up with me? I may need help on my project, and I can't hire a local yokel for reasons you can guess. Maybe you're in the same fix. How about it, huh?"

Chuen thought a while, then said: "I—ah—I think maybe you have reason, so here goes: I'm an agent for Chinese government with special commission from World Federation. I started out to try trace a shipment of fifty machine guns consigned from factory in Detroit to my government for their security police. These guns start out all right but don't arrive.

"Now, economically speaking, fifty machine guns is nothing at all to big government, but still nobody likes to have stolen guns floating around in hands of the criminal class. So, they put Chuen on job. Trail leads first to gangsters in Tientsin, who keep only twenty-six of guns and pass the other twenty-four on to an official of Viagens Interplanetarias.

"Things are obviously getting beyond national scope, so my government gets me a special commission from W. F. to run down missing guns. I find they've been brought to Krishna, to be smuggled out of Novorecife for delivery to some local potentate. The local potentate will use them to conquer the planet, or at least as much of it as can manage."

"Who was to do the smuggling out of Novorecife?" asked Hasselborg.

"Don't know. Somebody on the inside, no doubt."

Hasselborg nodded. "But who gets the guns? Don't tell me, let me guess. Anthony Fallon, right?"

"Right again."

Hasselborg lit a cigar. "Have one? No wonder I ran into you here. It seemed too good for a coincidence, but with you on the track of Tony's guns, and me after his girl, our paths were bound to cross. Where are the guns now?"

Chuen shrugged. "Wish I knew. I heard a story that a mysterious crate has been hidden in the Koloft Swamp by one of gangs of robbers that live there, but was no way for me to find them. Swamp not only big, but full of unpleasant monsters, too. However, since I felt sure they'd be delivered to Majbur for Fallon to pick them up, I came here to try intercept them. Been here days, checking boats and rafts that come down the river and trying to pick up a lead in bars and restaurants."

Hasselborg said: "I may be able to help you there," and told the rumor of Fallon's impending arrival in Majbur. "I imagine whoever's in charge of the guns will arrange to have them here when Fallon arrives."

"I imagine, too. What connections you got in Majbur?"

"King Eqrar gave me a letter to his envoy Gorbovast."

"Good. Can you ask Gorbovast when Fallon is expected?"

"Not very well; I'm supposed to be here on a short vacation and not to be interested in Fallon, and I suppose old Eqrar will check up on me through Gorbovast. Could you?"

"Maybe. I am friend of Chief Syndic, who know Gorbovast. Maybe the syndic knows. We see."

The following afternoon, Chuen came upon Hasselborg sitting on the top of a pile on the biggest pier and giving a convincing imitation of a congenital loafer. Chuen said:

"The syndic say Fallon due to arrive tomorrow night or early next day. Guns *must* arrive soon. Are you sure nothing's come in this morning?"

"Not a thing except a towboat with two passengers and no freight at all, and a timber raft from way upriver with nothing on it except a stove and a tent for the raftmen. *Tamates,* haven't we forgotten about Qadr? Any piers over there?"

"Yes, but they're only used for fishing boats and such. All big commercial traffic uses this side."

"Well, mightn't our mysterious friends be landing in Qadr for just that reason?"

"Maybe, now that you mention it. What shall we do about it?"

"Suppose you take over here, and I'll go across the river and look around."

"All right."

It transpired that the ferry was across the river and would not return for another hour. Hasselborg killed time by strolling about the piers and through nearby streets to orient himself and by pumping another sucker in a bar. Another empty sack. Fortunately impatience was not prominent among Hasselborg's vices.

When he returned to the ferry pier, it was to find a crowd watching the efforts of a crew in the uniform of railroad employees trying to keep a bishtar calm. The ferry was unloading. The spectators watched with a mixture of curiosity and apprehension, holding themselves poised for flight in case the huge animal got out of control.

When the last wagon rumbled off and the sails had been furled and reset, the ferry master signaled to board the boat. Some of those who had been intending to do so, seeing that they were to share the craft with the bishtar, changed their minds. Others got on, but huddled in the corners of the vessel, leaving as large a clear space as possible for the monster.

The bishtar, under the urging of its keepers, put out a foot and gingerly tried the deck of the ferry. Apparently not liking the yielding sensation, it shied back. The men yelled and whacked it with sticks and pulled on goads, which they hooked into its thick hide. The bishtar squealed angrily and rolled ugly little eyes this way and that but finally let itself be driven aboard, one foot after another. The ferry settled visibly as it took the weight.

Then the sailors cast off the lines and pushed off with poles. The oarsmen ran out their sweeps and set to their task, backing out from the pier and turning the scowlike vessel towards Qadr, grunting with every heave. As they came about, the sailors shook out the sails, whose flapping startled the bishtar. The animal set up an ominous squealing, swinging its head from side to side, shifting its feet, and lashing the air with its stubby trunks.

Hasselborg had stood on the wales, holding a stay, where he could leap ashore at the last minute if the animal ran amok. While wondering what all this portended, he noticed a bulge in one of his pockets and remembered that he still had one of the fruits he had bought on the ferry the day before. Some he had eaten, some he had fed to Avvaú, and the rest he had stowed in his pockets this morning for lunch. Now one was left, a thing that looked like a tangerine but tasted quite different.

Hasselborg stepped near the bishtar's head and called up to the mahout on its neck: *"Ohé* there! Will he eat this if I give it to him?"

"Yes, sir, that she will," the man said.

Hasselborg extended the fruit in gingerly fashion, fatalistically half expecting the beast to grab his arm in a trunk and beat him to bits against the nearest mast. The bishtar, however, after a wary look, put out a trunk and delicately took the fruit. Chomp. Then it stood quietly wagging its ears, since the sails, having filled, were no longer flapping.

"Thank you, sir," said the mahout.

"No trouble. What's she being taken over for?"

"That I know not. They do say we're to run a double-header to Hershid tomorrow, or perhaps the next day."

"A big load?"

"So I suppose. If ye'd really like to know, ask the station agent in Qadr."

So far, thought Hasselborg, he and Chuen had assumed that Fallon would simply come into Majbur in one of his ships, take delivery on his guns, and sail away again to Zamba unless stopped. Could it be that he was planning a lightning descent on Hershid to seize the whole Empire of Gozashtand? It was a little odd for an invading army to come in on the daily train. Come to think of it, however, Fallon's men would be sailors, as out of place on an aya or shomal as a horse on a house top. Moreover, such a sudden move by Fallon, outpacing even the rumor of his coming, would catch the dour entirely unprepared.

A fishy smell announced that they were drawing near to Qadr. When they docked at the ferry pier, Fallon watched the railroad men get the bishtar in motion again. The animal got off with much more alacrity than it had shown on the other side and lumbered up the main street, while small tame eshuna ran out of the sagging shacks that lined the street to yowl at it.

Hasselborg, after pleasantly greeting the dour's frontier guards loafing on the pier, followed the bishtar to the railroad yard, his boots squilching in the mud. Here he loafed around the station, smoking, until nobody would take him for an importunate inquirer. Finally he got into conversation with the station agent and said:

"That bishtar you fellows brought over on the ferry this afternoon nearly scared the daylights out of the passengers. She doesn't like boats."

"No, that's a fact, they don't," said the agent. "But with the river so wide here, we can't build a bridge, so we must needs use the ferry to move bishtars and rolling stock between Majbur and Qadr."

"Are you planning to run some big train soon?"

"So they tell us. Somebody's coming in with a great crew of men to take to Hershid. Yesterday a man comes up to buy twenty-six tickets in advance. Who he be I know not; howsomever, since he had the gold, we've no choice but to get ready."

They were still engaged in small talk when Hasselborg heard the warning bell from the ferry. Knowing that this was the last trip that day, he had to run to make it, arriving just as the lines were being case off.

He leaped the two-meter space between the barge and the pier and sat down to puff. He had not had time to snoop around for the guns, although this news about twenty-six tickets for Hershid was probably more urgent.

Chuen seemed to think so, too. "Nothing has come, sir. One large towboat with some baggage aboard, but nothing that could hold machine guns."

"There's no other way from the Koloft Swamp to Maj-bur?"

"Are roads from the swamp to Mishé. One runs straight south from Novorecife and the other from the village of Qou at edge of the swamp. So you could take these guns to Mishé and then by big highway from there to Majbur. I think that unlikely, because it's more roundabout, and also the Order of Qarar polices the Republic of Mikardand very thoroughly. So chances of getting them through would be less."

"It'll be dinner time soon," said Hasselborg, looking at another stunning Krishnan sunset.

"Do you want go eat while I watch river and then take my place?"

"Okay—say, what's that?"

Up-river, its one lateen sail pink in the sunset, a boat was approaching. Chuen, following Hasselborg's gaze, reached out and gave his companion's wrist a quick squeeze of warning. "It's type of boat I saw used around Qou," he murmured.

As the boat came closer, it resolved into a kind of wherry with a single mast stepped in the bow and eight or ten oars on a side.

"Better get back a little from the end of the pier," muttered Hasselborg.

"*Shi.* You take base of this pier; I take base of second pier up," said Chuen. "You got a cigar? I'm all out."

Hasselborg yawned, stretched, and sauntered back towards shore, to resume his loafing against a warehouse wall. Chuen departed up-river.

Hasselborg watched the boat with ostentatious lack of interest. Between the current, the breeze, and the efforts of the oarsmen, the boat soon arrived off their sections of the waterfront. Down came the sail with a rattle of blocks, and the boat crawled toward shore under oar-power alone. The crew were tough-looking types, and in front of the tillerman in the stern lay a large packing case.

The boat was pulling into the dock that Chuen had chosen to watch. Hasselborg strolled in that direction as the boat tied up and the crew manhandled the case ashore. Nobody paid them any heed as they rigged a sling with two carrying-poles through the loops. Two of them got under each end of each pole, put pads on their shoulders, and hoisted the case into the air with a simul-taneous grunt. The eight carriers set off briskly towards the base of the pier, the case bobbing slightly and the ropes creaking with every step. Two others of the crew went with them, while the rest sat on the pier, smoked, and waited.

Chuen followed the shore party, and Hasselborg fol-lowed a little behind Chuen. After a couple of turns in the narrow streets, they stopped at the door of a big featureless building with windows high up. Chuen kept right on walking past them, while Hasselborg became interested in the creatures displayed in the window of a wholesale sea food establishment, although the wobbly Krishnan glass made the things seem even odder than they were.

The man who had held the tiller plied the big iron knocker on the door of the house. Presently the door opened. There was a conversation, inaudible from where Hasselborg stood, and the bearers took up their burden and marched into the house. Slam!

After a while they came out again; or rather, nine of the ten came out. Hasselborg kept his eyes glued to the sea food, especially one thing that seemed to combine the less attractive features of a lobster, an octopus, and a centipede, as they walked past behind him. He drew a long breath of relief when they went by without trying to stab him in the back.

Chuen popped out of the alley into which he had

slipped and came towards Hasselborg, saying: "I looked around back of building. No windows on ground floor."

"Then how do we get in?"

"There's one window a little way up. Maybe two and a half meters. If we had something to stand on, could get in."

"If we had a ladder—and a crow."

"A crow? Bird?"

"No, a pry-bar—you know, a jimmy."

"Oh, you mean one of those iron things with hook on the end?"

"Uh-huh. I don't know what they call it in Gozashtandou."

"Neither do I, but can do lots with sign language. One of us must go buy while other one watches."

"Hm-m-m," said Hasselborg. "I suppose whatever they have in the way of hardware stores are closed up by now."

"Maybe some open. Majbur keeps very late hours."

"Okay, d'you want me to hunt while you watch? My legs are longer than yours."

"Thanks, but better you watch while I hunt. You got sword and know how to use. I don't."

Forebearing to argue, Hasselborg took up his post while Chuen toddled off on his short legs. The polychrome lights faded from the sky, and all three of the moons cast pyramidal shadows into the narrow, smelly streets. People passed occasionally, sometimes leading beasts of burden. A man whom Hasselborg did not recognize—not one of the boatmen, surely—came out of the building and pushed off on a scooter. Hasselborg was just wondering whether to give his second cigar one more puff or put it out when Chuen reappeared lugging a short ladder.

"Here," said Chuen, thrusting a pry bar with a hooked end into Hasselborg's hand.

They glanced about. As nobody seemed to be in sight

at the moment, they slipped into the alley that led to the rear of the warehouse.

Chuen had neglected to state that the medium-low window opened on a little court or backyard isolated by a substantial wall with spikes along the top. That, however, represented only a momentary check. They set the ladder against the wall, swarmed up it, and balanced themselves on top of the wall while they hauled the ladder up after them and planted it on the ground on the opposite side. Then down again; then to put the ladder against the wall of the warehouse itself.

Hasselborg mounted the ladder first. He attacked the window—a casement-type affair having a lot of little diamond-shaped panes—with the bar. Since he was an old hand at breaking and entering in line of duty, the window presently opened with a slight crunching of splintered wood. He stuck his head inside.

By the narrow beams of moonlight, which slanted in through the high windows, and the faint light reflected from a candle out of sight somewhere on the other side of the structure, he could see the tops of what looked like acres of bales, crates, and boxes. No movement; no sound.

Hasselborg whispered to Chuen: "I think we can get down to the floor level from here without hauling the ladder in. I'm going to drop down inside and scout around. If I find it's okay, I'll tell you to come down after me. If not, I'll ask you to hand me down the ladder, so we'll have a way out. Got my sword? Okay, here goes."

And Victor Hasselborg slid off the window sill into the darkness inside.

XII.

As Hasselborg's toes struck the wooden top of the nearest packing case, he thanked the local gods for the soft-leather Krishnan boots, which let him alight silently. The window sill was about the height of his chin, so that he should be able to get out without much trouble. He stalked catlike around the top of the case, peering about to plan his route. Da'vi was still with him, for an easy route led down by a series of crates and piles of sacks of diminishing heights.

"Chuen!" he whispered. "It's okay; we can leave the ladder where it is. Hand me my sword."

Chuen's bulk blocked the dim light through the window as he heaved himself over the sill with surprising quietness for one of his build. Together they stole down the piles of merchandise to the floor and walked stealthily towards the candlelight. Twice they got lost in the maze of aisles between the rows of crates. Finally they came to the corner of the building where the candle was located.

Looking around the corner of a pile of bags, Hasselborg espied a little cleared space, with a desk and a chair, and the candle burning in a holder on a shelf. Just outside the cleared space stood the packing case they were after. And, in the angle between the case and the wall, a man sat with legs asprawl, sleeping—one of the boat crew.

As Hasselborg moved to get a better view, his scabbard struck against the merchandise and gave forth a faint *tink*. Instantly the man's eyes opened. For two seconds these eyes swiveled before coming to rest on Hasselborg and his companion.

Instantly the man bounded to his feet, holding a scimitar that had lain on the floor beside him, and sprang towards the intruders. Hasselborg jumped away from the crates to get elbow room and drew his sword. The man, however, went for Chuen. The curved blade swished through the air and met the pry bar with a clank.

Hasselborg stepped toward them and cut at the man, who saw him coming and skipped away before the blow arrived. Then he came back again, light and fast, cutting right and left. Hasselborg parried as best he could, wishing he were an experienced swordsman so that he could skewer this slasher. *Clong, dzing, thump!* Chuen had stepped behind the man and conked him with the crow. The man's saber clanged to the floor and the man followed it, falling to hands and knees.

He shook his head, then reached for his sword.

"No you don't!" said Hasselborg. In his excitement he spoke English, but nevertheless got his meaning across by whacking the outstretched hand with the flat of his blade.

"Ao!" cried the man, nursing his knuckles.

"Shut up and back up," said Hasselborg, remembering his Gozashtandou.

The man started to comply, but Chuen landed heavily on his back, flattening him out, and twisted his arms behind him.

"Amigo," said the Chinese, "cut length of rope off one of these bales and give it to me."

Hasselborg did so, wondering if there were not some easier way of making a living. While during hot action he never had time to be afraid, it gave him a queasy feeling when he came to reckon up the odds afterwards.

When the man's wrists and ankles had been secured, they rolled him over and shoved him roughly back against the wall.

"Like to live?" asked Hasselborg, holding his point under the man's chin.

"Of course. Who be ye, thieves? I but guard the goods while—"

"Pipe down. Answer our questions, and in a low voice, or else. You're one of those who came down in the boat from Koloft, aren't you?"

"Yes."

"Wait," said Chuen. "What's become of the regular watchman?"

"Gone reveling. There's a place near here he's long craved to visit, but can't because their working hours be the same as his. Since I was to stay the night anyway, I told him to take himself off whilst I watched."

Chuen looked at Hasselborg, who nodded confirmation, saying: "I saw the man leave this building while I was waiting for you." Hasselborg then asked the riverman: "Where's the rest of your boatload?"

"Out on the town, even as the watchman, may Dupulán rot his soul!"

"When do they shove off?"

"Tomorrow, as soon after sunrise as their night's joys'll let 'em."

"D'you know whom this box is for?"

"The Dour of Zamba, so they say."

"Do you know this dour? Have you ever seen him?"

"No, not I."

"When's he due in Majbur?"

"Tomorrow ere sunset."

Chuen interposed: "Whom did you get this box from in the first place?"

"Earthman at Novorecife."

"What Earthman?"

"I—uh—know not his name; some unpronounceable *Ertso*—"

"You'd better remember," said Hasselborg, pricking the man's skin with his point. "I'm going to shove—"

"I know! I remember! 'Twas Master Julio Góis! Take away your sticker!"

Hasselborg whistled. "No wonder he tried to have me bumped off!"

"What's this?" asked Chuen.

Hasselborg told of his experiences with the Dasht of Rúz.

"Of course!" said Chuen. "Think I know. He didn't believe your story about Miss Batruni and took you for man after the guns. I wouldn't have believed it myself."

"But why should Góis go in for a smuggling scheme of this kind? What would he stand to gain from it?"

"No need for material gain. He's—ah—fanatic about progress."

"So that's why he said that no matter what happened, always to remember that he esteemed me! The twerp liked me well enough as a man, but since I threatened his world-changing scheme, as he thought, I'd have to be liquidated."

"Undoubtedly." Chuen turned back to the prisoner and switched to the latter's tongue, asking for more details. The few he got, however, were not such as to change the general outlines of what they already knew.

"I think you've pumped our friend dry," said Hasselborg at last. "Let's have a look at the crate."

With the pry bar they soon ripped the crate open. Inside, ranged in a double row in a rack, were twenty-four well-greased Colt-Thompson 6.5-millimeter light machines rifles. A compartment at the bottom of the crate held thousands of rounds of ammunition.

Hasselborg took one gun out and hefted its four kilos of weight. "Just look at these little beauties! You can adjust them for any reasonable rate of automatic or semi-automatic fire; you can set this doohickus to fire in bursts of two to ten shots. With one of these and plenty of ammunition I'd take on a whole Krishnan army."

"No doubt what friend Fallon has in mind," said Chuen. "Now that we got them, what shall we do with?"

"I was wondering myself. I suppose we could tote them an armful at a time down to the river and dump them in."

"That would fix Fallon's plans, all right, but then where would evidence be?"

"What evidence?"

"Evidence against smuggling ring. I don't care much about King Anthony. Lots of disguised Earthmen adventuring around Krishna, and if we get rid of him there will just be another soon. Main thing is to bust up gang inside Viagens Interplanetarias."

"Let me think," said Hasselborg. "By the way, now that we've drained this gloop, what'll we do with him? While we can't very well let him go, I don't like to kill the guy in cold blood."

"Why not? Oh, excuse, I forget you're an Anglo-Saxon. If not kill him, then what?"

Hasselborg felt in his pockets. "I think I've got it. Where's a pitcher and a glass?" He rummaged until he found a brass carafe and mug.

"What are you doing?" asked Chuen.

"See this? It's a trance pill that'll lay him out cold for a couple of weeks."

"I don't see how Novorecife authorities let you take that out."

Hasselborg grinned. "This is one they didn't know about. Or rather they thought it was an ordinary longevity pill. You might say it is, in a way, since I'll have a better chance of a long life on account of it."

"What are you going to do?"

"Knock him out, move the crates around to make a hiding place, and leave him there with enough air to keep him alive till he wakes up. In this mare's nest, we can hide him so it'll take a month to find him."

"All very well, but what when watchman come back? And what about the guns?"

Hasselborg had set down his water and was toying with the machine gun, working the bolt and squinting along the sights. He was careful to keep the muzzle pointed away from the others.

"Let's see—" he said. "I used to be able to strip and assemble these blindfolded." He unscrewed a wingnut and took out the bolt mechanism. "As I recall, one of the tricks they played on us in the Division of Investigation was to wait till we had the parts all laid out, then steal the firing pin while we were sitting there blind, and hope we'd put the gun back together without it. Maybe we could—"

"Take out firing pins—" said Chuen.

"And reassemble the guns—"

"Then let Fallon pick up guns—"

"Yes, while I tear back to Hershid and get my private army!"

Hasselborg and Chuen slapped each other's backs in sudden enthusiasm. Then the former said:

"But still we haven't disposed of the janitor. When he comes back and finds nobody—"

"He'll think his companion went off for fun too, yes?"

"Maybe—"

"I know," said Chuen. "We put this man to sleep, disarm the guns, nail crate back together. Then I disguise myself with this man's hat and sword like member of the boat crew. I look more like Krishnan than you. I tell watchman I'm member of the boat crew who relieved this man during night so he can have fun too. Then I leave in morning, saying I got to catch boat back to Koloft. Really I hang around to make sure Fallon get the guns. Meantime you take your buggy and ride back to Hershid like you said, catch Fallon, and turn him over to me."

"Yeah, but when the boat crew find a man missing—"

Chuen shrugged. "We hope they think he got lost in a dive and go off without. I'll be ready to duck if they come around looking for him anyway."

Hasselborg looked at his machine gun with narrowed eyes. "Chuen, how badly do you want Fallon?"

"Ah—so-so. Don't care much so long as I get Góis and other Viagens conspirators. I suppose since Fallon conspired to break regulations, I should bring him in, too. Why?"

"I was thinking that my need may be greater than thine."

"How so?"

"I'm supposed to bring Miss Batruni back to Earth. Now, I can't drag her aboard a spaceship; the minute I get her inside the wall at Novorecife she'll be under Earth law."

"Yes?"

"If you did bring Fallon in to Novorecife, what would happen then?"

"I'd present evidence at preliminary hearing before Judge Keshavachandra, who would order a trial. If he's convicted, go to jail. That's all."

"He'd be tried on Krishna?" said Hasselborg.

"Yes."

"How about appeals?"

"Interstellar Circuit Court of Appeals take care of that. Visit Krishna every couple years to hear appeals. What are you getting at?"

"I wondered if there were any way of having him tried on Earth. You see, if he were dragged back to Earth, Julnar Batruni would probably come back to Earth without urging. Follow me?"

"No chance. Fallon's offenses were all committed on Krishna."

"In that case, chum, I think I do need him more than you do. You see, I'll need some hold on Miss Batruni, and at the moment I can't think of a better one than to leave Fallon under duress here."

"Oh. Wouldn't that get you in trouble with Terran

law, being accessory to false imprisonment or something?"

"No it wouldn't, since the imprisonment would be on Krishna outside of Novorecife. If this were a planet with extradition, it might make me liable to trouble, but it isn't, since they haven't yet got habeas corpus and things like that."

"I see. But look, *companheiro,* maybe if Fallon is in jail at Novorecife, Miss Batruni would go back to Earth for not knowing what else to do, don't you think?"

"Might, or might not. Maybe she loves him enough to stick around Novorecife to be near him; or maybe she'd go back to her island and tell the Zambans: 'Your king's in the clink, so as queen I'm running the joint for him until he gets out.' Women rulers are fairly common on this part of Krishna. No, I think my scheme is the only one I can count on."

"How will you manage it?"

"I haven't worked it all out yet, but I've got an idea. With your help I'm sure we can put it across."

They sat looking at each other by candlelight silently for a full minute. Hasselborg hoped Chuen would accede without making an issue of the case. Chuen was a good man to work with, but by the same token would be a dangerous antagonist. He hoped he wouldn't have to resort to threats to elicit further coöperation.

Chuen finally said: "I'll—ah—make deal. I help you catch Fallon the way you said. Then if I can get deposition from him against Góis, to help my case there, I'll let him stew in own soup. If authorities at Novorecife want him, I'll try dissuade them; tell them they'd need an army to catch him, and anyway he's turned state's evidence, and things like that. If they insist I bring him in, I'll have to try. You understand?"

Hasselborg thought a while in his turn. He finally replied: "Okay. Let's go to work."

While Hasselborg forced his trance pill on the unwilling riverman, Chuen picked up the curved sword. "Thought I'd never use one of these, but since I stopped that cut with the pry bar, I begin think I'm born swordsman, too. How you say in the Old English? Ha, villain!" He swished the blade through the air.

XIII.

The keepers of the city gate at Hershid, knowing Victor Hasselborg as the savior of the Lady Fouri, waved him through without formal identification. It had rained almost continuously since he had left Majbur, and a few sneezes had filled him with more acute fear than all the fighters in Krishna. Although he wanted nothing so much as to curl up in bed with his pills until the threat of a cold disappeared, however, he drove straight to Hasté's palace and dashed in.

"Your Reverence," he told the high priest, "you told me when I first arrived here that you'd do anything I asked in return for my small services to your niece. Is that right?"

"Yes, my son?"

"Well then, here's where I foreclose." He smiled disarmingly. "It won't be too terrible and it won't cost the True Faith anything. First I'd like you to send one of your flunkies over to the royal palace and tell Ferzao bad-Qé, the leader of my men-at-arms, that I want them all to report over here on the double, with their arms and their ayas and a couple of spares."

"Master Kavir, the king has been asking after you. Hadn't you better pay your respects to him? He's impatient—"

"That's just the point! I don't want the king to know I'm in town, because he'll want me to paint his picture,

143

and I've got more urgent things to do. Second, will you have somebody go out and buy me some fireworks? The kind you light and hold out, and they shoot out colored fireballs."

"It shall be done, my son."

"Thanks. And finally, will you prepare one of those cells in your basement for an unwilling guest?"

"Master Kavir! What are you about? I trust that you seek not to lure me into sinful acts under the guise of gratitude."

The guy's beginning to waver, thought Hasselborg, remembering King Eqrar's remark about the priest's habit of promising anything and fulfilling nothing. He decided that the way to deal with Hasté was to be brisk and domineering. "You'll see. Nothing against the best interests of Gozashtand. And it's absolutely necessary; I have your promise, you know."

Fouri came out and greeted him formally. When Hasté occupied in giving orders, she murmured: "When can I see my hero alone? I'm aflame with longing for him! I cannot sleep—"

This is where I came in, thought Hasselborg. He managed to be brightly conversational and completely uninformative during the next half-hour while his preparations were being made.

He said: "If the king asks, tell him I've gone hunting with my men. It's no lie, either." And he strode out to his carriage.

Back on the road to Majbur they sped. Hasselborg, observing that the sun was lowering, hoped they would catch the invaders before sunset. He was driving one of the spare ayas he had bought for his little army, since he had nearly killed poor Avvaú to reach Hershid ahead of Fallon. They might meet the train any time, since, while the aya could outsprint the bishtar, the larger beast could keep up a higher average speed for long distances than any other domestic animal.

Presently Ferzao bad-Qé cantered up beside him and pulled down to a trot. "Master Kavir," he said, "methinks I see something far ahead on yonder track!"

Hasselborg looked. Sure enough the track, which stretched away across the plain on their left, parallel to the road, ended in a little spot. As they approached, the spot grew and grew until it became two bishtars in tandem pulling a dozen little cars.

"You've got your orders," said Hasselborg. "Go to it."

Ferzao halted and deployed his men. One of them handed him a Roman candle, which he lit with flint and steel. As the fuse fizzed, the sergeant galloped across the moss towards the leading bishtar, holding the firework in front of him like a lance. At the same time the other twenty-eight set up a yell, banging on their brass bucklers with their mailed hands to augment the din.

The Roman candle spat fireballs at the bishtar. A couple bounced off its slaty hide, while its mahout yelled in terror. The animal screamed and lumbered off across the plain away from its tormentors, dragging its fellow after it. Behind the second bishtar, the first of the little cars left the rails; the next teetered and fell over on its side.

A mighty chorus of yells arose from the train, and two dozen men in sailors' dress tumbled out of the remaining cars with Colt-Thompson machine guns. With a disciplined movement, the sailors dashed out and flung themselves down on the moss in a line of skirmishers.

Hasselborg's men galloped towards them with lances couched and arrows nocked. Up came the guns.

"*Pazzoi!*" shouted a voice from the train. A multiple click came from the twenty-four guns.

"Surrender!" shouted Ferzao. "Those things won't work!"

He pulled up a few feet in front of them. A couple of sailors worked their bolts and tried again with no better success. The rest, in the face of the lances and drawn bows, threw down their guns and rose to their knees, arms extended in token of surrender.

"What's all this?" yelled a voice, as a tall, gaudily-dressed person walked across the moss from the train.

Hasselborg recognized the handsome heartbreaker of the photographs under the Krishnan makeup. With him came a splendid-looking dark girl, and behind them the stocky form of Chuen Liao-dz. "What sort of reception—"

"Hello there, Fallon," said Hasselborg, who had secured his reins and, like Fallon, followed his army on foot to the scene of the battle.

"Who's speaking English? You? Are you—"

"Careful, chum; if you don't give me away I'll do the same for you. Officially I'm Kavir bad-Ma'lum, portrait painter by appointment to His Awesomeness King Eqrar of Gozashtand. Unofficially I'm Victor Hasselborg of London."

"Oh, really? Well, what do you think you're doing—"

"You'll learn. Meanwhile keep calm, because I've got the advantage. This is Miss Julnar Batruni, isn't it?"

"Our wife!" growled Fallon. "Her 'Resplendency Queen Julnar of Zamba, if you please!"

"Seems to me you already had one wife in London, didn't you? She sent her regards."

"You didn't come clear from Earth to tell us that! Anyway, it's not exactly true. We fixed things up."

"How?"

"Why, we divorced her and married Julnar under Zamban law."

"How convenient! I'll be judge, I'll be jury, said cunning old Fury. Delighted to know you, Queen. Mr. Batruni sent me to find out what had become of you."

"Oh, is that so?" said the girl. "Well, now that you know, why don't you go back to Earth and tell the old dear, and take your nose out of our affairs?"

"Uh—well, the fact is he commissioned me to bring you back if possible."

"You—" shouted Fallon, and tugged at his sword.

"Grab him!" said Hasselborg. Two of his men pounced on Fallon, twisted his arms behind him, and took his sword away.

"Naughty, naughty," said Hasselborg. "Now let's continue more calmly. As I was saying, Miss Batruni—pardon me, Mrs. Fallon—or Queen Julnar—your father's lonesome and would like to see you again."

"Well I—I do love the old fellow, you know, but one can't leave one's husband and run home half a dozen light-years for a week-end. Won't you please let us be? I'll write Father, or send a message, or anything like that—"

Hasselborg shook his head. "We'll have to go into this further. King Anthony, will you please mount this aya? One of my men will lead it for you, and don't try any breaks. Chuen, here's one for you—"

"Oh," said Chuen, looking apprehensive. "Is no other way to go?"

"No; I'm taking Miss Ba—the young lady with me."

"You know this fella?" said Fallon to Hasselborg. "Who is he?"

"He's Master Li-yau, who's looking into the disappearance of certain machine guns from—uh—from the mails, if you follow me. How did you get on the train with the rest, Chuen?"

"Bought ticket; told some lies about how my old uncle was dying in Hershid, so they let me ride in Fallon's special. What you doing with the Zambava?"

"Sending 'em back. Hey, you there!" Hasselborg called to the mahouts, who were just getting their beasts calmed. "Special's canceled. Break the train and hitch one of those bishtars to the Qadr end of the passenger coaches. Now, you!" He addressed the sailors, collected in a glum and muttering group. "You know you were caught invading Gozashtand with arms, don't you?"

They nodded.

"And it would go pretty hard with you if I turned you over to the dour?"

A sailor asked: "Don't you work for him, master?"

"As it happens I don't, though he and I are good friends. Wouldn't you like to be carried back to Qadr, and nothing said about this?"

"Aye, sir!" cried several of the Zambava with a sudden access of interest in life.

"Okay. Ferzao, detail a couple of men to see these boys off to Qadr in the train. Have somebody help get those derailed cars back on the track. Assign somebody to lead King Antané's aya, and a couple more to shoot him if he tries a break. We'll tell the guards at the gate that we're just back from the hunt, and hope they won't count us. You there, pick up those guns and load 'em into the carriage."

"I say," said Fallon, "what happened that those guns didn't shoot? We're told they were all right when they arrived on Krishna."

"Trade secret; tell you some day," said Hasselborg. "Queen Julnar, will you do me the honor? Don't look so scared, Chuen!"

"Is long way to the ground," said Chuen, peering down from his uneasy saddle.

"Not so far as it looks. And weren't you kidding me about being scared of germs?"

"Where are you taking us?" demanded Fallon. "To King Eqrar?"

"Not yet. Keep quiet and behave yourself and perhaps you won't have to meet him at all. *Hao!*"

Hasselborg cracked his whip, and his buggy headed back for Hershid at a canter through the sunset.

Hasté stroked the arm of his chair with long fingers. "No, I'll see the fellow not, until this matter's settled. Till then I've no official knowledge of his presence."

"Well," said Hasselborg, trying without complete success to conceal his exasperation, "will Your Reverence do what I ask, or won't you?"

"I know not, Master Kavir. I know not. 'Tis true I promised, but things have changed since then. I fain would help you, yet you ask a thing bigger than the Six Labors of Qarar. For look you, these sailors will arrive back in Majbur, and nothing on Krishna will stop them from talking. The talk will come to the ears of Gorbovast, who'll report back to the king, who will naturally wonder what befell him who led this strange invasion. He'll know you carried King Antané off, and the people of the city saw you drive up to my palace with your retinue. Therefore he'll come snooping around here with armed men at his back, and if he finds Antané locked in that old cell, there'll be awkward queries to answer."

Hasselborg said: "I think we can divert him. Tell him I took Antané with me to Novorecife. He won't be able to catch me to find out, I hope."

"Surely, you put a fair face on things. Still, I know not—"

"Well, there it is. If you want to carry out your promise—" Privately Hasselborg was more and more sharing the king's opinion of his vacillating high priest.

"I'll tell you. I'll do it on one condition."

"What's that?"

"It has not escaped your attention that my niece Fouri entertains for you feelings warmer than mere esteem?"

"Uh-huh."

"Well then, let you wed her by the rites of our most holy Church, and I'll undertake to keep your prisoner till you send me instructions for his disposal, as you demand."

Neither Hasté nor Fouri yet knew he was an Earthman, and moreover that he intended to return to Earth as soon as he perfected arrangements here. Legally it would not much matter. Once he got away from Gozashtand, he could nullify the marriage or ignore it, as Fallon had done with his.

Still, he disliked doing such a serious thing—serious to Fouri at least—under false pretenses.

"Well?" said Hasté.

Now Hasselborg was squirming on the horns of the dilemma, as Hasté had been previously. Should he balk at this point, throw up the game, turn his captives over to King Eqrar, or to Chuen, and report failure back to Batruni? It would simplify matters with Alexandra.

No, having come this close to success, he would not let himself be finessed out of it.

"Okay," he said. "How about as soon as I get back from where I'm going with the queen?"

"No; ere you leave. This night."

Away went that chance of escape. "All right. Whenever you say."

Hasté broke into a weary smile. "I had long hoped that the wedding of my niece would be a splendid affair. I should, for example, have consulted the ancient astrological archives to calculate the most auspicious date. However, Fouri insists upon an immediate ceremony. Therefore 'twill not even be necessary to compute your horoscopes." Hasté looked at the time candle. " 'Tis the hour for supper. What say you we perform it now, as soon as we and our friends can make ourselves presentable? Then to sup."

This was going to put Hasselborg in still more of a spot, unless he found a reason for setting off into the darkness right after supper. Yet, at this stage of the game it would not much matter if Fouri found out that he was an earthman.

"Very well," he said amiably, "but I'm afraid I'll have to get married the way I am, since all the rest of my clothes are over in Eqrar's shack."

He went to the room that Hasté assigned him, shaved, washed up, took a short nap, and then came out to prowl the palace. He knocked on Julnar's door.

"Yes?"

"Queen Julnar? This is the *soi-disant* Kavir bad-Ma'lum."

"What is it, fiend?" She opened the door.

"I thought you might like to attend the wedding."

"Wedding? Who? Where? When? How divine! I'd love to!"

"It seems that Hasté's niece Fouri and I are getting hitched in about fifteen minutes in His Reverence's private chapel."

"You are? But how can you if you're an earth—"

"*Sh!* That can't be helped, and I don't want it spread around. Just say, would you like to come?"

"I'd adore it! But—but—"

"But what?" asked Hasselborg.

"I couldn't very well accept while you're holding my husband in that wretched little cell, could I? That wouldn't be loyal."

"I'm sorry, but—"

"My idea was, why not let him out long enough to attend? Tony's a good sport, and I'm sure he'll behave."

"I'll see."

He went downstairs to Fallon's cell, finding the erstwhile king comfortably settled and playing Krishnan checkers with Ferzao. He said to the captive:

"Tony, I'm getting married to Hasté's niece in a few minutes, and your—uh—wife said she'd like to attend if I'd let you come, too. Would you like to?"

"We most certainly should!" said Fallon with such emphasis that Hasselborg looked at him in alarm.

Hasselborg warned: "Don't nourish ideas of making a break, chum; I'll have you well guarded."

"Oh, we won't bother *you*. Word of honor and all that."

"Okay. Ferzao, you and Ghum let King Antané out and take him up to the high priest's private chapel in a few minutes. Stick close to him and watch him."

Hasselborg then went to the chapel itself, finding Hasté, Fouri, Chuen, Fouri's maid, and Julnar. Fouri looked at him with a hungry expression that reminded him of those terran female spiders that ate their mates. Julnar, Hasselborg had decided, was just a healthy, normal girl, impressionable perhaps, but with a wonderful shape that the topless Krishnan evening dress made the most of.

Hasté said: "I will run through the forms once, to forewarn you of the responses you must make. You stand there and Fouri there. You take her hand in yours, so, I say— Who's this? Take that man away!"

Hasselborg turned to see Fallon and his two guards. "Which man?" he asked.

Fallon cut loose with a shout: "Hasté, you double-crossing—"

"Silence! I forbid you to speak!" cried Hasté.

Fallon paid no attention. "You double-crossing *zeft*, we'll see that you get—*ohé*, watch him!"

Hasselborg turned to see the high priest cock a little one-hand pistol crossbow and aim it in the general direction of Fallon. Fallon and his two guards ducked frantically. So did everybody else in the room except Hasselborg and Chuen.

While Chuen looked around for something to throw, Hasselborg, who was standing closer to Hasté, brought his right foot up in a terrific kick at Hasté's hand. The twang of the string mingled with the smack of Hasselborg's boot, the little crossbow flew high into the air, and the bolt struck the ceiling with a sharp sound and buried itself in the plaster.

Hasselborg threw himself upon Hasté in a tackle. Down went the priest, gorgeous robes and all. Hasselborg heard one of his men gasp at the sacrilege.

"Really, my son," said Hasté when he got his breath back, "be not so rough with one who is no longer young!"

"Sorry," said Hasselborg. "I thought you were reaching for a knife. Anyway, who told you you could plug Antané! He's my prisoner, see?" He got up with a grunt, feeling as if he had dislocated a hip joint. You are old, Father Victor, he thought, at least for football practice. "Say!"

"What?" Hasté sat up.

"This!" Hasselborg reached out and yanked off one of Hasté's antennae, which had become partly detached in the scuffle. "An Earthman, huh?"

Hasté felt his forehead. "Yes, now that you make mention thereof." Then as the significance of the event sank in, Hasté did a double-take. The rather stupid expression on his face changed to one of horror: "Speak it not, my s-s-son! I p-pray you! The results were dire! I were slain; the Established Church were overthrown; the bases of morality and justice were destroyed! Anything shall be yours, so that you betray not this dread s-s-secret!"

"Oho, so that's it? You were in on this smuggling deal too, eh? And you tried to murder Fallon just now because he was going to give you away?"

"That were a harsh interpretation, my boy. I—I c-can explain, though 'twere a lengthy tale—"

"Huh. No wonder you wouldn't see him when I brought him in! Well, that simplifies things. Sorry, Fouri, wedding's off."

"No! No! I love only you!"

He ignored her cries, not without a small internal pang. But then, he hoped to see Alexandra soon. He continued:

"Hasté, I'm pulling out tonight with Queen Julnar. You'll put Fallon back in his cell and hold him on pain of exposure. Moreover you'll carry out any instructions I send you with regard to him; meanwhile you'll make him as comfortable as possible. You'd also better pension Ferzao and Ghum to keep their mouths shut. Follow me?"

"I understand. But tell me one thing, my son—I've suspected that you, too, are of the race of earthmen. Be that the truth, or—"

"That's my business, chum. You understand, Julnar? You'll do just as I say, or I'll get word to Hasté to put your boy friend out of his misery?"

"I understand, you fiend."

"Chuen, you'll want to stick around, won't you?"

"Yes," said Chuen. "I got to collect depositions and other evidence."

"Okay, then—"

"But!" cried Julnar. "If I go back with you, it'll be years by Krishnan time before I can see Tony again, even though it seems only weeks to me!"

"I'll fix that," said Hasselborg, fishing out his precious pills. "Here, Tony. Trance pills. Know the formula?"

"Certainly we do," said Fallon sullenly.

"Fine. Hasté, before I go, I want to borrow the amount I left in my rooms in the royal place. I'll give you a note, and after I've left you can take it around to the palace. If King Eqrar's feeling honest, maybe he'll let you have the stuff. Ferzao, put King Antané back in his cell; then choose half the men to come with me to Novorecife. The other half I'm turning over to Master Li-yau, to do as he commands, together with the money to pay them. Then get my carriage ready, with food for a long fast journey. And cups of hot shurab for Queen Julnar and me before we start—"

Hasselborg was well away from Hershid, trotting briskly through the multiple moonlight, when Julnar asked: "Isn't this the road back to Majbur?"

"Uh-huh."

"Well, isn't that a roundabout way of getting to Novorecife?"

"Yes; we're going up the Pichidé by boat. The only other route lies via Rosid, and I'm afraid I'm not popular in Rúz just now."

She relapsed into gloom. The escort clop-clopped behind them. Hasselborg suddenly clapped a hand to his forehead.

"Tamates! It just occurred to me: if Hasté's an Earthman, Fouri can't be his niece, unless she's human too—say, d'you know anything about their background?"

"No," said Julnar, "and if I did I wouldn't tell you, you home-wrecker!"

Hasselborg subsided. As far as he was concerned, the many loose ends in this case would have to be left adrift. And he must remember to send Yeshram bad-Yeshram the jailer the other half of his bribe. He grinned as he thought how much easier it was to be scrupulous with Batruni's money than with his own.

Hasselborg walked down the ramp from the side of his ship at the Barcelona spaceport, followed by Julnar Batruni. Her suitcase had already gone down the chute; he insisted on carrying his own by hand rather than risk his professional equipment and medicines. In the other hand, he twirled the carved Gozashtando umbrella, an incongruous sight in this sunny city.

"What now?" she asked as they stood in line at the passport desk.

"First I'm going to wire your old man in Aleppo, and a—a friend of mine in London. Then I'll hunt up a doctor for a physical checkup."

"Why, are you sick? I thought the viagens doctor checked you."

"So he did," he said seriously, "but you can't be too careful. Then I thought we'd take in some of the high life. While most of it's *estincamente,* I know some good places over on the Montjuich."

"How simply divine! You're an extraordinary man, Victor," she said.

"How?"

"I don't seem to be able to loathe you as much as I should for breaking into my life."

"That's my insidious charm. Watch out for it." He handed over his passport.

He had just finished sending his telegrams when

somebody at his elbow said in Spanish: "Excuse me, but are you Señor Hasselborg?"

"Si, soy Hasselborg." The fellow was dressed in the uniform of an Iberian Federation cop, and flanked by two Viagens men.

"Lo siento mucho," said the Spaniard with an apologetic bow, "but I must place you under arrest."

"Huh? What for?"

"These gentlemen have a warrant. Will you explain, Señor Ndombu?"

One of the Viagens men, a Negro, said: "Violation of Regulation 368 of the Interplanetary Council rules, Section Four, Subsection Twenty-six, fifteenth paragraph."

Whew! Which is that?"

"The one relating to the introduction of mechanical devices or inventions on the planet Krishna."

"I never—"

"Queira, senhor, don't savage me about it! All I know is what's in this warrant. Something about putting a sight on a crossbow."

"Oh." Hasselborg turned to Julnar. "Here's some money. Take a cab to the Cristóbal Hotel. Call up the firm of Montejo and Durruti and tell 'em to bail me out of the *calabozo,* will you like a good kid?"

Then he went with the men.

Whether Julnar took the chance of getting even with him, or whether his Catalan colleagues were having an attack of *mañana,* nothing happened to get Hasselborg out of his cell as evening came on. This could be serious. They had the goods on him with respect to those sights, even if they were only a pair of corsage pins. The spectators had taken note at the time, and the imitative Krishnans were no doubt spreading the device all over their planet. Not that it was really important; a man is as dead when beaten to death with a club as when blown up with a plutonium bomb.

There would be a hearing, whenever the local magistrate got around to it, at which said magistrate would either dismiss the case or bind Hasselborg over and assign him to the court of first instance for trial. For an offense by an earthman on Krishna against an Interplanetary Council regulation enforced by the Viagens Interplanetarias security force, and arrested in Iberia on Earth, that would be—let's see—Lower Division, Earth World Court for the Third International Judicial District, which sat in—hm-m-m—Paris, didn't it? With appeal to— He'd have to dig out his old law texts when he got back to London. The maze of jurisdictions was so complicated that sometimes interplanetary cases simply got lost in the shuffle and never were tried at all, while the principals lived out their long lives on bail.

No, *if* he got back to London. This could result in a stiff sentence, especially if Chuen broke a big scandal inside the Viagens ranks about now, and the word was passed down to tighten up and make an example. And it did no good to have a trance pill smuggled in to knock yourself out with; Earth penal systems were wise to that one and simply added the time you spent in trance to your sentence.

Hasselborg reflected that he who acts as his own lawyer has a fool for a client. He had better round up some high-powered advice *muy pronto*. Lawyer though he was by training, he was too rusty to cope with this problem himself. Maybe he should have stuck to law in the first place, instead of getting involved in investigation. The glamour of detecting soon wore off. . . .

Obviously Montejo and Durruti were not going to call, whatever the reason. Although the jail people let him telephone, their office failed to answer, he did not know their home numbers, and the directory listed so many Montejos and Durrutis that he decided that it would take all night to go through them.

Next he tried the Cristóbal Hotel. No, they had no Miss Batruni. Nor any Señora Fallon either. Did they have the Queen of Zamba? Come, señor, you are joking with us and we do not appreciate . . . oh, wait a minute! We have a Hoolnar de Thamba; would that be the one?"

But Julnar's room did not answer. Hasselborg disgustedly went to bed. At least the Barcelona municipal clink, unlike many in the Peninsula, was a reasonably sanitary one, although Hasselborg doubted whether any Iberians could be trusted to display sufficient vigilance towards germs.

Hasselborg was at the telephone again next morning when a warden said: "A Señorita Garshin to see you."

He hung up unsteadily, missing the cradle with the handset twice, and followed the man to the visitors' room. There she was, looking just as he'd imagined her, only prettier if anything.

"Alexandra!" he said. "I—you—you're *Miss* Garshin now?"

"Yes. Why Victor, your *hair!*"

"It's green, isn't it?"

"You mean you see it, too? I thought I was having hallucinations."

"It's just the ends; it'll be gone the next haircut I get. You don't look different—not a day older."

"I've been in trance most of the time; that's why."

"You were?"

"Yes," she said.

"But—I'm afraid—I didn't bring back Tony after all."

"Oh, I didn't do it on Tony's account. I don't care anything about him any more."

"Then—uh—whose?"

"Can't you guess?"

"You mean you—uh—you—"

She nodded. He held out his arms, and the warden, who thought of Anglo-Saxons as cold fish, received a surprising enlightenment.

He brought out the little Krishnan god, which he had been carrying in his pocket for this moment, and gave it to her. Then they sat down holding hands. Hasselborg found that the paralysis of his vocal organs had vanished. They talked at a terrific pace of their past, present, and future until Hasselborg looked at his watch.

"Say," he cried, "I forgot I haven't even got a lawyer yet! Wait a minute, will you, chum?"

He dashed back to the telephone, this time getting Montejo and Durruti, who promised to send him a lawyer forthwith. The lawyer was arranging bail when the warden announced more visitors—a Señor Batruni and a lady.

Batruni practically slobbered over Hasselborg in gratitude. When the investigator finally wormed out of the emotional Levantine's embrace, he introduced Alexandra simply as "my fiancée, Miss Garshin." Then he asked Julnar:

"I thought I asked you to call Montejo and Durruti for me yesterday?"

"I would have, Victor, only—"

"Only what?"

"Well, you see, the stupid taxi driver must have misunderstood me and took me to the wrong place, so we got into an argument, and what with me not speaking any Spanish or Catalan and he not speaking any English or French or Arabic it was simply ghastly—and what with one thing and another, by the time I did get to the Cristóbal I'd forgotten the name!"

"Then why didn't you call me at the jail and find out?"

"I didn't think of that."

"Where were you during the evening, and again this morning when I called you?"

"In the evening I went to a movie, and when I got back to my room, Daddy called me by telephone from Aleppo to say he was chartering a special fast plane. So this morning I was so excited I left early to wait for him at the airport."

Hasselborg sighed. Nice girl, but too scatterbrained for his taste.

"Has Daddy told you the news?" she continued. "Of course not; he just arrived. Tell him, Daddy."

"I am going back to Krishna with Julnar," said Batruni.

"Why?" said Hasselborg.

"It is this way. While you were gone, the government socialized my factories. They paid me for them, so I need not starve, but there is no more fun in life. I even offered to act as manager; but they turned it down. They do not trust a wicked capitalist to run them without sabotaging them. There is no pleasure on Earth any more. Everything is too orderly, planned, regulated. You cannot move a meter without tripping over red tape.

"Therefore, if you will give me a letter directing that person who has Anthony in custody to let him go, I will go to Krishna and live with this wild son-in-law of mine in his island kingdom. I shall be a genuine prince, which you cannot be on Earth any more unless you are a Scandinavian."

"Isn't it just too divine?" squealed Julnar. "Now I'm really grateful to you for kidnaping me!"

"Swell," said Hasselborg. "I hope you're satisfied with the way I carried out the assignment, Mr. Batruni."

"Certainly, more than satisfied. In fact I am so pleased that I have an offer to make to you."

"Another job? said Hasselborg in slight alarm.

"Yes, but not the kind you think. In addition to my regular fee I am offering you a lectureship at the University of Beyrût, of which I am a trustee."

Hasselborg paused to let this sink in. "A lectureship in what?"

"Anglo-Saxon law."

"My word! I'd have to think, even if I beat this rap but my sincerest thanks. I'd have to brush up on my law and my Arabic. Say, how about seeing the sights of Barcelona? I promised Julnar but got pinched before I could deliver. Come on; 'tis a privilege high to have dinner and tea, along with the Red Queen, the White Queen, and me!"

The hearing took place the following morning. In the front row, like Alice between the two queens, sat Papa Batruni, showing signs of a hangover, with his daughter on one side and Alexandra on the other. The magistrate had just called the case when a bulky Oriental walked down the aisle.

"Chuen!" cried Hasselborg, then to his lawyer: "Señor Agüesar, there's the man we want!"

Chuen shook hands warmly. "I just arrived and learned you were in pokey. I left several days after you, but in faster ship."

"I always get the scows," said Hasselborg, and explained his plight.

When the Viagens officer, Ndombu, had explained the warrant, Agüesar called Chuen to the stand. Chuen, using an interpreter, told what had happened on Krishna, emphasizing the fact that only by a slight infraction of the anti-invention regulation had Hasselborg been able to survive to forestall another and much graver violation.

"Case dismissed," said the magistrate.

Hasselborg asked Chuen: "Could you stay over two days and act as my best men?" At Chuen's quizzical look he added: "Miss Garshin and I are getting married. We got our license yesterday, but they've got a three-day law in Iberia."

"I'm so sorry! I have my ticket for airplane to China; leave this afternoon. If I miss, won't be another seat for a week. Wish I knew sooner."

"Oh. Too bad. When are you going?"

Chuen looked at his watch. "Should start in a few minutes."

"I'll go with you. Can you dear, sweet people excuse me for an hour?"

In the taxi Chuen said: "Glad to get back to civilization?"

"Right! What did you do after I left?"

"Collected evidence for several days. I got those letters from Góis to Dasht of Rúz, for instance. Took doing."

"What happened to Góis?"

"Oh, he got ten years; couple of others who were in with him, shorter terms."

"Was Abreu in on it?"

"No; he's all right. He wouldn't believe Góis was a crook at first, but when I convinced him he helped me very much. But while I was still in Hershid, the most awful thing happened to *me!*"

"What?"

"Fouri made me marry her on threat of exposing me as Terran spy! Embarrassing, especially since I already got wife and eight children in Gweilin."

"What's the dope on Hasté and Fouri? She can't be his niece—"

"No."

"Mistress?"

"Think no. Hasté real old ascetic."

"She *is* a Krishnan?"

'Oh, yes," said Chuen.

"Then how—"

"Hasté was a deserter from one of earliest ships to land on Krishna. Pretty old then, over two hundred. Set himself up as holy hermit, lived in cave, became a power in their church in Gozashtand. Then when there was deadlock in election a few years ago, they picked him for high priest as compromise. Not bad man really, but too small for his job. Was owing to his weak leadership the Church was failing, I think, which is after all good thing if you don't believe that astrological nonsense."

"But Fouri?"

"She was young girl from caravan of Gavehona—you know, a wandering tribe, like our Gypsies. Went live with him while he was still hermit; don't know how much for religion, how much for regular meals. When he became high priest, she moved in with him—like father and daughter. Now Hasté getting really old, so Fouri start looking for another berth. Fall in love with you; genuine, I think. Made Hasté coöperate by threatening to expose him as Earthman.

"Meanwhile Hasté is looking for another berth too, since his Established Church is failing, so he entered plot with Fallon. He was going to hail Fallon as Messiah or something like that when Fallon took Hershid. We fixed that. But when you escaped, idea of getting married had become an obsession with Fouri. Hasté couldn't marry her, obviously, so she picked me; better than nothing, I suppose. Maybe she thought I'd fall in love with her and stay. Hard enough to tell what goes on in Earthwoman's mind."

Hasselborg brought his friend up to date on the Batruni affairs, adding: "I didn't mention that Alexandra was Fallon's ex; the Batrunis don't know it and it would only embarrass everybody. How's Fallon doing?"

"All right. Was planning to put himself in trance when I left; wanted to make sure you took off with Julnar first."

Hasselborg said: "It'll be years by objective time before they get back to Krishna, and anything might have happened by then. However, that's their lookout. You know, I'm sometimes bothered by the feeling that Góis and his gang were right and we and the Interplanetary Council wrong."

"I know, but not our business. We do our jobs. Speaking of jobs—you taking up this teaching offer?"

"I think so."

"Sounds dull."

"D'you like manhunting?"

"Of course. Why you think I work as a cop?"

"Well, I've had my fill. While I've usually taken things pretty much as they came, I pushed my luck on

Krishna as far as anybody could, what with being shot at with crossbows and slashed at with swords and stabbed with knives and almost eaten by yekis." Hasselborg, feeling expansive, drew on his cigar. "I remember in Plato's *Republic* where a character named Er gets knocked cold in a fight. His soul goes to Hades and later returns to his body, and Er comes to and tells how in Hades he saw the souls of other dead people picking their next incarnations. Ajax is choosing the life of a lion and so on. But Odysseus is smart. He figures he's had enough excitement in his last life, so he's selecting the life of an obscure private citizen leading a peaceful existence. And that's how I feel. Any time you're in Beyrût come see Professor and Mrs. Hasselborg and all the little Hasselborgs. We'll bore you to death with placid domesticity."

As Chuen waddled up the companionway into the fuselage, he turned to wave at Hasselborg, who waved back. A good guy, thought Hasselborg, but I hope I never have anything to do with the detective business again. That's that.

A young man brushed by Hasselborg, flashed him a quick glance, and ran up the companionway into the fuselage just before the door shut and the tractor towed the plane away to the catapult strip. Although Hasselborg had only a glimpse of the man's face, it was enough.

The man was the young Gozashtando priest who used to come in and murmur in Hasté's ear, disguised as an Earthman by a wig that came down over his forehead to hide the antennae. Fouri must have sent him to Earth to track down her fugitive and bigamous husband!

PERPETUAL MOTION

I.

"My good senhor," said Abreu, "where the devil did you get those? Raid half the Earth's pawnshops?" He bent closer to look at the decorations on Felix Borel's chest. "Teutonic Order, French Legion of Honor, Third World War, Public Service Award of North America, Fourth Degree of the Knights of St. Stephen, Danish Order of the Elephant, something-or-other from Japan, Intercollegiate Basketball Championship, Pistol Championship of the Policia do Rio de Janeiro . . . . Tamates, what a collection!"

Borel smiled sardonically down on the fat little security officer. "You never can tell. I might be a basketball champion."

"What are you going to do, sell these things to the poor ignorant Krishnans?"

"I might, if I ran short. Or maybe I'll just dazzle them so they'll give me whatever I ask for."

"Humph. I admit that in that private uniform, with all those medals and orders, you're an awe-inspiring spectacle."

Borel, amusedly watching Abreu fume, knew that the latter was sore because he had not been able to find any excuse to hold Borel at Novorecife. Thank God, thought Borel, the universe is not yet so carefully organized that personal influence can't perform a trick or two. He would have liked to do Abreu a bad turn if for no better reason than that he harbored an irrational prejudice against Brazzies, as though it were Abreu's fault that his native country was the Earth's leading power.

Borel grinned at the bureaucrat. "You'd be surprised how helpful this—uh—costume of mine has been. Flunkeys at spaceports assume I'm at least Chief of Staff of the World Federation. 'Step this way, senhor! Come to the head of the line, senhor!' More fun than a circus."

Abreu sighed. "Well, I can't stop you. I still think you'd have a better chance of survival disguised as a Krishnan, though."

"And wear a green wig, and false feelers on my forehead? No thanks."

"That's your funeral. However, remember Regulation 368 of the Interplanetary Council rules. You know it?"

"Sure. 'It is forbidden to communicate to any native resident of the planet Krishna any device, appliance, machine, tool, weapon, or invention representing an improvement upon the science and technics already in existence upon this planet. . .' Want me to go on?"

"*Não,* you know it. Remember that while the Viagens Interplanetarias will ordinarily let you alone once you leave Novorecife, we'll go to any length to prevent and punish any violation of that rule. That's Council orders."

Borel yawned. "I understand. If the type has finished X-raying my baggage, I'll be pushing off. What's the best route to Mishé at present?"

"You could go straight through the Koloft Swamps, but the wilder tribes of the Koloftuma sometimes kill travelers for their goods. You'd better take a raft down the Pichidé to Qou, and follow the road southwest from there to Mishé."

"*Obrigado.* The Republic of Mikardand is on a gold standard, isn't it?"

"*Pois sim.*"

"And what's gold at Novorecife worth in terms of

World Federation dollars on Earth?"

"Oh, *Deus meu!* That takes a higher mathematician to calculate, what with freight and interest and the balance of trade."

"Just approximately," persisted Borel.

"As I remember, a little less than two dollars a gram."

Borel stood up and shook back his red hair with a characteristic gesture. He gathered up his papers. *"Adeus,"* Senhor Cristovão; you've been most helpful."

He smiled broadly as he said this, for Abreu had obviously wanted to be anything but helpful and was still gently simmering over his failure to halt Borel's invasion of Krishna.

The next day found Felix Borel drifting down the Pichidé on a timber raft under the tall clouds that paraded across the greenish sky of Krishna. Next to him crouched the Kolofto servant he had hired at Novorecife, tailed and monstrously ugly.

A brisk shower had just ended. Borel stood up and shook drops off his cloak as the big yellow sun struck them. Yerevats did likewise, grumbling in broken Gozashtandou: "If master do like I say, put on poor man clothes, could take towboat and stay close to shore. Then when rain come, could put up tarpaulin. No get wet, no be afraid robbers."

"That's my responsibility," replied Borel, moving about to get his circulation going again. He gazed off to starboard, where the low shore of the Pichidé broke up into a swarm of reedy islets. "What's that?" he asked, pointing.

"Koloft Swamps," said Yerevats."

"Your people live there?"

"No, not by river. Further back. By river is all *ujero.*" (He gave the Kolofto name for the quasi-human people of the planet, whom most Earthmen thought of simply as Krishnans because they were the dominant species.) "Robbers," he added.

Borel, looking at the dark horizontal stripe of reeds

between sky and water, wondered if he had been wise to
reject Yerevats's advice to buy the full panoply of a
garm or knight. Yerevats, he suspected, had been hoping
for a fancy suit of armor for himself. Borel had turned
down the idea on grounds of expense and weight; suppose one fell into the Pichidé in all that stove-piping?
Also, he now admitted to himself, he had succumbed to
Terran prejudice against medieval Krishnan weapons,
since one Terran bomb could easily wipe out a whole
Krishnan city and one gun mow down a whole army.
Perhaps he had not given enough weight to the fact that,
where he was going, no Terran bombs or guns would be
available.

Too late now for might-have-beens. Borel checked
over the armament he had finally bought: a sword for
himself, as much a badge of status as a protection. A
cheap mace with a wooden handle and a star-shaped
iron head for Yerevats. Sheath knives of general utility
for both. Finally, a crossbow. Privately Borel, no
swashbuckler, hoped that any fighting they did would be
at as long a range as possible. He had tried drawing a
longbow in the Outfitting Shop at Novorecife, but in his
unskilled grip it bobbled about too much and would
have required more practice than he had time for.

Borel folded his cloak, laid it on his barracks bag, and
sat down to go over his plans again. The only flaw he
could see lay in the matter of getting an entré to the
Order of Qarar after he arrived at Mishé. Once he had
made friends with members of the Brotherhood, the rest
should be easy. By all accounts, the Mikardanduma
were natural-born suckers. But how to take that first
step? He would probably have to improvise after he got
there.

Once he had gotten over that first hurdle, his careful
preparation and experience in rackets like this would see
him through. And the best part would be that he would
have the laugh on old Abreu, who could do absolutely
nothing about it. Since Borel considered honesty a sign

of stupidity, and since Abreu was not stupid for all his pompous ways, Borel assumed that Abreu must be out for what he could get like other wise joes, and that his moral attitudes and talk of principles were mere hypocritical pretence.

"Ao!" The shout of one of the raftmen broke into Borel's reverie. The Krishnan was pointing off towards the right bank, where a boat was emerging from among the islets.

Yerevats jumped, up, shading his eyes with his hairy hand. "Robbers!" he said.

"How can you tell from here?" asked Borel, a horrid fear making his heart pound.

"Just know. You see," said the Koloftu, his tail twitching nervously. He looked appealingly at Borel. "Brave master kill robbers? No let them hurt us?"

"Sh-sure," said Borel. He pulled out his sword halfway, looked at the blade, and shoved it back into its scabbard, more as a nervous gesture than anything else.

"Ohé!" said one of the raftmen. "Think you to fight the robbers?"

"I suppose so," said Borel.

"No, you shall not! If we make no fight, they will slay only you, for we are but poor men."

"Is that so?" said Borel. The adrenalin being poured into his system made him contrary, and his voice rose. "So you think I'll let my throat be cut quietly to save yours, huh? I'll show you *baghana!"* The sword whipped out of the scabbard, and the flat slapped the raftman on the side of the head, staggering him. "We'll fight whether you like it or not! I'll kill the first coward myself!" he was screaming at the three raftmen, now huddled together fearfully. "Make a barricade of the baggage! Move that stove forward!" He stood over them, shouting and swishing the air with his sword, until they had arranged the movables in a rough square.

"Now," said Borel more calmly, "bring your poles and crouch down inside there. You too; Yerevats. I'll try to hold them off with the bow. If they board us anyway, we'll jump out and rush them when I give the signal. Understand?"

The boat had been slanting out from the shore on a course converging toward that of the raft. Now Borel, peering over the edge of his barricade, could make out the individuals in it. There was one in the bow, another in the stern, and the rest rowing—perhaps twenty in all.

"Is time to cock bow," muttered Yerevats.

The others looked nervously over their shoulders as if wondering whether the river offered a better chance of safety than battle.

Borel said: "I wouldn't try to swim ashore. You know the monsters of the Pichidé." This only made them look unhappier.

Borel put his foot into the stirrup at the muzzle end of the crossbow and cocked the device with both hands and a grunt. Then he opened the bandoleer he had bought with the bow and took out one of the bolts: an iron rod a span long, with a notch at one end, and at the other a flattened, diamond-shaped head with a twist to make the missile spin in its flight. He inserted the bolt into its groove.

The boat came closer and closer. The man in the front end called across the water: "Surrender!"

"Keep quiet," said Borel softly to his companions. By now he was so keyed up that he was almost enjoying the excitement.

Again the man in the boat hailed: "Surrender and we'll not hurt you! 'Tis only your goods we want!"

Still no reply from the raft.

"For the last time, give up, or we'll torture you all to death!"

Borel shifted the crossbow to cover the man in the front. Damn, why hadn't these gloops put sights on their gadgets? He'd taken a few practice shots at a piece of paper the day before and thought himself pretty good. Now, however, his target seemed to shrink to mosquito size every time he tried to draw a bead on it, and something must be shaking the raft to make the weapon waver so.

The man in the bow of the boat had produced an object like a small anchor with extra flukes, tied to the end of a rope. He held this dangling while the grunting oarsmen brought the boat swiftly towards the raft, then whirled it around his head.

Borel shut his eyes and jerked the trigger. The string snapped loudly and the stock kicked back against his shoulder. One of the raftmen whooped.

When Borel opened his eyes, the man in the front of the boat was no longer whirling the grapnel. Instead he was looking back towards the stern, where the man who had sat at the tiller had slumped down. The rowers were resting on their oars and jabbering excitedly.

"Great master hit robber captain!" said Yerevats. "Better cock bow again."

Borel stood up to do so. Evidently he had missed the man he aimed at and instead hit the man in the stern. He said nothing, however, to disillusion his servant about his marksmanship.

The boat had reorganized and was coming on again, another robber having taken the place of the one at the tiller. This time there were two Krishnans in front, one with the grapnel and the other with a longbow.

"Keep your heads down," said Borel, and shot at the archer; the bolt flew far over the man's head. Borel started to get up to reload, then realized that he would be making a fine target. Could you cock these damned things sitting down? The archer let fly his shaft, which passed Borel's head with a frightening *whisht*. Borel hastily found that he could cock his crossbow in a sitting position, albeit a little awkwardly. Another arrow thudded into the baggage.

Borel shed his military-style cap as too tempting a target and sighted on the boat again. Another miss, and the boat came closer. The archer was letting off three

arrows to every one of Borel's bolts, though Borel sur-
mised that he was doing so to cover their approach rather than with hope of hitting anybody.

Borel shot again; this time the bolt banged into the
planking of the boat. The man with the grapnel was
whirling it once more, and another arrow screeched
past.

"Hey," said Borel to one of the raftmen, "you with
the hatchet! When the grapnel comes aboard, jump out
and cut the rope. You other two, get ready to push the
boat off with your poles."

"But the arrows—" bleated the first man spoken to.

"I'll take care of that," said Borel with more confidence than he felt.

The archer had nocked another arrow but was holding it steady instead of releasing it. As the boat came
within range of the grapnel, the man whirling it let go. It
landed on the raft with a thump. Then the man who had
thrown it began to pull it in hand over hand until one of
the flukes caught in a log.

Borel looked around frantically for some way of
tempting the archer to shoot, since otherwise the first to
stand up on the raft would be a sitting duck. He seized
his cap and raised it above the edge of the barricade.
Snap! and another arrow hissed by.

"Go to it!" shrieked Borel, and sighted on the archer.
His crew hesitated. The archer reached back to his
quiver for another arrow, and Borel, forcing himself to
be calm, drew a bead on the man's body and squeezed.

The man gave a loud animal cry, between a grunt and
a scream, and doubled over.

"Go on!" yelled Borel again, raising the crossbow as
if to beat the raftmen over the head with it. They sprang
into life. One severed the rope with a chop of his
hatchet, while the other two poked at the boat with their
poles.

The remaining man in the front of the boat dropped
his rope, shouted something to the rowers, and bent to

pick up a boathook. Borel shot at him, but let himself
get excited and missed, though it was practically spitting
distance. When the boathook caught in the logs, the
man hauled the bow of the boat closer, while a few of
the forward rowers stopped rowing to cluster around
him with weapons ready.

In desperation Borel dropped his crossbow, grabbed
the end of the boathook, wrenched it out of the wood,
and jerked it towards himself. The man on the other end
held on a second too long and toppled into the water,
still gripping the shaft. Borel pulled on it with some idea
of wrenching it away and reversing it to spear the man
in the water. The latter held on, however, and was
hauled to the edge of the raft, where he made as though
to climb aboard. Meanwhile the raftmen had again
pushed the boat away with their poles, so that those who
had been gathering themselves to jump across thought
better of the idea.

Thump! Yerevats brought his mace down on the head
of the man in the water, and the mop of green hair sank
beneath the surface.

The raftmen were now yelling triumphantly in their
own dialect. A robber, however, had picked up the longbow from the bottom of the boat and was fumbling with
an arrow. Borel, recovering his crossbow, took pains
with his next shot and made a hit just as the new archer
let fly. The arrow went wild and the archer disappeared,
to bob up again a second later cursing and holding his
shoulder.

Borel cocked his crossbow again and aimed at the
man in the boat. This time, however, instead of shooting, he simply pointed it at one man after another. Each
man in turn tried to duck down behind the thwarts, so
that organized rowing became impossible.

"Had enough?" called Borel.

The robbers were arguing again, until finally one
called out: "All right, don't shoot; we'll let you go." The
oars resumed their regular rhythm, and the boat swung

away towards the swamp. When it was safely out of range, some of the robbers yelled back threats and insults, which Borel could not understand at the distance.

The raftmen were slapping each other's backs, shouting: "We're good! Said I not we could lick a hundred robbers?" Yerevats babbled about his wonderful master.

Borel felt suddenly weak and shaky. If a mouse, or whatever they had on Krishna that corresponded to a mouse, were to climb aboard and squeak at him, he was sure he would leap into the muddy Pichidé in sheer terror. However, it would not do to show that. With trembling hands, he inserted a cigarette into his long jewelled holder and lit it. Then he said:

"Yerevats, my damned boots seem to have gotten scuffed. Give them a shine, will you?"

II.

They tied up at Qou that evening to spend the night. Felix Borel paid off the raftmen, whom he overheard before he retired telling the innkeeper how they had (with some help from the Earthman) beaten off a hundred river pirates and slain scores. Next morning he bade them goodby, as they pushed off down the river for Majbur at the mouth of the Pichidé, where they meant to sell their logs and catch a towboat back home.

Four long Krishnan days later, Borel was pacing the roof of his inn in Mishé. The capital of the Republic of Mikardand had proved a bigger city than he had expected. In the middle rose a sharp-edged, mesa-like hill surmounted by the great citadel of the Order of Qarar. The citadel frowned down upon Borel, who frowned right back as he cast and rejected one plan after another for penetrating not only the citadel but also the ruling caste whose stronghold it was.

He called: "Yerevats!"

"Yes, master?"

"The *Garma Qararuma* toil not, neither do they spin, do they?"

"Guardians work? No sir! Run country, protect common people from enemies and from each other. That enough, not?"

"Maybe, but that's not what I'm after. How are these Guardians supported?"

"Collect taxes from common people."

"I thought so. Who collects these taxes?"

"Squires of Order. Work for treasurer of Order."

"Who's he?" asked Borel.

"Is most noble *garm* Kubanan."

"Where could I find the most noble Sir Kubanan?"

"If he in citadel, no can see. If in treasury office, can."

"Where's the treasury office?"

Yerevats waved vaguely. "That way. Master want go?"

"Right. Get out the buggy, will you?"

Yerevats disappeared, and presently they were rattling over the cobblestone towards the treasury office in the light one-aya four-wheeled carriage Borel had bought in Qou. It had occurred to him at the time that one pictured a gallant knight as pricking o'er the plain on his foaming steed rather than sitting comfortably behind the steed in a buggy. However, since the latter procedure promised to be pleasanter, and Yerevats knew how to drive, Borel had taken a chance on the Mikardanders' prejudices.

The treasury office was in one of the big, graceless rough-stone buildings that the Quararuma used as their official architectural style. The doorway was flanked by a pair of rampant stone yekis: the dominant carnivores of this part of the planet, something like a six-legged mink blown up to tiger size. Borel had had the wits scared out of him by hearing the roar of one on his drive down from Qou.

Borel gathered up his sword, got down from the buggy, assumed his loftiest expression, and asked the doorman: "Where do I find the receiver of taxes, my good man?"

In accordance with the doorman's directions, he followed a hall in the building until he discovered a window in the side of the hall, behind which sat a man in the drab dress of the commoners of Mikardand.

Borel said: "I wish to see whether I owe the Republic

any taxes. I don't wish to discuss it with you, though; fetch your superior."

The clerk scuttled off with a look compounded of fright and resentment. Presently another face and torso appeared at the window. The torso was clad in the gay coat of a member of the Order of Qarar, but judging from the smallness of the dragonlike emblem on the chest, the man was only a squire or whatever you'd call the grade below the true *garma*.

"Oh, not you," said Borel. "The head of the department."

The squire frowned so that the antennae sprouting from between his brows crossed. "Who are you, anyhow?" he said. "The receiver of taxes am I. If you have anything to pay—"

"My dear fellow," said Borel, "I'm not criticizing you, but as a past Grand Master of an earthly order and a member of several others, I'm not accustomed to dealing with underlings. You will kindly tell the head of your department that the *garm* Felix Borel is here."

The man went off shaking his head in a baffled manner. Presently another man with a knight's insignia stepped through a door into the corridor and advanced with hand outstretched.

"My dear sir!" he said. "Will you step into my chamber? 'Tis a pleasure extraordinary to meet a true knight from Earth. I knew not that such lived there; the *Ertsuma* who have come to Mikardand speak strange subversive doctrines of liberty and equality for the commonality—even those who claim the rank, like that Sir Erik Koskelainen. One can tell you're a man of true quality."

"Thank you," said Borel. "I knew that one of the *Garma Qararuma* would know me as spiritually one of themselves, even though I belong to another race."

The knight bowed. "And now what's this about your wishing to pay taxes? When I first heard it I believed it not; in all the history of the Republic, no man has ever offered to pay taxes of his own will."

Borel smiled. "I didn't say I actually *wanted* to pay them. But I'm new here and wanted to know my rights and obligations. That's all. Better to get them straightened out at the start, don't you think?"

"Yes—but—are you he who came hither from Quo but now?"

"Yes."

"He who slew Ushyarian the river pirate and his lieutenant in battle on the Pichidé?"

Borel waved a deprecating hand. "That was nothing. One can't let such rogues run loose, you know. I'd have wiped out the lot, but one can't chase malefactors with a timber raft."

The Qararu jumped up. "Then the reward is due you!"

"Reward?"

"Why, knew you not? A reward of ten thousand *karda* has lain on the head of Ushyarian for years! I must see about the verification of your claim. . ."

Borel, thinking quickly, said: "Don't bother. I don't really want it."

"You don't *wish* it?" The man stared blankly.

"No. I only did a gentleman's duty, and I don't need it."

"But—the money's here—it's been appropriated—"

"Well, give it to some worthy cause. Don't you have charities in Mishé?"

The knight finally pulled himself together. "Extraordinary. You must meet the treasurer himself. As for taxes—let me see—there is a residence tax on metics, while on the other hand we have treaties with Gozashtand and some of the other states to exempt each other's gentlefolk. I know not how that would affect you —but concern yourself not, in view of your action in the matter of the reward. I'll put it up to the treasurer. Can you wait?"

"Sure. Mind if I smoke?"

"Not at all. Have one of these." The knight dug a bunch of Krishnan cigars out of a desk drawer.

After a few minutes, the official returned and asked Borel to come to the treasurer's office, where he introduced the Earthman to the treasurer of the Order. Sir Kubanan was that rarity among Krishnans, a stout man, looking a little like a beardless Santa Claus.

The previous conversation more or less repeated itself, except that the treasurer proved a garrulous old party with a tendency to ramble. He seemed fascinated by Borel's medals.

"This?" said Borel, indicating the basketball medal. "Oh, that's the second degree of the Secret Order of Spooks. Very secret and very powerful; only admits men who've been acquitted of a murder charge. . ."

"Wonderful, wonderful," said Kubanan at last. "My dear sir, we will find a way around this tax matter, fear not. Perish the thought that one so chivalrous as yourself should be taxed like a vulgar commoner, even though the Order be sore pressed for funds."

This was the opening Borel had been waiting for. He pounced. "The Order would like additional sources of revenue?"

"Why, yes. Of course we're all sworn to poverty and obedience." (he contemplated his glittering assortment of rings) "and hold all in common, even our women and children. Nevertheless, the defense of the Republic puts a heavy burden upon us."

"Have you thought of a state lottery?"

"What might that be?"

Borel explained, rattling through the details as fast as his fair command of the language allowed.

"Wonderful," said Kubanan. "I fear I could not follow your description at all times, though; you do speak with an accent. Could you put it in writing for us?"

"Sure. In fact I can do better than that."

"How mean you?"

"Well, to give you an example, it's much easier to tell how to ride an aya than to do it, isn't it?"

"Yes."

"Just so, it's easy to tell you how a lottery works—but it takes practical experience to run one."

"How can we surmount that difficulty?"

"I could organize and run your first lottery."

"Sir Felix, you quite take my breath away. Could you write down the amounts involved in this scheme?"

Borel wrote down a rough estimate of the sums he might expect to take in and pay out in a city of this size. Kubanan, frowning, said: "What's this ten percent for the director?"

"That's the incentive. If you're going to run this thing in a businesslike manner after I've left, we'd better set it up right. And one must have an incentive. The first time I'd be the director, naturally."

"I see. That's not unreasonable. But since members of the Order aren't allowed private funds beyond mere pocket money, how would the commission act as incentive?"

Borel shrugged. "You'd have to figure that one out. Maybe you'd better hire a commoner to run the show. I suppose there are merchants and bankers among them, aren't there?"

"True. Amazing. We must discuss this further. Won't you come to my chambers this evening to sup? I'll pass you into the citadel."

Borel tried to hide his grin of triumph as he said: "It's my turn to be overwhelmed, Your Excellency!" The Borel luck!

At the appointed hour, Borel, having presented his pass at the gate of the citadel, was taken in tow by a uniformed guide. Inside Mishé's Kremlin stood a lot of huge plain stone buildings wherein the Guardians led their antlike existence. Borel walked past playgrounds and exercise grounds, and identified other buildings as apartment houses, armories, office buildings, and an auditorium. It was just as well to memorize such details in case a slip-up should require a hasty retreat. Borel had once spent six months as a guest of the French Republic in consequence of failing to observe this precaution. He passed hundreds of gorgeously arrayed *garma* of both sexes. Some look at him sharply, but none offered interference.

For the quarters of one sworn to poverty, the treasurer's apartment was certainly sumptuous. Kubanan cordially introduced Borel to a young female Mikardandu who quite took his breath away. If one didn't mind green hair, feathery antennae, and a somewhat flat-featured Oriental look, she was easily the most beautiful thing he'd seen since Earth, especially since the Mikardando evening dress began at the midriff.

"Sir Felix, my confidential secretary, the Lady Zerdai." Kubanan lowered his voice in mock-confidence. "I *think* she's my own daughter, though naturally one can never know for sure."

"Then family feeling does exist among the Guardians?" said Borel.

"Yes, I fear me it does. A shameful weakness, but natheless a most pleasant one. Heigh-ho, at times I envy the commoners. Why, Zerdai herself has somehow bribed the women in charge of the incubator to show her which is her own authentic egg."

Zerdai sparkled at them. "I was down there but today, and the maids tell me it's due to hatch in another fifteen days!"

"Ahem," said Borel. "Would it be good manners to ask who's papa? Excuse me if I pull a boner occasionally; I'm not entirely oriented yet."

Kubanan said: "No offense, sir. He was Sir Sardu, the predecessor of Sir Shurgez, was he not, Zerdai?"

"Yes," she agreed. "But our petty affairs must seem dull to a galaxy-traveller like you, Sir Felix. Tell us of the Earth! I've long dreamed of going thither; I can fancy nought more glamorous than seeing the New Moscow Art Theater, or the Shanghai night clubs with my own eyes. It must be wonderful to ride in a power vehicle! To talk to somebody miles distant! And all those marvelous inventions and factories. . ."

Kubanan said dryly: "I sometimes think Lady Zerdai shows an unbecoming lack of pride in her Order, young though she be. Now about this lottery: will you see to having the certificates printed?"

"Certainly," said Borel. "So you do have a printing press here?"

"Yes; from the Earthmen we got it. We'd have preferred a few Earthly weapons to smite our enemies; but no, all they'll let us have is this device, which bodes ill for our social order. Should the commoners learn reading, who knows what mad ideas this ill-starred machine may spread among them?"

Borel turned on the charm, thankful that supper consisted of some of the more palatable Krishnan dishes. On this planet you were liable to have something like a giant cockroach set before you as a treat. Afterwards all three lit cigars and talked while sipping a liqueur.

Kubanan continued: "Sir Felix, you're old enough in the ways of the world to know that a man's pretext is often other than his true reason. Your Earthmen tell me they hide their sciences from us because our culture is yet too immature—by which they mean our gladiatorial shows, our trials by combat, our warring national sovereignties, our social inequalities, and the like. Now, I say not that they're altogether wrong—I for one should be glad had they never introduced this accursed printing press. But the question I'd ask you is: What's their real reason?"

Borel wrinkled his forehead in the effort of composing a suitable reply. Being an adventurer and no intellectual, he had never troubled his head much about such abstract questions. At last, he said:

"Perhaps they're afraid the Krishnans, with their warlike traditions, would learn to make space ships and attack their neighboring planets."

"A fantastic idea," said Kubanan. " 'Tis not so long since there was a tremendous uproar over the question of whether the planets were inhabited. The churches had been assuring us that the planets were the very gods and crucifying heretics who said otherwise. No wonder we hailed as gods the first beings from Earth and the other planets of your sun!"

Borel murmured a polite assent, privately thinking that the first expedition to this system ought, if they had any sense, to have been satisfied with being gods and not go disillusioning the Krishnans. That's what came of letting a bunch of sappy do-gooders. . .

Kubanan was going on: "Our problem is much more immediate. We're hemmed and beset by enemies. Across the Pichidé lies Gozashtand, whose ruler has been taking an unfriendly line of late; and Majbur City is a veritable hotbed of plots and stratagems. If a way could be found to get us—let's say—one gun, which our clever smiths could copy, there's nothing the Order would not do. . ."

So, thought Borel, that's why the old boy is so hospitable to a mere stranger. He said: "I see your point, Excellency. You know the risks, don't you?"

"The greater the risk, the greater the reward."

"True, but it would require most careful thought. I'll let you know when I've had time to think."

"I understand." Kubanan rose, and to Borel's surprise said: "I leave you now; Kuri will think I've forgotten her utterly. You'll stay the night, of course?"

"Why, I—thank you, Your Excellency. I'll have to send a note out to my man."

"Yes, yes, I'll send you a page. Meanwhile the Lady Zerdai shall keep you company, or if you've a mind to read there are ample books on the shelves. Take the second room on the left."

Borel murmured his thanks, and the treasurer departed, his furred robe floating behind him. Then, having no interest whatever in Kubanan's library, he sat down near Zerdai.

Eyes aglow, Zerdai said: "Now that we need talk finance no more, tell me of the Earth. How live you? I mean, what's your system of personal relationships? Have you homes and families like the commoners, or all in common as we Guardians do?"

As Borel explained, the girl sighed. With a faraway look she said: "Could I but go thither! I can imagine nought more romantic than to be an Earthly housewife with a home and a man and children of my own! And a telephone!"

Borel reflected that some Terran housewives sang a different tune, but said gently: "Couldn't you resign from the Order?"

"In theory, yes—but 'tis hardly ever done. 'Twould be like stepping into another world, and what sort of welcome would the commoners give? Would they not resent what they'd call one's airs? And to have to face the scorn of all Guardians. . . No, it would not do. Could one escape this world entire, as by journeying to Earth. . ."

"Maybe that could be arranged too," said Borel cautiously. While he was willing to promise her anything to enlist her coöperation and then ditch her, he did not want to get involved in more schemes at once than he could handle.

"Really?" she said, glowing at him. "There's nought I wouldn't do. . ."

Borel thought, they all say there's nothing they wouldn't do if I'll only get them what they want. He said: "I may need help on some of my projects here. Can I count on your assistance?"

"With all my heart!"

"Good. I'll see that you don't regret it. We'd make a wonderful team, don't you think? With your beauty and my experience, there's nothing we couldn't get away with. Can't you see us cutting a swath through the galaxy?"

She leaned toward him, breathing hard. "You're wonderful!"

He smiled. "Not really. You are."

"No, you."

"No, you. You've got beauty, brains, nerve— Oh well, I shall have plenty of chance to tell you in the future, when I get this lottery organized."

"Oh." This seemed to bring her back to Krishna again. She glanced at the time candle and put out her cigar, saying: "Great stars, I had no idea the hour was so late! I must go to bed, Sir Felix the Red. Will you escort me to my room?"

III.

At breakfast, Sir Kubanan said: "Thanks to the stars, the Grand Council meets this forenoon. I'll bring up your lottery suggestion, and if they approve, we can start work on it today. Why spend you not the morning laying your plans?"

"A splendid idea, Excellency," said Borel, and went to work after breakfast, on the design of lottery tickets and advertising posters. Zerdai hung around, asking if she could not help, trying to cuddle up beside him and getting in the way of his pen arm, all the time looking at him with such open adoration that even he, normally as embarrassable as a rhinoceros, squirmed a little under her gaze.

However, he put up with it in a good cause, to wit: the cause of making a killing for Felix Etienne Borel.

By the middle of the day Kubanan was back, jubilant. "They approved! At first Grand Master Juvain boggled a little, but I talked him round. He liked not letting one not of our Order so deep into our affairs, saying, how can there be a secret Order if all its secrets be known? But I bridled him. How goes the plan?"

Borel showed him the layouts. The treasurer said: "Wonderful! Wonderful! Carry on, my boy, and come to me for aught you need."

"I will. This afternoon I'll arrange for printing this

stuff. Then we shall need a booth. How about setting it up at the lower end of that little street up to the gate of the citadel? And I shall have to train a couple of men as ticket sellers and some more to guard the money."

"All shall be done. Harken, why move you not hither from your present lodgings? I have ample room, and 'twould save time as well as augment comfort, thus slaying two unhas with one bolt."

"Do come," sighed Zerdai.

"Okay. Where can I stable my aya and quarter my servant?"

Kubanan told him. The afternoon he spent making arrangements for printing. Since Mishé had but two printers, each with one little hand press, the job would not be finished for at least twenty days.

He reported this to Kubanan at supper, adding: "Will you give me a draft on the treasury of the Order for fifteen hundred *karda* to cover the initial costs?" (This was more than fifty percent over the prices the printers had quoted, but Kubanan assented without question.)

"And now," continued Borel, "let's take up the other matter. If Zerdai's your confidential secretary, I don't suppose you mind discussing it in front of her."

"Not at all. You've found a way to get around the technological blockade?"

"Well—yes and no. I can assure you it'll do no good for me to go to Novorecife and try to smuggle out a gun or plans for one. They have a machine that looks right through you, and they make you stand in front of it before letting you out."

"Have they no regard for privacy?"

"Not in this matter. Besides, even if one did succeed, they'd send an agent to bring one back dead or alive."

"Of those agents I've heard," said Kubanan with a slight shudder.

"Moreover I'm no engineer—a base-born trade—so I can't carry a set of plans in my head for your people to work from. Guns are too complicated for that."

"What then?"

"I think the only way is to have something they want so badly they'll ease up on the blockade in return for it."

"Yes, but what have we? There's little of ours that they covet. Even gold, they say, is much too heavy to haul billions of miles to Earth with profit, and almost everything we make, they can make more cheaply at home once they know how. I know; I've discussed it with the Viagens folk at Novorecife. Knight though I be, my office requires that I interest myself in such base commercial matters."

Borel drew on his cigar and remarked: "Earthmen are an inventive lot, and they'll continue thinking up new things for a long time to come."

Kubanan shuddered. "A horrid place must this Earth of yours be. No stability."

"So, if we had an invention far ahead of their latest stuff, they might want the secret badly enough to make a deal. See?"

"How can we? We're not inventive here. No gentleman would lower himself by tinkering with machines, while the common people lack the wit."

Borel smiled. "Suppose *I* had such a secret?"

"That would be different. What is it?"

"It's an idea that was confided to me by a dying old man. Although the earthmen had scorned him and said his device was against the laws of nature, it worked. I know because he showed me a model."

"But what *is* it?" cried Kubanan.

"It would not only be of vast value to the Earthmen, but also would make Mikardand preëminent among the nations of Krishna."

"Torture us not, Sir Felix!" pleaded Zerdai.

"It's a perpetual-motion machine."

Kubanan asked: "What's that?"

"A machine that runs forever, or at least until it wears out."

Kubanan frowned and twitched his antennae. "Not sure am I that I understand you. We have water wheels for operating grain mills, which run until they wear out."

"Not quite what I mean," Borel concentrated on putting a scientific concept into words, a hard thing to do because he neither knew nor cared about such matters. "I mean, this machine will give out more power than is put into it."

"Wherein lies the advantage of that?"

"Why, Earthmen prize power above all things. Power runs their space ships and motor vehicles, their communications equipment, and factories. Power lights their homes and milks their cows. . . I forget, you don't know about cows. And where do they get their power? From coal, uranium, and things like that. Minerals. They get some from the sun and the tides, but not enough, and they worry about exhaustion of their minerals. Now, my device takes power from the force of gravity, which is the very fundamental quality of matter." He was striding up and down in his eagerness. "Sooner or later, Krishna is bound to have a scientific revolution like that of Earth. Neither you nor the Viagens Interplanetarias can hold it off forever. And when—"

"I hope I live not to see it," said Kubanan.

"When it comes, don't you want Mikardand to lead the planet? Of course! No need to give up your social system. In fact, if we organize the thing right, it'll not only secure the rule of the Order in Mikardand, but extend the Order's influence over all Krishna!"

Kubanan was beginning to catch a little of Borel's fire. "How propose you to do that?"

"Ever heard of a corporation?"

"Let me think—is that not some vulgar scheme earthmen use in trade and manufacture?"

"Yes, but there's more to it than that. There's no limit to what you can do with a corporation. The Viagens is

a corporation, though all its stock is owned by
governments. . ." Borel plunged into corporation finance, not neglecting to say: "Of course, the promoter
of a corporation gets fifty-one percent of the stock in
consideration of his services."

"Who would the promoter be in our case?"

"I, naturally. We can form this corporation to finance
the machine. The initial financing can come from the
Order itself, and later the members can either hold—"

"Wait, wait. How can the members buy stock when
they own no money of their own?"

"Unh. That's a tough one. I guess the treasury'll have
to keep the stock; it can either draw profits from the
lease of the machines, or sell the stock at an enormous
profit—"

"Sir Felix," said Kubanan, "You make my head to
spin. No more, lest my head split like a melon on the
chopping-block. Enticing though your scheme be, there
is one immovable obstacle."

"Yes?"

"The Grand Master and the other officers would never permit—you'll not take offense?—would never permit
an outsider such as yourself to acquire such power over
the Order. 'Twas all I could do to put over your lottery
scheme, and this would be one thing too many, like a
second nose on your face."

"All right, think it over," said Borel. "Now suppose
you tell me about the Order of Qarar."

Kubanan obliged with an account of the heroic deeds
of Qarar, the legendary founder of the Order who had
slain assorted giants and monsters. As he talked, Borel
reflected on his position. He doubed if the Qararuma
would want to take in a being from another planet like
himself. Even if they did, the club rules against private
property would handicap his style.

He asked: "How do Mikardanduma become members? By being—uh—hatched in the official incubator?"

"Not always. Each child from the incubator is tested

at various times during its growth. If it fail any test, 'tis let out for adoption by some good commoner family. On the other hand, when membership falls low, we watch the children of commoners, and any that show exceptional qualities are admitted to training as wards of the Order." The treasurer went on to tell of the various grades of membership until he got sleepy and took his leave.

Later Borel asked Zerdai: "Love me?"

"You know I do, my lord!"

"Then I have a job for you."

"Aught you say, dearest master."

"I want one of those honorary memberships."

"But Felix, that's for notables like the King of Gozashtand only! I know not what I could accomplish—"

"You make the suggestion to Kubanan, see? And keep needling him until he asks me. He trusts you."

"I will try, my dearest. And I hope Shurgez never returns."

While ordinarily Borel would have investigated this last cryptic remark, at the moment his head was too full of schemes for self-aggrandizement. "Another thing. Who's the most skilled metal-worker in Mishé? I want somebody who can make a working model that really works."

"I'll find out for you, my knight."

Zerdai sent Borel to one Henjaré bad-Qavao the Brazier, a gnomish Mikardandu whom Borel first dazzled with his facade and then swore to secrecy with dreadful-sounding oaths of his own invention.

He then presented the craftsman with a rough plan for a wheel with a lot of rods with weights on their ends, pivoted to the circumference so that they had some freedom to swing in the plane of rotation of the wheel. There was also a trip arrangement so that as the wheel rotated, each rod as it approached the top was moved from a position leaning back against a stop on the rim to a straight-out radial position. Hence the thing looked as though at any time the weights on one side stood out farther from the center than those on the other, and therefore would overbalance the latter and cause the wheel to turn indefinitely.

Borel knew just enough about science to realize that the device would not work, though not enough to know why. On the other hand, since these gloops knew even less than he did, there should be no trouble in selling them the idea.

That night Kubanan said: "Sir Felix, a brilliant thought has struck me. Won't you accept an honorary membership in our proud Order? In truth, you'll find it a great advantage while you dwell in Mikardand, or even when you journey elsewhere."

Borel registered surprise. "Me? I'm most humbly grateful, Excellency, but is an outsider like myself worthy of such an honor?" Meanwhile he thought: good old Zerdai! If I were the marrying kind . . . For a moment he wavered in his determination to shake her when she had served her turn.

"Nonsense, my lad; of course you're worthy. I'd have gone farther and proposed you for full membership, but the Council pointed out that the constitution allows that only to native-born Mikardanders of our own species. As 'tis, honorary membership will provide you with most of the privileges of membership and few of the obligations.

"I'm overcome with happiness."

"Of course there's the little matter of the initiation."

"What?" Borel controlled his face.

"Yes; waive it they would not, since no king are you. It amounts to little; much ceremony and a night's vigil. I'll coach you in the ritual. And you must obtain ceremonial robes; I'll make you a list."

Borel wished he had hiked the printing charges on the lottery material by another fifty percent.

*   *   *

The initiation proved not only expensive, but also an interplanetary bore as well. Brothers in fantastic robes and weird masks stood about muttering a mystic chant at intervals. Borel stood in front of the Grand Master of the Order, a tall Krishnan with a lined face, which might have been carved from wood for all the expression it bore. Boral responded to interminable questions; since the language was an archaic dialect of Gozashtandou, he did not really know what he was saying half the time. He was lectured on the Order's glorious past, mighty present, and boundless future, and on his duties to protect and defend his interests. He called down all sorts of elaborate astrological misfortunes on his head should he violate his oaths.

"Now," said the grand master, "art thou ready for the vigil. Therefore I command thee: strip to thy underwear!"

Wondering what he was getting into now, Borel did so.

"Come with me," said Grand Master Sir Juvain.

They led him down stairs and through passages, which got progressively narrower, darker, and less pleasant. A couple of the hooded brethren carried lanterns, which soon became necessary in order to see the way. We must be far below the ground level of the citadel, thought Borel, stumbling along in his socks and feeling most clammy and uncomfortable.

When they seemed to have descended into the very bowels of the earth, they halted. The Grand Master said: "Here shalt thou remain the night, O aspirant. Danger will come upon thee, and beware how thou meetest it."

One of the brothers was measuring a long candle. He cut it off at a certain length and fixed it upright to a small shelf in the rough side of the tunnel. Another brother handed Borel a hunting spear with a long, broad head.

Then they left him.

So far, he had carried off his act by assuring himself

that all this was a lot of bluff and hokum. Nothing serious could be intended. As the brothers' footfalls died away, however, he was no longer so sure. The damned candle seemed to illuminate for a distance of only about a meter in all directions. Fore and aft, the tunnel receded into utter blackness.

His hair rose as something rustled. As he whipped the spear into position, it scuttled away; some ratlike creature, no doubt. Borel started pacing. If that damned dope Abreu had only let him bring his watch! Then he would at least have a notion of the passage of time. It seemed he had been pacing for hours, although that was probably an illusion.

Borel became aware of an odd irregularity in the floor beneath his stockinged feet, and he bent down and explored it with his fingers. Yes, a pair of parallel grooves, two or three centimeters deep, ran lengthwise along the tunnel. He followed them a few steps each way, but stopped when he could no longer see what he was doing. Why should there be two parallel grooves like a track along the floor?

He paced until his legs ached from weariness, then tried sitting on the floor with his back against the wall. When he soon found his eyelids drooping, he scrambled up lest his initiators return to find him asleep. The candle burned slowly down, its flame standing perfectly still for minutes at a stretch and then wavering slightly as some tiny air current brushed it. Still silence and darkness.

The candle would soon be burned down to nothing. What then? Would they expect him to stand here in complete darkness?

A sound made him jump violently. He could not tell what sort of sound it was; merely a faint noise from down the tunnel. There it came again.

Then his hair really rose at a low throaty vocal noise, the kind one hears in the carnivore cage of the zoo before feeding time. A sort of grunt, such as a big cat makes in tuning up for a real roar. It came again, louder.

The dying candle flame showed to Borel's horrified gaze something moving fast towards him in the tunnel. With a frightful roar a great yeki rushed into the dim light with gleaming eyes and bared fangs.

For perhaps a second (although it seemed an hour) Felix Borel stood helplessly holding his spear poised, his mouth hanging open. In that second, however, his mind suddenly worked with the speed of a tripped mousetrap. Something odd about the yeki's motion, together with the fact of the grooves in the floor, gave him the answer: the animal was a stuffed one pushed towards him on wheels.

Borel bent and laid his spear diagonally across the floor of the tunnel, and stepped back. When the contraption struck the spear, it slewed sideways with a bang, rattle, and thump and stopped, its nose against the wall.

Borel recovered his spear and examined the derailed yeki at close range. It proved a pretty battered-looking piece of taxidermy, the head and neck criss-crossed with seams where the hide had been slashed open and sewn up again. Evidently it had been used for initiations for a long time, and some of the aspirants had speared it. Others had doubtless turned tail and run, thus flunking the test.

Footsteps sounded in the corridor and lanterns bobbed closer just as the candle on the shelf guttered out.

The Grand Master and the masked brethren swarmed around Borel, including one with a horn on which he had made the yeki noises. They slapped him on the back and told him how brave he was. Then they led him back up many flights to the main hall, where he was allowed to don his clothes again. The Grand Master hung a jewelled dragon insigne around his neck and welcomed him with a florid speech in archaic style:

"O Felix, be thou hereby accepted into this most noble, most ancient, most honorable, most secret, most puissant, most righteous, most chivalrous, and most fraternal Order, and upon thee be bestowed all the rights, privileges, rank, standing, immunities, duties, liabilities, obligations, and attributes of a knight of this most noble, most ancient, most honorable. . ."

The long Krishnan night was two-thirds gone when the hand-shaking and drinking were over. Borel and Kubanan, arms about each other's necks, wove their way drunkenly to the latter's apartment, while Borel sang what he could remember of a Terran song about a king of England and a queen of Spain, until Kubanan shushed him, saying:

"Know you not that poetry's forbidden in Mikardand?"

"I didn't know. Why?"

"The Order decided it was bad for our—*hic*—martial spirit. B'sides, poets tell too damned many lies. What's the nex' stanza?"

IV.

Next morning Sir Felix, as he tried to remember to think of himself, began to press for consideration of his perpetual-motion scheme. He obtained an interview with Grand Master Juvain in the afternoon and put his proposal. Sir Juvain seemed puzzled by the whole thing, and Borel had to call in Kubanan to help him explain.

Juvain finally said: "Very well, Brother Felix, tell me when your preparations are ready and I'll call a general meeting of the members in residence to pass upon your proposal."

Then, since the working model was not yet ready, Borel had nothing to do for a couple of days except breathe down the neck of Henjaré the Brazier and superintend the building of the lottery ticket booth. The printing job was nowhere near done.

Therefore he whistled up Yerevats to help him pass the time by practicing driving the buggy. After a couple of hours, he could fairly well manage the difficult art of backing and filling to turn around in a restricted space.

"Have the carriage ready right after lunch," he ordered.

"Master go ride?"

"Yes. I shan't need you though; I'm taking it myself."

"Unk. No good. Master get in trouble."

"That's my lookout."

"Bet master take girl out. Bad business."

"Mind your own business!" shouted Borel, and made a pass at Yerevats, who ducked and scuttled out. Now, thought Borel, Yerevats will sulk and I'll have to spend a day cajoling him back into a good humor or I'll get no decent service. Damn it, why didn't they have mechanical servants with no feelings that their masters had to take into account? Somebody had tried to make one on Earth, but the thing had run amok and mistaken its master for a cord of firewood. . .

The afternoon saw him trotting down the main avenue of Mishé with Zerdai by his side, looking at him worshipfully. He could not get quite used to the curious sound made by the six hooves of the aya when it trotted.

He asked: "Who has the right of way if somebody comes in from the side?"

"Why, you do, Felix! You're a member of the Order, even if not a regular Guardian!"

"Oh." Borel, although he had about as little public spirit as a man can have, had been exposed to the democratic institutions of Earth long enough so as to find these class distinctions distasteful. "In other words, because I'm now an honorary knight, I can tear through the town at full gallop hollering '*byant-hao!*' and if anybody gets run over that's too bad?"

"Naturally. What think you? But I forget you're from another world. 'Tis one of your fascinations that beneath your hard adventuresome exterior you're more gentle and considerate than the men of this land."

Borel hid a smile. He'd been called a lot of things before, including thief, swindler, and slimy double-crossing heel, but never gentle and considerate. Maybe that was an example of the relativity the long-haired scientists talked about.

"Where would you like me to drive you?" he asked.

"To Earth!" she said, putting her head on his shoulder. For a moment he was almost tempted to renege on his plan to leave her behind. Then the resolute selfishness, which was the adventurer's leading trait, came to his rescue. He reminded himself that on a fast getaway, the less baggage the better. Love 'em and leave 'em. Anyway, wouldn't she be happier if they parted before she learned he was no do-gooder after all?

"Let's to the tournament ground outside the North Gate. Today's the battle betwixt Sir Voljah and Sir Shusp."

"What's this? I hadn't heard of it."

"Sir Shusp forced a challenge on Sir Volhaj; some quarrel over the love of a lady. Shusp has already slain three knights in affrays of this kind."

Borel said: "If you Guardians are supposed to have everything in common, like the Communists we used to have on Earth, I don't see what call a knight has to get jealous. Couldn't they both court her at once?"

"That's not the custom. A maid should dismiss the one before taking another; to do otherwise were in bad taste."

They reached the North Gate and ambled out into the country. Borel asked: "Where does this road go?"

"Know you not? To Koloft and Novorecife."

Beyond the last houses, where the farmed fields began, the tournament grounds lay to the right of the road. It reminded Borel of a North American high-school football field: same small wooden grandstands, and tents at the ends where the goal posts should be. In the middle of one stand, a section had been built out into a box, in which sat the high officers of the Order. Hawkers circulated through the crowd, one crying:

"Flowers! Flowers! Buy a flower with the color of your favorite knight! Red for Volhaj, white for Shusp. Flowers!"

The stands were already full of people who, from the predominant color of the flowers in their hats, seemed to favor Shusp. Borel ignored Zerdai's suggestion, that he pitch some commoner out of his seat and claim it for himself, and led her to where the late arrivals clustered

standing at one end of the field. He was a little annoyed
with himself for not having come in time to lay a few
bets. This should be much more exciting than the ponies
on Earth, and by shaving the odds and betting both
ways he might put himself in the enviable position of
making a profit on these saps no matter who won.

As they took their places, a trumpet blew. Nearby,
Borel saw a man in Moorish-looking armor, wearing a
spiked helmet with a nose-guard and a little skirt of
chain mail; he was sitting on a big tough-looking aya,
also wearing bits of armor here and there. This Qararu
now left his tent to trot down to the middle of the field.
From the red touches about his saddle and equipment,
Borel judged him to be Sir Volhaj. Volhaj as the challenged party had his sympathy, in line with his own dis-
taste for violence. Why couldn't the other gloop be a
good fellow about his girl friend? Borel had done that
sort of thing and found nobody the worse for it.

From the other end of the field came another rider,
similarly equipped but decorated in white. The two met
at the center of the field, wheeled to face the Grand
Master, and walked their mounts forward until they
were as close as they could get to the booth. The Grand
Master made a speech, which Borel could not hear, and
then the knights wheeled away and trotted back to their
respective ends of the field. At the near end, Sir Volhaj's
squires or seconds or whatever they were handed him up
a lance and a small round shield.

The trumpet blew again, and the antagonists galloped
towards each other. Borel winced as they met with a
crash in the middle of the field. When Borel opened his
eyes again, he saw that the red knight had been knocked
out of the saddle and was rolling over and over on the
moss. His aya continued on without him, while the
white knight slowed gradually as he approached Borel's
end of the field, then turned and headed back.

Volhaj had meanwhile gotten up with a visible effort
in his weight of iron and clanked off to where his lance

lay. He picked it up, and as Shusp bore down on him he planted the butt-end in the ground and lowered the point to the level of the charging aya's chest, where the creature's light armor did not protect it. Borel could not see the spear go in, but he judged that it had when the beast reared, screamed, threw its rider, and collapsed kicking. Borel, who felt strongly about cruelty to animals, thought indignantly that there ought to be an interplanetary S. P. C. A. to stop this sort of thing.

At this point, the crowd began to jostle and push with cries of excitement, so Borel had to take his eyes off the fight long enough to clear a space with his elbows for Zerdai. When he looked back again, the knights were at it on foot, making a tremendous din, Shusp with a huge two-handed sword, Volhaj with his buckler and a sword of more normal size.

They circled around one another, slashing, thrusting, and parrying, and worked their way slowly down to Borel's end of the field, until he could see the dents in their armor and the trickle of blood running down the chin of Sir Volhaj. By now, both were so winded that the fight was going as slowly as an honest wrestling match, with both making a few swipes and then stopping to pant and glare at each other for a while.

Then, in the midst of an exchange of strokes, Sir Volhaj's sword flew up, turning over and over until it came down at Shusp's feet. Sir Shusp instantly put a foot on it and forced Sir Volhaj back with a swing of his crowbarlike blade. Then he picked up the dropped sword and threw it as far away as he could.

Borel asked: "Hey, is he allowed to do that?"

"I know not," said Zerdai. "Though there be few rules, mayhap that's against them."

Shusp now advanced rapidly on Volhaj, who was reduced to a shield battered all out of shape and a dagger. The latter gave ground, parrying the swipes as best he could.

"Why doesn't the fool cut and run?" asked Borel.

Zerdai stared at him. "Know you not that for a knight of the Order the penalty for cowardice is flaying alive?"

At the rate Volhaj was backing towards them, he would soon be treading on the toes of the spectators, who in fact began to spread out nervously. Volhaj was staggering, disheartening Borel, who hated to see his favorite nearing his rope's end.

On a sudden impulse, Borel drew his own sword and called: "Hey, Volhaj, don't look now but here's something for you!" With that he threw the sword as if it had been a javelin, so that the point stuck into the ground alongside of Volhaj. The latter dropped his dagger, snatched up the sword, and tore into Shusp with renewed vigor.

Then Shusp went down with a clang. Volhaj, standing over him, found a gap in his armor around the throat, put the point there, and pushed down on the hilt with both hands. . . When Borel opened his eyes again, Shusp's legs were giving their last twitch. Cheers and the paying of bets.

Volhaj came back to where Borel stood and said: "Sir Felix the Red, I perceive you succored me but now."

"How d'you know that?"

"By your empty scabbard, friend. Here, take your sword with my thanks. I doubt the referee will hold your deed a foul, since the chief complainant will no longer be present to press his case. Call on me for help any time." He shook hands warmly and walked wearily off to his wigwam.

" 'Twas a brave deed, Felix," said Zerdai, squeezing his arm as they walked back to the buggy through the departing crowd.

"I don't see that it was anything special," said Borel truthfully.

"Had Sir Shusp won, he'd have challenged you!"

"*Gluk!*" said Borel. He hadn't thought of that.

"What is it, my dearest?"

"Something caught in my throat. Let's get back to

dinner ahead of the crowd, huh? Giddap, Galahad!"

Zerdai retired after dinner, however, saying she would not be back for supper; the excitement had given her a headache.

Kubanan said: " 'Tis a rare thing, for she's been in better spirits since your arrival than was her wont since Sir Shurgez departed."

"You mean she was grieving for a boy-friend until I came along and cheered her up?" Borel thought, Kubanan's a nice old wump; too bad he'll have to be the fall guy for the project. But business is business.

"Yes. Ah, Felix, it's sad you're of another species, so that she'll never lay you an egg! For the Order can use offspring inheriting your qualities. Even I, sentimental old fool that I am, like to think of you as a son-in-law and Zerdai's eggs as my own grandchildren, as though I were some simple commoner with a family."

Borel asked: "What's this about Shurgez? What happened to him?"

"The Grand Master ordered him on a quest."

"What quest?"

"To fetch the beard of the King of Balhib."

"And what does the Order want with this king's beard? Are you going into the upholstery business?"

Kubanan laughed. "Of course not. The King of Balhib has treated the Order with scorn and contumely of late, and we thought to teach him a lesson."

"And why was Shurgez sent?"

"Because of his foul murder of Brother Sir Zamrán."

"Why did he murder Zamrán?"

"Surely you know the tale—but I forget, you're still new here. Sir Zamrán was he who slew Shurgez's lady."

"I thought Zerdai was Shurgez's girl."

"She was, but afterward. Let me begin at the beginning. Time was when Sir Zamrán and the Lady Fevzi were lovers, all right and decorous in accord with the customs of the Order. Then for some reason Lady Fevzi cast off Zamrán, as she had every right to do, and took Sir Shurgez in his stead. This made Sir Zamrán wroth, and instead of taking his defeat philosophically like a true knight, what does he do but come up behind Lady Fevzi at the ball celebrating the conjunction of the planets Vishnu and Ganesha, and smite off her head just as she was presenting a home-made pie to the Grand Master!"

"Wow!" said Borel with an honest shudder.

"True, 'twas no knightly deed, especially in front of the Grand Master, not to mention the difficulty of cleansing the carpet. If he had to slay her, he should at least have taken her outside. The Grand Master, most annoyed, would have rebuked Zamrán severely for his discourtesy, but he's hardly past the preamble when Sir Shurgez comes in to ask after his sweetling, sees the scene, and leaps upon Zamrán with his dagger before any can stay him. So then we have two spots on the rug to clean and the Grand Master in a fair fury. The upshot was that he ordered Shurgez on this quest to teach him to issue his challenges in due form and not go thrusting knives among the ribs of any who incur his displeasure. No doubt he half hoped that Shurgez would be slain in the doing, for the King of Balhib is no effeminate."

Borel was sure now that nothing would ever induce him to settle permanently among such violent people. "When did Shurgez get time to—uh—be friends with Zerdai?"

"Why, he couldn't leave before the astrological indications were favorable, to wit for twenty-one days, and during that time he enjoyed my secretary's favor. Far places have ever attracted her, and I think she'd have gone with him if he'd have had her."

"What's the word about Shurgez now?"

"The simplest word of all, to wit: no word. Should he return, my spies will tell me of his approach before he arrives."

Borel became aware that the clicking sound that had

puzzled him was the chatter of his own teeth. He resolved to ride herd on Henjaré the next day to rush the model through to completion.

"One more question," he said. "Whatever became of Lady Fevzi's pie?" Kubanan could not tell him that, however.

The model was well enough along so that Borel asked the Grand Master for the perpetual-motion meeting the following day. Although he expected an evening meeting, with all the knights full of dinner and feeling friendly, it turned out that the only time available on the Grand Master's schedule was in the morning.

"Of course, Brother Felix," said Sir Juvain, "if you prefer to put it off a few days. . ."

"No, most mighty potentate," said Borel, thinking of the Shurgez menace. "The sooner the better for you, me, and the Order."

Thus it happened that the next morning, after breakfast, Felix Borel found himself on the platform of the main auditorium of the citadel, facing several thousand knights of the Order of Qarar. Beside him on a small table stood his gleaming new brass model of the perpetual-motion wheel. A feature of the wheel not obvious to the audience was a little pulley on the shaft, around which was wound a fine but strong thread made of hairs from the tails of shomals, which led from the wheel off into the wings where Zerdai stood hidden from view. It had taken all Borel's blandishments to get her to play this role.

He launched into his speech: ". . . what is the purpose and function of our noble Order? Power! And what is the basis of power? First, our own strong right arms; second, the wealth of the Order, which in turn is derived from the wealth of the commons. So anything that enriches the commons increases our power, does it not? Let me give you an example. There's a railroad, I hear, from Majbur to Jazmurian along the coast, worked by bishtars pulling little strings of cars. Now, mount one of my wheels on a car and connect it by a belt or chain to the wheels. Start the wheel revolving, and what happens? The car with its wheel will pull far more cars than a bishtar, and likewise it never grows old and dies as an animal does, never runs amok and smashes property, and when not in use stands quietly in its shed without needing to be fed. We could build a railroad from Mishé to Majbur and another from Mishé to Jazmurian, and carry goods faster between the coastal cities than it is now carried by the direct route. There's a source of infinite wealth, of which the Order would of course secure its due share.

"Then there is the matter of weapons. I cannot go into details because many of these are confidential, but I have positive assurance that there are those who would trade the mighty weapons of the Interplanetary Council for the secret of this little wheel. You know what that would mean. Think it over.

"Now I will show you how it actually works. This model you see is not a true working wheel, but a mere toy, an imitation to give you an idea of the finished wheel, which would be much larger. This little wheel will not give enough power to be very useful. Why? Friction. The mysterious sciences of my native planet found centuries ago that friction is proportionately larger in small machines than in large ones. Therefore the fact that this little wheel won't give useful power is proof that a larger one would. However, the little wheel still gives enough power to run itself without outside help.

"Are you watching, brothers? Observe: I release the brake that prevents the wheel from turning. Hold your breaths, sirs—ah, it moves! It turns! The secret of the ages comes to life before you!"

He had signalled Zerdai, who had begun to pull on the thread, reeling in one end of it while paying out the other. The wheel turned slowly, the little brass legs going click-click-click as they reached the trip at the top.

"Behold!" yelled Borel. "It works! The Order is all-rich and all-powerful!"

After letting the wheel spin for a minute or so, Borel resumed: "Brothers, what must we do to realize on this wonderful invention? One, we need funds to build a number of large wheels to try out various applications: to power ships and rail cars, to run grist mills, and to turn the shafts of machines in workshops. No machine is ever perfect when first completed; there are always details to be improved. Second, we need an organization to exploit the wheel: to make treaties with other states to lease wheels from us and to give us the exclusive right to exploit wheels within their borders; and to negotiate with the powers that be to exchange the secret of the wheel for—I need go no further!

"On Earth we have a type of organization called a corporation for such purposes. . ." And he launched into the account he had previously given Kubanan and Juvain.

"Now," he said, "what do we need for this corporation? The officers of the Order and I have agreed that to start, the treasury shall advance the sum of 245,000 karda, for which the Order shall receive forty-nine percent of the stock of the company. The remaining fifty-one percent will naturally remain with the promoter and director of the company; that's the arrangement we've found most successful on Earth. However, before such a large sum can be invested in this great enterprise, we must in accordance with the constitution let you vote on the question. First I had better stop our little wheel here, lest the noise distract you."

The clicking stopped as Borel put his hand against the wheel. Zerdai broke the thread with a quick jerk, gathered it all in, and slipped away from her hiding place.

Borel continued: "I therefore turn the meeting back to our friend, guide, counsellor, and leader, Grand Master Sir Juvain."

The Grand Master put the vote, and the appropriation passed by a large majority. As the knights cheered, Kubanan led a line of pages staggering under bags of coins to the stage, where the bags were ranged in a row on the boards.

Borel, when he could get silence again, said: "I thank you one and all. If any would care to examine my little wheel, they shall see for themselves that no trickery is involved."

The *Garma Qararuma* climbed up *en masse* to congratulate Borel. The adventurer, trying not to seem to gloat over the money, was telling himself that once he got away with this bit of swag he would sell it for World Federation dollars, go back to Earth, invest his fortune conservatively, and never have to worry about money again. Of course he had promised himself the same thing on several previous occasions, but somehow the money always seemed to dissipate before he got around to investing it.

V.

Sir Volhaj was pushing through the crowd, saying: "Sir Felix, may I speak to you aside?"

"Sure. What is it?"

"How feel you?"

"Fine. Never better."

"That's good, for Shurgez has returned to Mishé with his mission accomplished."

"What's that?" said Kubanan. "Shurgez back, and my spies haven't told me?"

"Right, my lord."

"Oh-oh," said the treasurer. "If he challenges you, Sir Felix, you will, as a knight, have to give him instant satisfaction. What arms own you besides that sword?"

"Gluk," said Borel. "N-none. Doesn't the challenged party have a choice of weapons?" he asked with some vague idea of specifying boxing gloves.

"According to the rules of the Order," said Volhaj, "each fighter may use what weapons he pleases. Shurgez will indubitably employ the full panoply: lance, sword, and a mace or ax in reserve, and will enter the lists in full armor. As for you—well, since you and I are much of a size, feel free to borrow aught that you need."

Before Borel could say anything more, a murmur and a head-turning apprised him of the approach of some interest. As the crowd parted, a squat, immensely muscular, and very Mongoloid-looking knight came forward. "Are you he whom they call Sir Felix the Red?" asked the newcomer.

"Y-yes," said Borel, icicles of fear running through his viscera.

"I am Sir Shurgez. It has been revealed to me that in my absence you've taken the lady Zerdai as your companion. Therefore I name you a vile traitor, scurvy knave, villainous rascal, base mechanic, and foul foreigner, and shall be at the tournament grounds immediately after lunch to prove my assertions upon your diseased and ugly body. Here, you thing of no account!" And Sir Shurgez, who had been peeling off his glove, threw it lightly in Borel's face.

"I'll fight you!" shouted Borel in a sudden surge of temper. *"Baghan! Zeft!"* He added a few more Gozashtandou obscenities and threw the glove back at Shurgez, who caught it, laughed shortly, and turned his back.

"That's that," said Kubanan as Shurgez marched off. "Sure am I that so bold and experienced a knight as yourself will make mincemeat of yon braggart. Shall I have my pages convey the gold to your chamber while we lunch?"

Borel felt like saying: "I don't want any lunch," but judged it impolitic. His wits, after the first moment of terror-stricken paralysis, had begun to work again. First he felt sorry for himself. What had he done to deserve this? Why had he joined this crummy club, where instead of swindling each other like gentlemen, the members settled differences by the cruel and barbarous methods of physical combat? All he'd done was to keep Zerdai happy while this blug was away. . .

Then he pulled himself together and tried to think his way out of the predicament. Should he simply refuse to fight? That meant skinning alive. Could he sprain an ankle? Maybe, but with all these people standing around. . . Why hadn't he told that well-meaning sap Volhaj that he was sick unto death?

And now how could he get away with the gold? It was probably too heavy for the buggy; he would need a big two-aya carriage, which could not be obtained in a matter of minutes. How could he make his getaway at all before the fight? With his dear damned friends clustering round. . .

They were filling him with good advice: "I knew a man who'd begin a charge with lance level, then whirl it around his head as 'twere a club. . ."; "When Sir Vardao slew that wight from Gozashtand, he dropped his lance altogether and snatched his mace. . ."; "If you can get him around the neck with one arm, go for his crotch with your dagger. . ."

What he really wanted was advice on how to sneak out of the acropolis and make tracks for Novorecife with a third of the Order's treasury. When he had gulped the last tasteless morsel, he said: "Good sirs, please excuse me. I have things to say to those near to me."

Zerdai was crying on her bed. He picked her up and kissed her. She responded avidly; this was a Terran custom on which the Krishnans had eagerly seized.

"Come," he said, "it's not that bad."

She clung to him frantically. "But I love only you! I couldn't live without you! And I've been counting so on going with you to far planets. . ."

Borel's vestigial conscience stirred, and in a rare burst of frankness he said: "Look, Zerdai, it'll be small loss no matter how the fight comes out. I'm not the shining hero you think I am; in fact some people consider me an unmitigated heel."

"No! No! You're kind and good. . ."

". . . and even if I get through this alive I may have to run for it without you."

"I'll die! I could never companion with that brute Shurgez again. . ."

Borel thought of giving her some of the gold, since he couldn't hope to get it all away himself. But then with the Guardians' communistic principles she couldn't keep it, and the Order would seize all he left in any case. Finally he unpinned several of his more glittery decorations and handed them to her, saying:

"At least you'll have these to remember me by." That seemed to break her down completely.

He found Yerevats in his own room and said: "If the fight doesn't go my way, take as much of this gold as you can carry, and the buggy, and get out of town fast."

"Oh, wonderful master must win fight!"

"That's as the stars decide. Hope for the best but expect the worst."

"But master, how shall pull buggy?"

"Keep the aya too. Volhaj is lending me his oversized one for the scrap. Tell you what: when we go out to the field, bring one of those bags inside your clothes."

An hour later, Yerevats buckled the last strap of Borel's borrowed harness. The suit was a composite, chain mail over the joints and plate armor elsewhere. Borel found that it hampered him less than he expected, considering how heavy it had seemed when he hefted before putting it on.

He stepped out of the tent at his end of the field. Volhaj was holding the big aya, which turned and looked at him suspiciously from under its horns. At the far end, Shurgez already sat his mount. Borel, although outwardly calm, was reviling himself for not having thought of this and that: he should have hinted that *his* weapon would be a gun; he should have bought a bishtar and sat high up on its elephantine back, out of reach of Shurgez, while he potted his enemy with his crossbow. . . .

Yerevats, bustling about the animal's saddle, secured the bag he had brought with him. Although he tried to do so secretly, the jingle of coin attracted the attention of Volhaj, who asked: "A bag of gold on your saddle? Why do you that, friend?"

"Luck," said Borel, feeling for the stirrup. His first

effort to swing his leg over his mount failed because of the extra weight he was carrying, and they had to give him a boost. Yerevats handed him up his spiked helmet, which he carefully wiggled down onto his head. At once the outside noises acquired a muffled quality as the sound was filtered through the steel and the padding. Borel buckled his chin strap.

A horn blew. As he had seen the other knights do the day of the previous battle, Borel kicked the animal into motion and rode slowly down the field towards his opponent, who advanced to meet him. Thank the Lord he knew how to ride a Terran horse! This was not much different, save that the fact that the saddle was directly over the aya's intermediate pair of legs caused its rider to be jarred unpleasantly in the trot.

Borel could hardly recognize Shurgez behind the nasal of his helmet, and he supposed that his own features were equally hidden. Without a word they wheeled towards the side of the field where the Grand Master sat in his booth. They walked their animals over to the stand and listened side by side while Sir Juvain droned the rules of the contest at them. Borel thought it an awful lot of words to say that, for all practical purposes, anything went.

Beside the Grand Master sat Kubanan, stony-faced except at the last, when he tipped Borel a wink. Borel also caught a glimpse of Zerdai in the stands; catching his eye, she waved frantically.

The Grand Master finished and made motions with his baton. The fighters wheeled away from each other and trotted back to their respective tents, where Volhaj handed Borel his lance and buckler, saying: "Hold your shaft level; watch his. . ." Borel, preoccupied, heard none of it.

"Get you ready," said Volhaj. The trumpet blew.

Borel, almost bursting with excitement said: "Goodbye, and thanks."

The hooves of Shurgez's mount were already drum-

ming on the moss before Borel collected his wits enough
to put his own beast into motion. For a long time, it
seemed, he rode towards a little figure on aya-back that
got no nearer. Then all at once the aya and its rider
expanded to life-size and Borel's foe was upon him.

Since Shurgez had started sooner and ridden harder,
they met short of the mid-point of the field. As his enemy bore down, Borel rose in his stirrups and threw his
lance at Shurgez, then instantly hauled on the reins
braided into the aya's mustache to guide it to the right.

Shurgez ducked as the lance hurtled toward him, so
that the point of his own lance wavered and missed
Borel by a meter. Borel heard the thrown spear hit sideways with a clank against Shurgez's armor. Then he was
past and headed for Shurgez's tent at the far end. He
leaned forward and spurred his aya mercilessly.

Just before he reached the end of the field, he jerked
a look back. Shurgez was still reining in to turn his
mount. Borel switched his attention back to where he
was going and aimed for a gap on one side of Shurgez's
tent. The people around the tent stood staring until the
last minute, then frantically dove out of the way as the
aya thundered through. Yells rose behind.

Borel guided his beast over to the main road towards
Novorecife, secured the reins to the projection on the
front of the saddle, and began shedding impedimenta.
Off went the pretty damascened helmet, to fall with a
clank to the roadway. Away went sword and battle ax.
After some fumbling, he got rid of the brassets on his
forearms and their attached gauntlets, and then the
cuirass with its little chain sleeves. The iron pants would
have to await a better opportunity.

The aya kept on at a dead run until Mishé dwindled
in the distance. When the beast began to puff alarming-
ly, Borel let it slow to a walk for a while. However, when
he looked back he thought he saw little dots on the road
that might be pursuers, and spurred his mount to a
gallop once more. When the dots disappeared he slowed
again. Gallop—trot—walk—trot—gallop—that was

how you covered long distances on a horse, so it should work on this six-legged equivalent. After this, he would confine his efforts to Earth, where at least you knew the score.

He looked scornfully down at the bag of gold clinking faintly at the side of his saddle. One bag was all he had dared to take for fear of slowing his mount. It was not a bad haul for small-time stuff and would let him live and travel long enough to case his next set of suckers. Still, it was nothing compared to what he would have made if the damned Shurgez hadn't popped up so inopportunely. If, now, he had been able to get away with the proceeds both of the stock sale and of the lottery. . .

Next morning found Borel still on the aya's back, plodding over the causeway through the Koloft Swamps. Flying things buzzed and bit; bubbles of stinking gas rose through the black water and burst. Now and then some sluggish swamp-dwelling creature roiled the surface or grunted a mating call. A shower had soaked Borel during the night, and in this dank atmosphere his clothes seemed never to dry.

With yelping cries, the tailed men of Koloft broke from the bushes and ran towards him: Yerevats's wild brethren with stone-bladed knives and spears, hairy, naked, and fearful-looking. Borel spurred the aya into a shambling trot. The tailed men scrambled to the causeway just too late to seize him; a thrown spear went past his head with a swish.

Borel threw away his kindness-to-animals principle and dug spurs into the aya's flanks. They pounded after him. In fact, by squirming around, he could see that they were actually gaining on him. Another spear came whistling along. Borel flinched, and the spear-head struck the cantle of his saddle and broke, leaving a sliver of obsidian sticking into the saddle as the shaft clattered to the causeway. The next one, he thought gloomily, would be a hit.

Then inspiration seized him. If he could get his

money-bag open and throw a handful of gold to the roadway, these savages might stop to scramble for it. His fingers tore at Yerevats's lashings.

And then the twenty-kilo weight of the gold snatched the whole bag from his grasp. Clank! Gold pieces spilled out of the open mouth of the sack and rolled in little circles on the causeway. The tailed men whooped and pounced on them, abandoning their chase. While Borel was glad not to have to dodge any more spears, he did think the price a little steep. However, to go back to dispute possession of the money now would be merely a messy form of suicide, so he rode wearily on.

He reeled into Novorecife about noon. He was no sooner inside the wall than a man in the uniform of Abreu's security force said: "Is the senhor Felix Borel?"

"Huh?" He had been thinking in Gozashtandou so long that in his exhausted state the Brazilo-Portuguese of the spaceways at first was meaningless to him.

"I said, is the senhor Felix Borel?"

"Yes. Sir Felix Borel to be exact. What—"

"I don't care what the senhor calls himself; he's under arrest."

"What for?"

"Violation of Regulation 368. *Vamos, por favor!*"

Borel demanded a lawyer at the preliminary hearing. Since he could not pay for one, Judge Keshavachandra appointed Manual Sandak. Abreu presented his case.

Borel asked: "Senhor Abreu, how the devil did you find out about this little project of mine so quickly?"

The judge said: "Address your remarks to the court, please. The Security Office has its methods, naturally. Have you anything pertinent to say?"

Borel whispered to Sandak, who rose and said: "It is the contention of the defense that the case presented by the Security Office is *prima facie* invalid, because the device in question, to wit: a wheel allegedly embodying the principles of perpetual motion, is inherently inoperative, being in violation of the well-known law of conservation of energy. Regulation 368 specifically states that it's forbidden to communicate a device 'representing an improvement upon the science and technics already existing upon this planet'. But since this gadget wouldn't work by any stretch of the imagination, it's no improvement on anything."

"You mean," sputtered Abreu, "that it was all a fake, a swindle?"

"Sure," said Borel, laughing heartily at the security officer's expression."

Abreu said: "My latest information says that you actually demonstrated the device the day before yesterday in the auditorium of the Order of Qarar at Mishé. What have you to say to that?"

"That was a fake too," said Borel, and told of the thread pulled by Zerdai in the wings.

"Just how is this gadget supposed to work?" asked the judge. Borel explained. Keshavachandra exclaimed: "Good Lord, that form of perpetual-motion device goes back to the European Middle Ages! I remember a case involving it when I was a patent lawyer in India." He turned to Abreu, saying: "Does that description check with your information?"

"*Sim, Vossa Excelencia.*" Abreu turned on Borel. "I knew you were a crook, but I never expected you to brag on the fact as part of a legal charge!"

"Bureaucrat!" sneered Borel.

"No personalities," snapped Judge Keshavachandra. "I'm afraid I can't bind him over, Senhor Cristovão."

"How about a charge of swindling?" said Abreu hopefully.

Sandak jumped up. "You can't, your honor. The act was committed in Mikardand, so this court has no jurisdiction."

"How about holding him until we see if the Republic wants him back?" said Abreu.

Sandak said: "That won't work either. We have no extradition treaty with Mikardand, because their legal code doesn't meet the minimum requirements of the Interplanetary Juridical Commission. Moreover, the courts hold that a suspect may not be forcibly returned to a jurisdiction where he'd be liable to be killed on sight."

The judge said: "I'm afraid he's right again, senhor. We still, however, have some power over undesirables. Draw me a request for an expulsion order and I'll sign it quicker than you can say *'non vult.'*. There are ships leaving in a few days, and we can give him his choice of them. I dislike inflicting him on other jurisdictions, but I don't know what else we can do." He added with a smile: "He'll probably turn up here again like a bad anna, with a cop three jumps behind him. Talk of perpetual motion, he's it!"

Borel slouched into the Nova Iorque Bar and ordered a double comet. He fished his remaining money out of his pants pocket: about four and a half karda. This might feed him until he took off. Or it might provide him with a first-class binge. He decided on the binge; if he got drunk enough, he wouldn't care about food in the interim.

He caught a glimpse of himself in the mirror back of the bar, unshaven, with eyes as red as his hair and his gorgeous private uniform unpressed and weather-beaten. Most of the bravado had leaked out of him. If he had avoided the Noverecife jail, he was still about to be shipped, God knew where, without even a stake to get started again. The fact that he was getting his transportation free gave him no pleasure, for he knew space travel for the ineffable bore it was.

Now that Zerdai was irrevocably lost to him, he kidded himself into thinking that he had really intended to take her with him as he had promised. He wallowed in self-pity. Maybe he should even go to work, repugnant though the idea appeared. (He always thought of reforming when he got into a jam like this.) But who would employ him around Novorecife when he was in Abreu's black books? To go back to Mikardand would be silly. Why hadn't he done this, or that. . .

Borel became aware of a man drinking down the bar; a stout middle-aged person with a look of sleepy good-nature.

Borel said: "New here, senhor?"

"Yes," said the man. "I just came in two days ago from Earth."

"Good old Earth," said Borel.

"Good old Earth is right."

"Let me buy you a drink," said Borel.

"I will if you'll let me buy you one."

"Maybe that can be arranged. How long are you here for?"

"I don't know yet."

"What do you mean, you don't know yet?"

"I'll tell you. When I arrived, I wanted a good look at the planet. But now I've finished my official business and seen everything in Novorecife, and I can't go wandering around the native states because I don't speak the languages. I hoped to pick up a guide, but everybody seems too busy at some job of his own."

Borel, instantly alert, asked: "What sort of tour did you have in mind?"

"Oh, through the Gozashtandou Empire, perhaps touching the Free City of Majbur, and maybe swinging around to Balhib on my way back."

"That would be a swell tour," said Borel. "Of course it would take you through some pretty wild country, and you'd have to ride an aya. No carriages. Also there'd be some risk."

"That's all right, I've ridden a horse ever since I was a boy. As for the risk, I've had a couple of centuries already, and I might as well have some fun before I get really old."

"Have another," said Borel. "You know, we might be able to make a deal on that. I just finished a job. My name's Felix Borel, by the way."

"I'm Semion Trofimov," said the man. "Would you be seriously interested in acting as a guide? I thought from your rig that you were some official. . ."

Borel barely heard the rest. Semion Trofimov! A big-shot if ever there was one; a director of Viagens Interplanetarias, member of various public boards and commissions, officer of various enterprises back on Earth. . . At least there would be no question of the man's ability to pay well, and to override these local bureaucrats who wanted to ship Borel anywhere so long as it was a few light-years away.

"Sure, Senhor Dom Semion," he said. "I'll give you a tour such as no Earthman ever had. There's a famous waterfull in northern Rúz, for instance, which few Earthmen have seen. And then do you know how the Kingdom of Balhib is organized? A very interesting set-up. In fact, I've often thought a couple of smart Earthmen with a little capital could start an interprise there, all perfectly legal, and clean up. I'll explain it later. Meanwhile we'd better get our gear together. Got a sword? And a riding outfit? I know an honest Koloftu we can get for a servant, if I can find him, and I've got one aya already. As for that Balhib scheme, an absolutely sure thing. . ."

If you enjoyed the first book in deCamp's classic KRISHNA SERIES, *you won't want to miss Book #2, coming from Ace Science Fiction in August:* THE SEARCH FOR ZEI/THE HAND OF ZEI. *Here's a free peek at what's to come. . . .*

On a fine clear morning, the sun rose redly over the rim of the Banjao Sea. The three moons of Krishna, which—as happens but seldom on that planet—were all in opposition to the sun at once, slipped one by one below the western horizon.

The rising sun, which the Krishnans call Roqir and the Earthmen call Tau Ceti, cast its ruddy rays slantwise across a vast floating swamp. Near the northern margin of this marine morass, these rays picked out a movement. A small ship crept eastward along the ragged edge of the swamp, where the floating continent of terpahla sea vine frayed out into streamers and floating islands.

A high-peaked, triangular lateen sail, barely filled by the faint dawn breeze from the north, flew from the single mast. To speed the little craft along, seven heavy-shouldered Krishnans sat in a row down each side of the deck, each man heaving on an oar. At the stern a stocky, gnarled old Krishnan, looking like some barnacled sea monster, gripped the tiller. A pair of staring eyes were painted upon the bow; while, across the transom of the

221

stern, a row of hooked characters gave the ship's name as *Shambor*.

Driven by its sail and its fourteen oars, the *Shambor* forged ahead into the sunrise, now and then altering its course to dodge a patch of terpahla. After each swerve, however, the steersman swung his vessel back towards a single objective: a primitive seagoing raft, with a tattered sail flapping feebly in the faint breeze. This derelict floated awash a few bowshots ahead.

Two persons lay prone on the rotting planks of this craft, peering towards the approaching ship from under their hands. At first sight they looked like Krishnans, a man and a woman. That is, they were of much the same size and shape as Earthmen, but with minor differences.

Thus their skins had a faint olive-greenish tinge, and the woman's dark hair was decidedly green. The man's head, however, was shaven, although a coarse bronze fuzz had begun to sprout from his scalp. Their ears were larger than those of Terrans, rising to points that gave them an elfin look. From the forehead of each, just above the inner ends of the eyebrows, rose a pair of the feathery antennae, like extra eyebrows, which served Krishnans as organs of smell.

The woman was young, tall, and superbly proportioned, with dark eyes and a prominent aquiline nose. She wore only the remains of a gown of gauze, shortened to knee-length by pulling up through her girdle. The garment, however, was so tattered that it was hardly better than none at all. The right shoulder strap had parted, exposing more of the girl's beauty than many Earthmen would consider seemly. Her bare feet had been chafed raw in places.

The man was tall and muscular, although his large-boned form, with knobby joints and oversized hands and feet, would not have been deemed a thing of beauty. He wore a stained and faded suit of pale blue, with short baggy breeches and a jacket with silver buttons. Thin leather boots rose to his calves. Beside him, on the deck, lay a dented ornamental helmet of thin silver, from which sprouted a pair of batlike silver wings.

The costume was, in fact, the uniform of the Mejrou Qurardena, which may be translated as Reliable Express Company. In this disguise, the man had sought to enter the Sunqar—the floating swamp—and snatch away two persons whom the pirates of that sinister place held captive. He had succeeded with one, the girl beside him.

Also on the planks of the raft lay four boards, a little over six feet long and whittled into crude skis, together with the ropes that had served as lashings and the oars the fugitives had used as balancing poles. It was on these skis that the man and the woman had escaped the previous night from the settlement of the Morya Sunqaruma—the freebooters of the Sunqar. In all the many centuries of Krishnan history, nobody had ever before thought of using this method of passage over the otherwise impassable mat of terpahla vine.

The terpahla lay all around the raft: a tangle of brown seaweed upheld by grapelike clusters of purple bladders. Peering over the side, one could sometimes catch a flash of motion where the fondaqa, the large venomous eels of the Sunqar, pursued their prey.

The man, however, was not studying the sea life of the Sunqar. He was frowning towards the approaching ship, which showed a faint whitish triangle of sail above the swampy surface. Now and then he cast a glance to southward, towards the main body of the floating continent of terpahla. A vast congeries of derelict vessels broke the horizon in that direction. Here the beaked galleys of Dur and the tubby roundships of Jazmurian slowly rotted in the unbreakable grip of the vine.

Even the violent storms of the Krishnan subtropics could no more than ruffle the surface of the Sunqar. From time to time, however, the swamp heaved and bubbled with the terrible sea life of the planet, the most fell of which was the gvám or harpooner.

But no monsters now broke the sluggish surface. Here

in the growing light reigned silence and haze and the stench of the strangling vine.

Here, also, rose the works of man. The Morya Sunqaruma had built a floating city of derelicts. They kept a passage clear from the margins of the vine to their settlement, whence from time to time they sallied forth in reconditioned derelicts, or ships made from the sounder timbers of such, to work their will upon the nations and mariners of the Triple Seas.

Now, as the man on the raft looked towards the settlement, faint plumes of blue smoke arose from the ramshackle cluster of improvised houseboats. Along with domestic doings, the Morya were beginning the day's run of janru—that amazing drug which, extracted from the terpahla and incorporated in perfumery, gave any woman, either Krishnan or Terran, what power she wished over any man. By devious routes the stuff was smuggled from the Sunqar to Earth, where it wrought much social havoc.

Looking back towards the approaching *Shambor,* the man on the raft muttered: "It's our ship, all right, but. . ."

"But what, O Snyol?" said the girl.

"Because, Zei darling, it shouldn't have that sail up. Anybody with a telescope could see the sail from the settlement. So either my boys are being stupid, or they're not my boys."

The man had spoken Gozashtandou, the common speech of the western shores of the Triple Seas. He spoke with a marked accent, which he asserted to be that of Nyamadze, the antarctic Krishnan land he claimed as his home. One skilled in such matters, however, would easily have recognized his dialect for that of an Earthman.

For the man was neither Synol of Pleshch, an exiled officer and adventurer from cold Nyamadze, nor yet the expressman Gozzan, both of which he had at various times pretended to be. He was Dirk Cornelius Barnevelt,

a native of New York State, United States of America,
Terra. The points on his ears, the antennae on his brow,
and the faint greenish flush to his skin were all artificial,
wrought upon his person by the skill of the barber at
Novorecife, the outpost on Krishna of the Viagens Interplanetarias.

Moreover, Barnevelt was an employee of the firm of
Igor Shtain, Limited. He was in fact the ghost writer for
the firm. The corporation included the explorer Shtain
himself, who traveled in far places and brought back
reels of data; Barnevelt, who composed articles and lectures about these travels; and an actor, made up to look
like Shtain, who delivered the lectures. In this age of
specialization, the firm also kept a xenologist, who told
the others what to think about the data that the intrepid
Shtain had gathered.

Zei said: "When yestereve the brabble broke forth
upon the ship, you would fain have trussed an Earthman
who dwelt among the Sunqaruma, tossed him into the
treasure chest, and born him forth. You recall the man
—a stubby wight with wrinkled, ruddy face, blue eyes,
and stiff gray hair, growing upon his upper lip as well as
on his pate?"

"Yes."

"Well, at that time, you said you'd vouchsafe me
anon the reason for this antic. Methinks the time has
come for full confession. So answer, sir: wherefore this
caprice?"

Barnevelt took so long about answering that she said:
"Well, dear my lord?"

"That man," said Barnevelt carefully, "is Igor Shtain,
a Terran who disappeared from the ken of his kind. I
promised the Earthmen at Novorecife—for a consideration—to try to find and rescue him. Well, as you saw, he
doesn't want to be rescued. Evidently that dinosaur
thing who heads the gang—Sheafasé—has put the
Osirian hex on friend Shtain, so he no longer knows who
he is but thinks he's just another Sunqaro buccaneer. At

the time I signed up, of course, I didn't know I'd be called upon to rescue you, too."

"How sad that my poor self should thus by inadvertence clog the cogwheels of your worthy enterprise!"

"Oh, don't talk nonsense, darling. I'd rather rescue one of you than a dozen Shtains. Give me a kiss!"

Again, Barnevelt demonstrated the Earthly custom that he had taught Zei while they waited on the raft for dawn. Aside from the natural pleasure of making love to this gorgeous creature, he hoped thus to distract her mind from further questions.

Moreover, he was more than half in love with her and suspected that—as nearly as one could tell in dealing with one of another species—she felt the same towards him. They had become good friends during the time that he and George Tangaloa, the xenologist, had stayed at Ghulindé, capital of Qirib. Although Zei was the only daughter of Queen Alvandi, a combination of circumstances had caused Barnevelt and Tangaloa to be welcomed at the palace as distinguished and sought-after guests while they abode in Ghulindé. They had been outfitting an expedition, supposedly for hunting gvám stones but actually for seeking the missing Shtain.

Then the pirates of the Sunqar had raided Ghulindé and carried off Zei. In the fracas, Tangaloa had been wounded. Fierce old Queen Alvandi had seized the genial Samoan as a hostage to force Barnevelt, still under his alias of Synol, to try to recover her daughter. Although he had succeeded with Zei, two rescues at once had proved too many. So Shtain, still believing himself a Sunqaruma, remained behind in the settlement.

The daring rescue and the brilliant improvisation of skis to cross the uncrossable weed had naturally enlarged Barnevelt still further in the eyes of the princess. In fact, an hour earlier, when they had removed their soaking garments and hung them on the mast stay to dry, they had come perilously close to consummating their mutual desire.

Two natures had struggled for supremacy in Barnevelt. One was the healthy young animal, which was all for it; the other was the cautious, calculating man of affairs. The latter nature had warned that such intimacy might cost Barnevelt his head.

For Qirib was a matriarchate, where the queen took a new consort every year. At the end of the year, the old king was executed and ceremonially eaten at a solemn religious festival. It was this festival, the *kashyo*, which the piratical raid had interrupted. In the confused fighting, old King Káj had perished, struck down while wielding the executioner's axe, in a last-minute recovery of his manhood, against the raiders.

Barnevelt, knowing that Queen Alvandi meant to abdicate in favor of her daughter, foresaw a year of bliss for himself—followed, however, by the chopping block and the stew pan. While his impulses contended, the sight of the *Shambor* had tipped the scale in favor of cautious self-restraint.

Zei kissed him briefly but continued to ask questions. After all, even though hers was a mild and friendly nature, as a princess she was used to having her own way with everybody except her mother.

"Then," said she, "that tale of the search for gvám stones was but a taradiddle wherewith to cozen us?"

"Not entirely. I hoped to pick up some of the stones, too, in case I failed with Shtain." (Always, he told himself, mix enough truth with your lies and vice versa to make it hard to separate the true from the false.)

"Then neither of us is wholly what he seems." She looked back at the *Shambor,* slowly meandering towards them. "Will they never come nigh enough to settle our doubts?"

"They have to zigzag to avoid the weed, so it takes much longer than you'd think."

She glanced towards the settlement, springing into full view in the strengthening light. "Is there no shift whereby we could get word of young Zakkomir's fate?"

" 'Fraid not. He's on his own."

Zakkomir was a young Qiribu, a ward of the crown, who had come with Barnevelt on his expedition out of admiration for the heroic deeds of the supposed General Snyol of Pleshch. In the fight of the ships they had become separated. Zakkomir fled in one direction, and Zei and Barnevelt in the other.

Barnevelt peered again at the *Shambor*. "By Bákh, that's Chask, my boatswain, at the tiller!" He stood up, waved, and whooped: "O Chask! Ship ahoy! Here we are!

"It'll take them some time yet," he told Zei. "Let's hope the Sunqaruma don't see us."

" 'Tis a wonder they returned to rescue us, once they'd won free. Snyol of Pleshch must command deathless loyalty from his men."

"I'm not so good as all that, darling. In fact, Chask is the only one I'd really trust, and I daresay it was his doing that the ship's here."

Barnevelt then confessed to having spoiled his sailors at the start of the voyage by treating them in too familiar and democratic a manner. After one of them had been snatched from the deck by a sea monster, the rest in terror wished to turn back, and he had almost had to quell a mutiny.

"That smart young squirt Zanzir's at the bottom of the trouble," he growled. "Instead of encouraging him, I should have gotten rid of him the first chance I had."

As the *Shambor* nosed through the weed a few meters from the raft, Barnevelt remembered one of his duties. He stood up and pointed his fist at the ship, moving it slowly back and forth. For the big ring on his finger was really a Hayashi motion-picture camera, and he was filming the approach of the *Shambor*.

Igor Shtain, Limited, had a contract with Cosmic Features for 50,000 meters of film about the Sunqar. One task of Barnevelt and Tangaloa had been to shoot as much of this film as possible to keep the firm from going bankrupt. Although the regulations of the Interplanetary Council forbade the importation into Krishna of inventions not already known there, an exception was made for the Hayashi camera, because it was so small and inconspicuous that it could hardly upset Krishnan culture. Besides, a destructor spring would make it fly apart in a fine mist of tiny wheels and lenses if a tyro tried to open it up.

"What's that?" said Zei. "Dost cast a spell?"

"Of sorts. Get your sandals on. Here we go."

He boosted Zei over the rail and climbed aboard himself, grumpily telling himself that he had been lucky to escape from forming an intimate connection with the princess and ending up as an Earthburger at the next kashyo festival. But, at the same time, the less practical side of his nature—the romantic-dreamer side—whispered: *Ah, but you do love her! And some day, perhaps, you and she will be united somehow, somewhere. Some day. Some day. . .*

—*from THE HAND OF ZEI*
Copyright © 1963 by L. Sprague de Camp

CONAN

☐ 11577-2	**CONAN, #1**	$2.50
☐ 11595-0	**CONAN OF CIMMERIA, #2**	$2.50
☐ 11614-0	**CONAN THE FREEBOOTER, #3**	$2.50
☐ 11596-9	**CONAN THE WANDERER, #4**	$2.50
☐ 11634-5	**CONAN THE ADVENTURER, #5**	$2.25
☐ 11635-3	**CONAN THE BUCCANEER, #6**	$2.25
☐ 11636-1	**CONAN THE WARRIOR, #7**	$2.25
☐ 11637-X	**CONAN THE USURPER, #8**	$2.25
☐ 11638-8	**CONAN THE CONQUEROR, #9**	$2.25
☐ 11639-6	**CONAN THE AVENGER, #10**	$2.25
☐ 11640-X	**CONAN OF AQUILONIA, #11**	$2.25
☐ 11641-8	**CONAN OF THE ISLES, #12**	$2.25

Available wherever paperbacks are sold or use this coupon.

THIEVES' WORLD

ADVENTURES

edited by Robert Asprin